SOLOMON KANE

THE OFFICIAL MOVIE NOVELISATION

SOLOMON KANE

THE OFFICIAL MOVIE NOVELISATION

A NOVEL BY
RAMSEY CAMPBELL

BASED ON THE SCREENPLAY WRITTEN BY
MICHAEL J. BASSETT

BASED ON THE CHARACTER CREATED BY
ROBERT E. HOWARD

Solomon Kane:
The Official Movie Novelisation
Print edition ISBN: 9781848567269
E-book edition ISBN: 9780857685322

Published by
Titan Books
A division of
Titan Publishing Group Ltd
144 Southwark St
London
SE1 0UP

First edition June 2011
10 9 8 7 6 5 4 3 2 1

Visit our website: **www.titanbooks.com**

Did you enjoy this book? We love to hear from our readers. Please email
us at readerfeedback@titanemail.com or write to us at Reader Feedback at
the above address.

A CIP catalogue record for this title is available from the British Library.

Printed and bound in the United States

For Kate and John –
invite no sorcerer within your castle!

Sections of this novel were written at the Aloni Apartments in Pefkehori (thank you for the provisions, Jim and Naomi Gurr!), at the British Fantasy Convention in Nottingham, at the Festival of Fantastic Films in Manchester and at Tammy and Sam's Brockley mansion.

ONE

"Stay close to Captain Kane!"

As the men of the *Relentless* fought their way across the drawbridge of the castle, Martin was never more than yards behind his captain. More than once he came so close that he was sprayed with the blood of guards that Kane cut down. The blood was as hot as the African night – as hot as the rage for victory with which Kane filled his men. Fighting in his wake felt like following a storm of blood, and now their nearness to the treasure seemed to have rendered him indomitable. Martin saw him gut two adversaries at once, pausing only long enough to snatch his blades out of their vitals. Another guard took that chance to rush him, but Kane thrust his rapier so deep between the man's ribs that he had to kick the dying man free of the weapon. A defender seemed to think this left Kane vulnerable, but as he ran at the captain the point of the rapier skewered his throat. "Yes?" Kane enquired of his screams, and Martin saw him gaze into the man's eyes as though he was seeking some truth. When he found none he held the man up with the sword like a specimen he was examining before he pulled the blade out, letting the body crumple to the bridge. At that moment the doors at the end of the drawbridge shut with a thunderous slam.

It seemed to shiver the obsidian minarets that towered against the suffused black sky. Martin heard a massive bar rumbling ponderously into its sockets, and then a stampede of footsteps made it clear that many defenders had added their weight to the barrier. Martin saw Kane's eyes glitter, not only with the flames with which the bombardment of the castle had scattered the drawbridge. "Aside," said Kane, and beckoned behind him.

At once four men pushed a cart onto the bridge. It was loaded with barrels of gunpowder. Martin felt the bridge vibrate beneath his feet as the cart trundled towards him. He and his fellows cleared the way, kicking scraps of fire aside or stamping on them. At last the cart reached the end of the bridge, and the men piled the barrels against the doors before setting a trail of powder. One of them lit it and ran back to safety while Kane stood his ground, challenging the explosion to harm him.

The bridge quaked, and the doors caved in as if the wood were rotten. The doorway was blocked by a dense flood of smoke, through which could be heard the clatter of falling rubble and the screams of men. Kane was already stalking towards it, swords held high. His mirthless grin made his lean face wolfish. As he strode through the insubstantial barrier, Martin was close behind him.

Beyond the doorway a wide corridor of amber stone was strewn with men and parts of men and blazing chunks of wood. Not a guard had been left standing, and those who could still move were almost indistinguishable from their dead comrades. Kane strode among them with his swords crossed behind his shoulders, his long black cloak flapping like a vulture's wings, and peered at each face or remnant of a face. He might have been examining pieces of meat on a slab. All at once he stooped closer to a guard whose body was a mass of torn flesh and tattered armour but whose eyes turned fearfully to meet his. "Where is the throne room?" Kane said through his bared teeth.

The man's face worked as though he would have dragged himself away from Kane if his shattered limbs had let him, but he gave no answer. His eyes rolled in the sockets, more wildly as Kane traced the guard's cheek with the point of his dagger. The point came to rest a fingertip's breadth short of the man's left eye. "Ajna tudgadur ghurfatul arsh?" said Kane, and Martin understood that he was repeating the question in Arabic.

Either this or his fear of the blade gave the guard back his voice. "Hunaak, hunaak," he gasped and raised a shaky finger to point along the corridor. "Tafadzal, tafadzal."

"Good lad." For a moment Kane's Devonshire accent made him sound as gentle as a lover. "Good lad," he repeated and stroked the man's cheek. He straightened up, shaking his long black greasy locks out of his face, and sheathed the dagger. The guard must have had time to conclude he would be spared before Kane took his musket from his belt and levelled it at the man's head. "Let not one of these putrid heathen live," he shouted.

The shot added the man's brains to the rubble on the floor, and seemed to infect Kane's companions with a lust to kill. They thrust their swords into the hearts of every fallen guard, even those who betrayed no sign of life. Martin drove his blade between the ribs of a man whose last breath seemed to shape a word that might have been a protest or a warning. As Martin dragged the sword out of the corpse Kane shouted "Follow me."

Had they slain every one of the defenders? None challenged them as Kane led the way through corridor after broad corridor supported by circular arches, past enormous halls where towering columns effloresced against ceilings encrusted with elaborate mosaics. The deserted amber corridors put Martin in mind of tramping through gigantic veins of gold, and the prospect of treasure helped him quieten his indefinable doubts about the absence of any guards. Then Kane held up one hand, saying "It is here."

Martin raised his sword as he saw movement beyond a rounded arch, but the silhouettes lined up to face each other across an antechamber were not guards, or even human. Only the flickering of torches set in brackets on the walls granted them the illusion of life. They were oval mirrors taller than he was, and he and his companions would have to pass between them. They must be the paraphernalia of some kind of African magic, but no God-fearing man need be afraid of such things. As soon as Kane stepped across the threshold Martin strode after him.

He disliked the antechamber more with every step he took. Was it only the restless light that had made it seem to harbour some form of life? Each mirror was supported by two pairs of thin splayed limbs that might have been the legs of monstrous insects. Or perhaps they resembled bones, because they and the scrawny oval frames were covered in tatters of material unpleasantly reminiscent of human skin. When Martin glanced into a mirror he was unsure what he saw. The figure silhouetted by flickering dimness could only be his reflection, but he retreated to the middle of the way between the mirrors as a chill seemed to reach for him out of the glass. "What is this place?" one of his fellows muttered behind him.

"There's dark magic," another man whispered. "We shouldn't be here."

Kane swung around to glare at his followers. "Silence, you dogs," he snarled.

When he stalked forward Martin did his best to imitate his carelessness. Either every guard was slain or any survivors had fled. That was why the throne room was unguarded, unless the guards themselves were fearful of the antechamber. As the thought overtook Martin he heard a murmur at his back, apparently too muted for Kane to catch. "There's something in here with us."

"No treasure is worth this," came a response.

It was, Martin wanted to protest; it had to be. It would make up for the months of rough voyaging, of sleeping on the bare deck, of breathing in the stenches of the bilge, of drinking fetid water and wine turned to vinegar, of subsisting on putrid meat and biscuit infested with weevils. It had even to be worth the sense of dread that had begun to dog him – a dread for which he did his best to blame his companions, although it felt capable of stealing his breath. He glimpsed movements in the mirrors and glanced at one in search of reassurance, but his reflection appeared to be obscured by another shape. Was that simply a flaw in the mirror, which would also explain why the glass was blurred as if it had been breathed upon? Just behind him Daniel whispered "What's that, in God's name?"

Martin looked back to see several of his companions peering at the mirrors, more than one of which was blurred by condensation now. As he saw the grey mist fade from one glass oval he realised how unnatural it was. The moisture that looked far too much like evidence of surreptitious breaths was beneath the surface of the glass. The other men had hesitated at the whisper, but now they advanced, and Martin saw breaths swell up within the mirrors to greet them. He was opening his mouth to shout a warning when his voice retreated into his throat. More than breath had come to the surface of the mirrors.

Alongside Daniel a pair of hands had planted themselves on either side of the patch of moisture, and Martin saw that the blur was masking a head.

The hands were dreadful enough. Their fingers were abominably long, and grey as death. Their gnarled segments were so prominent that they resembled insect legs more than anything remotely human. Their cruelly pointed tips scraped over the inside of the mirror, and a face loomed into view between them, searching blindly for its prey. It was bald as a worm and almost as featureless, except for a round voracious mouth low down on the long head. In a moment the shape found its way out of the mirror.

The glass did not shatter. It bulged like an egg composed of some material softer than shell, and two elongated fleshless arms sprang forth. As the claws fastened on Daniel's shoulders, the circular mouth gaped as though the absence of a face had been designed to let it stretch unnaturally wide. It seized like a leech on Daniel's head. He barely had the chance to scream as he was snatched into the mirror, which closed over him like a pool too deep for light to penetrate.

A second man was dragged off his feet and vanished struggling. A third had no time to cry out before a mirror engulfed him and the shape that had clutched him in a demonic embrace. The remaining men glared about, lifting their swords as they backed away from the mirrors, forgetful of the mirrors at their backs. To Martin the swords looked powerless, no longer weapons but simply talismans his companions were brandishing in a vain attempt to ward off unimaginable evil. He raised his own in a desperate gesture of defence as he stumbled to Kane's side. "Captain," he begged and heard his voice shake.

Kane's eyes blazed beneath a scowl like the onset of a storm. "Hold steady," he growled and put out a hand to take Martin by the shoulder.

Martin disengaged himself and stepped back out of reach. "Stay close to Captain Kane" – but the advice that every man heard before they fought alongside him seemed to have no power in this place. "There's deviltry," Martin said louder and turned to flee. "Let the devil take my share."

"I said hold steady," Kane told him in a voice as chill as steel, but Martin was already running between the mirrors. He saw some of his fellows think of imitating him, and then their faces betrayed a different kind of fear. Before Martin had a chance to draw another breath he was thumped with great force on the back.

For the briefest instant he thought a denizen of one of the mirrors had tried and failed to capture him, and then the impact exploded through him. It felt as though his heart had been punched from behind. As he heard the shot, his ribs splintered and his chest burst outwards. He was thrown to the floor, which was splashed with blood – his own. "I am the only devil here," he heard Kane shout. Then he heard and felt nothing, but a final thought accompanied him into the dark: his captain was wrong. There was worse in this place than Kane.

TWO

"Captain..."

Kane heard the fear in Martin's voice and saw it flicker in his eyes. The other men had only murmured their disquiet for fear of Kane himself, but now it was daring to speak up. It could be the first sign of mutiny, and Kane gripped Martin by the shoulder hard enough to bruise him – to drag him back from wherever his panic had sent him. "Hold steady," Kane said through his teeth.

Martin pulled free of his grasp. "There's deviltry," he protested and whirled around to face his companions. "Let the devil take my share."

"I said hold steady," Kane snarled, but the fury in his voice fell short of halting Martin. The man bolted down the avenue of mirrors, jerking up his sword to repel whatever he saw in the glass. Did he fear his own reflection? Not so Kane, who had looked into the depths of himself and made that darkness part of him. Before the fellow could infect his comrades with cowardice Kane brought him down with a single shot. "I am the only devil here," Kane declared.

He had faced many devils in his life, and the common name of all of them was fear. He had learned not to fear to kill any more than he feared death. Fear was the greatest demon, because it could possess a man and steal his spirit, just as it had done to Martin. Kane had cast it out of the man, and the fear he could see in the eyes of the survivors was of him and his authority. "Now," he said, though he hardly needed to voice the command, "follow me."

As if the words had more power than he knew – as if he had uttered a magical formula – he heard a massive groan of wood and metal at his back. Beyond the antechamber a pair of doors twice his height had swung inwards far enough to admit a man. In the tremulous darkness beyond them Kane thought he saw a glint of precious metal. Without hesitation he strode up a broad flight of amber steps into the throne room.

It was circular, and so vast that the light from torches held by colossal figures carved out of the dark stone of the walls barely reached the domed ceiling. The flames clothed the figures with restless shadows, so that Kane could not judge whether they were meant for gods or some form of guardian. Otherwise the room was illuminated only by circular windows patterned in blue and purple stained glass, tints rendered just visible by the approaching dawn. On the far side of the room a throne had been hewn from a single monumental block of swarthy stone. Sprawled before it, as if the weight of all his finery had proved too much for his thin frame, was the corpse of a king with a withered face. His fallen crown resembled an overturned goblet, for a dark stain glistened beside it on the amber marble around his head. Kane spared none of this more than a glance, because the middle of the room was heaped with gold. "I've found it," he shouted. "Here it is, boys."

Once again his words seemed to conjure a response, but none he would have wished for. The great hinges groaned again, and the doors shut behind him with a slam like a clap of thunder. It muffled other noises – the screams of men, a clash of blades, a solitary gunshot. He thought he was hearing the start of another skirmish until, in the silence that swiftly followed the clamour, he realised that the clatter of metal he had mistaken for a swordfight was the sound of swords falling to the floor. He strode to the doors and pounded on them, shouting to his men, but there was no answer, only a hush like a giant's held breath. The unyielding doors kept whatever secret lay beyond them, but he knew he was alone. If a man could not go back he must go on, and he turned to cross the throne room.

The torchlight flickered on the mound of gold, which was broader than his arms could stretch. As he made for it he seemed to hear an exhalation like a chorus of stealthy breaths, but glaring about showed him no adversary, just the colossal obsidian torch-bearers. It must have been a wind in the crevices of the fortress, Kane decided, and its significance dwindled as he gazed upon the mass of wealth.

Midas might have laid his aurifying hands on every item. Golden swords lay among shields and armour of the same substance. Heavy necklaces were draped over plates of gold and aureate masks that seemed to frown at their own abduction. What ancient ceremonies might they have seen? Countless doubloons added to the riches, and Kane thought they alone could have ransomed a royal dynasty. He stooped to gather handfuls, and as he let the coins slip through his fingers he felt as if the fortune had transformed him into a colossus, able to play with golden coins as a child plays with grains of sand. The last doubloon fell with a delicate chink on the hilt of a sword decorated with a circular face that seemed immersed in its own mystery, and as Kane made to sift the wealth afresh he heard another sound.

It might have been an echo of the tinkling of coins. It was thin and chill, little more than an inhuman whisper. It was somewhere beyond the treasure, closer to the throne. Was it among the fallen king's regalia? As Kane peered towards the corpse, wondering if a rat was feasting on the dead flesh, he saw the prone form begin to shift as though it was preparing to crawl to reclaim its wealth. This was simply a trick of the treacherous light, but in a moment Kane saw what he was hearing: the formation of crystals. The stain beside the head and the crown was no longer red. It was white.

A shiver passed through Kane. Some change had overtaken the room, sucking out all the stagnant heat of the African night. He raised one hand to breathe into the palm. Not only did he see his breath, but for an instant his fingertips glimmered white, outlining every whorl. The gelid clutch of the air felt too similar to fear, and Kane glared about the room in search of some more substantial adversary to challenge than shadows and ice. As though in answer to his unvoiced wish, something came at him.

It resembled breath turned black. It streamed from the mouths of the stone colossi and whirled in ebon skeins around him. With it came a Babel of shrieks and shrill whispers. Kane felt surrounded by a whirlwind that spoke, though in no words that he could comprehend. He spun about, slashing at the ropy darkness, but his swords could discover no substance. As he staggered to a halt the blackness rushed away from him.

It raced in two tattered streams over the fallen king, whose robes were furred with frost now, and converged on his throne. Kane saw a shadow seated there, drawing its shape from the blackness. The thin shrieks and the insidious whispers and whatever remnants of humanity had emitted them were engulfed by the presence, as if they were assuaging some inhuman hunger. The last scraps of the unnatural darkness vanished like wisps of mist in sunlight, but it was not the sun that turned the throne room pale as death. It was ice.

The presence seated on the throne was flanked by bodies that might have been unholy tributes – almost a dozen crucified men. They had been flayed as well, and stalactites of blood dangled from the exposed flesh. Their faces were distorted by grimaces of agony and terror, so that even in the sourceless icy light that had overwhelmed the flickering of torches, Kane did not immediately recognise the corpses of his men. Rage blazed through him as he turned his gaze on the figure enthroned between them.

It was abnormally tall, and robed from head to foot in black. If it had a face, that was concealed in the depths of a hood. Just the hands were visible, their long pallid fingers tipped with claws as cruel as any predator's. Was it bone that glimmered within the hood, and was there a glint of pitiless eyes? Kane was not to be daunted. He took a step forward, lifting his rapier to point at any heart his adversary had. "What are you?" he demanded.

The figure reared up like a wave of blackness. It threw out one splayed hand, which resembled bone imperfectly transformed into flesh, and then it spoke. The roar that emerged from the depths of the cowl contained no words. The onslaught of sound was so thunderous that although Kane saw the mound of gold quake with it, he could not hear the movement for the aching of his eardrums. The roar grew louder and less bearable as its breath reached him. It smelled as though an ancient sepulchre had been opened – it smelled of things so long dead that they ought to have been dust. It was so frigid that the air in front of Kane visibly shuddered like thin ice. The breath threatened to render his bones as brittle as shell, and it leached all the power from his muscles, which trembled like the air. As he collapsed to the floor Kane barely avoided falling prone by supporting himself with both hands on the hilt of the rapier.

He crouched like a beast at bay and glared his hatred at his assailant. At last the lethal breath relented as the figure towering before the throne gave Kane his answer. "I am the Devil's reaper," it pronounced in a voice that resonated like the tolling of a great bell. "I am here to claim you, Solomon Kane," it said, and other voices whispered its words as though souls trapped in the hooded darkness were compelled to imitate their master. "Your deal is done."

"What deal?" At least Kane was capable of speech, even if his limbs were no more use to him than an infant's. "I made no deal," he snarled.

"There was a deal." The edges of the cowl fluttered as if whatever face lurked within was about to appear from its lair. "And your soul is the price," the voice decreed. "It was signed away in the blood of the first man you killed."

For a terrible instant Kane remembered who that had been. The voice and its words seemed to resonate deep in his guts as it proclaimed "Your life of murder and greed is over."

The imminence brought Kane back from his memory, and he struggled to lever himself to his feet. "You cannot take my soul," he said in outraged disbelief.

"Bow your head before me!" Once more the figure thrust out its hand, and a freezing gale assaulted Kane, shivering through every limb. "The Devil will have his due," the figure vowed, and the enslaved voices whispered confirmation.

Kane had been forced to lower his head, which felt

weighed down by ice. He fought to lift it as he saw an elongated flame reflected dimly by the amber stone on which he knelt. He sensed heat as fierce as the cold had been. His head wavered erect, and he saw what confronted him. It was worse than fire. The hooded figure held a sword that might have been withdrawn that very moment from a furnace.

The blade was molten, yet it retained its shape. As it dripped gouts that flared on the stone floor it constantly renewed its substance. It could have been forged only in Hell, and perhaps it had been designed as a hint of the eternal torments it presaged. Kane felt the infernal heat settle on him before the cowled figure raised the blade high to cleave Kane's skull.

Not just rage but the heat gave Kane back his strength. He rose on one knee and brought up his crossed swords to meet the descending blade. The impact shook him, but he held his stance. "You may tell your master," he shouted, "I am not yet ready for Hell."

His faith raised him to his feet, still parrying the blade. "The Lord protects me," he cried.

"Fool!" The syllable seemed to vibrate through the flaming blade, and Kane felt the heat spread through his own swords. "He has abandoned you," the hooded figure told him, and within the cowl Kane seemed to glimpse the grin of gleeful bone.

The words felt like a wound too deep for any earthly weapon to deal. The diabolical heat coursed through the hilts of Kane's swords, searing his fists. He fought to maintain his grip even as he saw the blades begin to drip metal. He struggled to hold back the blazing sword of his adversary, but at last, with a bellow of pain, he had to open his hands. The distorted remains of his weapons clattered to the floor, and the molten blade swooped down at him.

A backward lurch saved him. White-hot drops of metal spattered the mound of gold and blackened the floor where Kane had just stood. The point of the flaming blade slashed through the air scant inches from his face, and he felt as though Hell was reaching for him. "On your knees," the hooded figure thundered, and a single stride brought it far too close to him, swinging the sword in a great arc.

Kane ducked but would not look away. As he felt the heat of the blade pass over his scalp like an infernal benediction, he saw the dawn touch the window beyond the throne, limning the image in the stained glass. It was universal and eternal – an angel battling a demon. The hint of the dawn reminded Kane how high the window must be. He thought of a man falling from a height, and all at once he seemed to be facing his destiny. "You will never take my soul," he vowed and sprinted for the window.

The hooded figure whirled about, and the blade slashed at Kane, dripping fire. It missed him by inches, and at once he heard his pursuer at his back, trampling over the strewn gold. Kane's desperate leap carried him through the stained glass. The peacock colours shattered before his face, and there was no knowing which had belonged to the angel, which to the demon. The sliver of sun that had cleared the horizon shone in his eyes, and then he plummeted into darkness, where waves tossed like a sleeper in the throes of a nightmare. Above him he heard a voice so huge that it might have been using the throne room for a mouth. "You cannot escape us," it said. "Your soul is damned."

THREE

As the last amen of matins echoed through the cloisters, Kane gazed out of his cell. Beyond the window, around which a few sprigs of holly were pale with frost, the world resembled a charcoal sketch. Mist lay on the lake that surrounded the island on which the monastery stood. Leafless trees protruded from the water, where the only signs of life were two immobile silent crows perched among the gnarled branches. A scattering of snowflakes drifted through the air to lie for a breath on the water before vanishing. They might have been scraps of the sky, which hid the sun and which was as white as the mist that masked the land on the far side of the lake. The view reminded Kane that the world was only God's sketch for perfection. It seemed as austere as the monastery itself, and austerity was where God was to be found most in the world.

A discreet bell began to peal, and Kane turned away from the window. Stripping to the waist, he plunged his hands into the basin that stood next to his unadorned bed. The frigid water felt like not just a penance but an essence of the rigours of monastic life. Both its isolation and its simplicity – the absence of any hint of idolatry, or anything that could have been construed as such by the investigators of the Reformation – had enabled the monastery to survive. Its remoteness was as comforting to

Kane as his sense of the unemphasised presence of God. He was bathing his face when he heard a knock at the door of the cell, and a voice spoke his name.

He turned to see Brother Fletcher and a young monk, who bore a tray of simple fare – bread, cheese, beer. The youth was visibly nervous. His gaze ranged about the cell, taking in the piles of scrolls and the bulky theological volumes Kane pored over late into the night with only a candle for illumination. He seemed to gain some necessary reassurance from the large stone crucifix beneath which Kane had placed the bed. "Who's the novice?" Kane enquired.

"This is Brother Thomas," Brother Fletcher said. "He joined us only a few days ago."

"Welcome," Kane said, which failed to nerve the youth to look directly at him. "Welcome, Brother Thomas."

He had grown used to calling these men brother, although it was a word he had believed for many years that he would never choose to utter. The novice laid the tray down on the solitary table, beside the heavy tome that had been Kane's midnight reading, and then he ventured to face Kane. In a moment he was staring openly at the prayers and symbols – some occult, some religious – that were inscribed on Kane's chest, and the tattoo of a cross that spanned his back. "Those marks," he breathed. "Do they really protect you from Satan?"

Kane prayed they did – they and the sanctity that surrounded him. Before he could speak he was forestalled. "Mind what you name in this holy place," a new voice said.

Brother Thomas's hand flew to his mouth, where he made a hasty sign of the cross. His dismay was fleeting, almost schoolboyish, but Kane's was more profound. The abbot had appeared in the doorway, and his warning seemed to imply that the monastery was less sacrosanct than Kane yearned to believe. "I would like to speak to Solomon alone," the abbot said.

Brother Thomas hurried out of the cell without a backward glance, and Brother Fletcher followed more sedately. For a moment the abbot only gazed at Kane, who saw pity and determination in his eyes. "Walk with me, Solomon," the abbot said.

He was silent while he waited in the corridor for Kane to finish dressing. He said no word as they walked through the cloisters, where the undecorated columns and the simple arches of the windows seemed to betoken an age that had been closer to God. The abbot remained mute as they emerged from the monastery and crossed the grounds. Throughout the seasons Kane had sought peace beneath the trees – in the renewal of foliage that surely symbolised a promise of eternal life, in the grassy summer shade that elaborated on the promise, among the countless autumnal tints of leaves that seemed to whisper of serenity as breezes that heralded winter found them. Now the ground was hard and white as the marble of a sepulchre, and icy winds had picked the trees clean of leaves. Their twigs resembled twisted icicles, and their branches were mossy with snow, which filled the cracks in the bark of the trunks as though to emphasise their more than human age. It seemed to Kane that even the abbot's face – gaunt and pale with his advancing years, and stubbled with a thin white beard – had been gripped by the uncommonly severe winter. The abbot halted beside the perimeter wall, which was encrusted with snow, and gazed at him until Kane wondered if he was expected to speak. At last the abbot said "Once again we heard your cries at matins, Solomon."

"My dreams," Kane said. "They haunt me still."

"You would do well to heed what your dreams tell you. I do," the abbot said.

He turned along a barren avenue, and Kane could only follow in the hope of solace. In his waking hours the monastery gave him a refuge from his dreams, but now the abbot's exhortation had brought them to the surface of his mind. The most dreadful of them showed two figures at the edge of a high place – the kind of height where Satan had brought Christ to tempt Him. In every re-enactment one of the figures was thrown from the cliff. Sometimes it was Kane who pushed him, and sometimes the falling man was Kane, but one element was constant: worse than jagged rocks brought the fall to an end – Satan was waiting to claim the souls of both men. "My dreams tell me only that I am damned," Kane muttered.

The abbot glanced sharply at him as a monk with a lidded basket passed close to them, on his way to grub any vegetables he could extract from the stiffened earth. "God protects his own," the abbot said.

"But I am not one of his own, am I?" Kane saw the monk tramp through the gateway to the vegetable plots, and might have thought he was watching his own future retreat from him – a potential future that he could have grown to deserve. "My enemies are ever watchful of me," he said.

"You still defile our sacred texts." The abbot's frown was etched as deep as cracks in bark. "You corrupt your flesh with them," he said. "Men are being burned for less."

"This place and these prayers..." Kane touched his breast as if he were laying his hand on a holy object. "These symbols," he said. "They are all that keep me from that gaze."

The abbot hesitated and then took hold of Kane's

shoulder. His grip was firm but impersonal, and there was regret as well as purpose in his eyes. He guided Kane along the rough path into the gardens, where the blades of two axes were buried in a block of wood. The sight was unwelcomely reminiscent of battle, and even the trellises that flanked the path put Kane in mind of an encampment, of frameworks awaiting tents. He was attempting to recapture his sense of sanctuary when the abbot moved to face him. "These months you have been here, Solomon," he said, "I've felt a shadow growing over us."

Nothing in the gardens cast a shadow now, and all at once it seemed unnatural, as if shadows were secretly massing while the sun was buried by the impenetrable clouds. "These are dark times," Kane said uneasily.

"I have prayed for guidance, and I was answered." The abbot fixed Kane's gaze with his, not unkindly but resolutely. "You must leave us, Solomon," he said.

"Leave?" Surely the abbot could be placated; Christ had been merciful to sinners such as Kane, after all. "But why?" Kane said. "I live here in solitude. I do no harm to any man."

The abbot inclined his head. "I've renounced my power, my evil ways," Kane reminded him. "I am learning to be a man of peace."

"I believe that to be so." The corners of the old man's eyes winced, as if he had been troubled by an unexpected ache. "But your future is not here with us," he said.

"How can you do this to me?" Perhaps another species of reminder would succeed where pleading failed. "I have given all my wealth to the church," said Kane.

"And of course we are all grateful for your generosity." Nevertheless the abbot seemed offended by Kane's attempt to buy redemption – to make his gift into a price.

The traces of regret were fading from his eyes as he said "But you must understand – "

"Father." It was a word Kane had thought he might never use again. He seized the abbot's arm, remembering barely in time how frail the old bones must be. "Father," he repeated like a prayer. "Do not make me beg. This place is a sanctuary to me."

He saw that the abbot needed no reminding – that he might even resent it. His gaze was unwavering, and Kane could only make a final plea. "Where would you have me go?"

"You must go home."

The abbot frowned at Kane's reaction – he might almost have recoiled from Kane. "Home," Kane said in disbelief.

"You are of noble birth," the abbot said. "You have lands in the west. You must return to your inheritance."

"Father," Kane protested, but the word seemed to have lost its power. He was struggling not to clench his fist around the frail arm. "I cannot return home," he pleaded.

Was there a glimmer of remorse in the abbot's eyes? It failed to prevent him from saying "Nor can you remain."

It was as final and as immutable as the words that ended every mass. The old man stood mute until Kane released his arm, and then he left Kane at the edge of the frozen garden, beside an elevated crucifix that watched over the growth of the fruits of the earth. Kane heard a monk's hoe scraping at the soil, and the harsh derisive call of a crow. For a moment he thought the shadow of the crucifix had fallen on him, but the sun was still muffled by the clouds. No holy object had cast that harbinger of darkness, as invisible as it was unmistakable and chill, over him.

FOUR

As Kane followed Brother David out of the grounds of the monastery he heard the abbot's voice behind him. For a moment he hoped that he was about to be called back to his refuge, and then he realised that the abbot was speaking to a monk. They were at the parapet that overlooked the path to the ferry across the lake. The winter stillness and the silence of Kane's guide left their voices absolutely clear. "I was told in my dreams that he was to be sent from here," the abbot said. "I listen to what I am told."

"Does Kane know his purpose?" the abbot's companion said.

"Every man must discover his own destiny." Kane was close to turning to demand more of an answer when the abbot said "Kane must find his purpose."

Kane thought this was closer a condemnation than to any kind of valediction. As he trudged after his guide the abbot's voice seemed to pursue him. "There are many paths to redemption, and not all of them are peaceful."

The early mist had retreated across the lake, where snowflakes hovered like seeds of ice. Otherwise the only movement beyond the path was the flapping of wings as a crow sighted Kane and his guide. As Kane settled himself on a bench in the small boat, lifting over his head the straps of a water-bottle and of a heavy bag,

Brother David untied the rope from the ring in the post on the overgrown margin of the lake. The ring struck the post with a clunk that resembled the note of a bell so old and rusty it was robbed of meaning. The monk dropped the rope on the floor of the boat and began to pole the ferry across the lake. He had uttered no word since summoning Kane from his cell with a gesture that had seemed reluctant if not wary. Perhaps he had taken a vow of silence – perhaps it was a penance – but Kane was assailed by the notion of a silent ferryman. Surely it was too ancient a belief to trouble him, and yet he found it ominous.

The crows grew restless in the branches of the drowned trees as the ferry sent lethargic ripples across the lake. When the water lapped against a supine bole one crow emitted a raucous cry that was answered by its mate. Kane could have thought their eyes glinted at him before the birds left their perches. As they flapped away from him Kane glimpsed their dim reflections, ill-defined winged shapes that appeared to glide just beneath the surface of the water like some unknown species of predator. The crows vanished into the trees that surrounded the lake, and Kane could have taken them to be leading him if not awaiting him.

Soon the ferry bumped against the far margin of the lake. Here the path was almost indistinguishable to the untrained eye, and wholly so where it led among the trees. The ring on this side of the lake was sealed to the wooden post by ice, so that Brother David had to lever it up with both hands. He refrained from tying the ferry to it, instead holding onto the ring while Kane resumed his burdens and stepped ashore. Kane might have thought the monk was eager to be rid of him. "My thanks to you, Brother David," he said.

The monk inclined his head without speaking. He let go of the ring, which stayed raised in the air like an emblem of silence, and made a sign of the cross in front of Kane. While it could have been a blessing, it might equally have been designed to ward off Kane or what he represented. Brother David pushed the ferry clear of the bank and turned away at once to pole the boat across the lake. Perhaps he was making greater speed because the boat was lighter, but it seemed to Kane that the monk was fleeing him if not the world. He watched the boat grow dim and then invisible in the mist that had returned to the lake; he saw the last ripples stray out of the mist and merge with the still water. Then it was as if the island and the monastery no longer existed – for Kane, at any rate.

FIVE

Kane had almost reached the crossroads when he saw two long-beaked creatures standing there. They wore sombre headgear, and they were as tall as Kane. In front of them a pyre blazed at the meeting of the lonely roads between the icy barren fields. The flames confused his vision, so that for a moment the funereal bird-headed figures appeared to flex wings as if they were preparing to take to the air and swoop to meet him. They were doctors masked against the plague, with medicine secreted in the beaks of their masks. They were performing no cures here, miracles being outside their scope. They were presiding over a funeral.

Kane passed by as discreetly as he could. If he had been an emissary from the island in the lake he could at least have bestowed a blessing or offered a prayer. Instead he did his best to hide his face in the hood of his heavy robe as a women cried out with grief. The shrouded body that two men were laying on the pyre scarcely needed both of them to lift the crude stretcher. Kane raised his staff so as not to strike the earth as he trudged behind the Celtic cross that marked the junction of the roads, but the bereaved mother lifted her head to watch him. Surely just the tears that blurred her eyes made them look accusing. Kane strode onwards twenty paces before he yielded to a compulsion to glance back. The beaked heads were turned towards him, and he could have thought the inhuman eyes were observing him.

How tainted was the land? Into what state had the world fallen during his time on the island? Little news had reached the monastery, and in any case discussion of such worldly matters was frowned upon. Kane did not slacken his pace until the crossroads were out of sight and he saw a solitary oak ahead of him, beside a track across a heath. He sat against the venerable trunk and quenched his thirst, and then he wrapped his robe about him against the chill that blanched the heath. He hoped to rest for a few minutes, but he had scarcely closed his eyes when he heard movement above him. A crow had alighted on a leafless branch.

Whatever it was holding in its beak, the object looked torn and raw. A drop of dull red dangled from it and then spattered a fallen leaf beside Kane. He sprang to his feet and struck at the crow with his staff, but the scavenger flapped away across the heath. Kane had no more liking for the place it had marked, and he set off along the track. He appeared to be travelling west, so far as he could judge with no sight of the sun. The oak was far behind him when he saw the crow ahead.

He had the unpleasant notion that it was the same bird, no longer perched in a tree. Structures reminiscent of the trellises in the monastery garden towered on either side of the road. Three hanged men, or as much of them as the crows had left intact, dangled from each. As Kane strode between the gibbets, refusing to be daunted, the crow flapped down from the crosspiece to settle on the shoulder of a man with half a face. While the greatest delicacies had been consumed, the nose between the empty sockets was there for the taking. The beak pecked and tore and gouged at the grisly titbit to reveal the cavity beneath.

Kane set his gaze resolutely on the way ahead and struck the rough road again and again with his staff. The gibbets would have been in sight, if he had any reason to look back, when he heard movement behind him, growing louder. It was too large for a crow. It might have belonged to a flock of them, but he had the unwelcome fancy that the ravaged bodies of the hanged men had taken it into their minds to jig in mid-air on the gibbets, unless they were struggling to free themselves and drop to the road and scuttle on all fours or shamble after him. But the noise was made by rain, which quickly found him.

It was almost as icy as hail, but worse. Its chill penetrated Kane's garb at once, and soon the onslaught drenched him. The cold clung to him, reaching for his bones. The downpour cloaked the land, so that he might have been trudging along a road through a grey void, from which it only gradually emerged. Nothing was clear apart from the shaggy verges of the road and the hedges separating them from the obscured fields. The only hint of life was the activity of rain in the hedges, trickling down the pallid twigs to dangle from the icy leaves. Once Kane thought he saw a raindrop turn to ice.

There was no shelter to be seen. Kane almost wished he had sought refuge in whatever settlement the gibbets served, but he suspected that travellers could expect no hospitality. The downpour drove him onwards until he lost all sense of time and almost of himself. He seemed to have become merely a plaything of the elements. It must be God's will, and he knew God's will often to be pitiless.

At last the rain slackened without having softened the earth or even thinned the clouds. As it trailed away to the horizon it revealed fields where a few leafless trees stood sentinel. Its enervating chill stayed with Kane, whose garments felt laden with water. He cast back the sodden hood and was striding doggedly along the road, which was defined largely by uneven ruts as hard and cold as iron beneath his feet, when he heard a sound like an omen of another storm.

It was the rumbling of wheels. He turned to see a small covered wagon drawn by two horses. As it trundled alongside Kane the driver reined it to a halt. Under the conical wide-brimmed hat of a Puritan his pockmarked face was weather-beaten, but his large nose seemed to lend humour to his eyes. "Can we offer you a ride, pilgrim?" he said.

Kane had an instinct that his destiny was best sought without the distractions of companionship. "Thank you, no."

The man's wife touched her husband's arm. Beneath a headscarf her face was weathered too, but still delicate. Like his, her garments were as sombre as the depths of winter. Kane saw that she was mutely urging her husband, who said "These roads should not be travelled alone."

"A man who fears God need fear no man." This silenced the driver while Kane added "Thank you for your offer, but I'll be walking."

"As you wish," the driver said. "God be with you."

"And with you too, sir," said Kane.

The driver jerked the reins, and the wagon left Kane behind. Then the flaps at the rear of the vehicle were parted, and a boy's face gazed out at him. Was there a glimpse of red fabric beyond him – the only hint of brightness in the wagon? The boy watched Kane as the wagon pulled further ahead, and Kane could have fancied that he was seeing his own boyhood retreat from him. He put those memories away from him as the wagon swayed over the ruts into a wood. The wagon and the sounds of hooves and wheels disappeared among the trees, and Kane strode towards his fate.

FOUR

It took Kane the best part of an hour to find sufficient wood that was dry enough for building even a meagre fire. He struck the flint again and again until his fingers ached. He had prayed too by the time a grudging flame sputtered up from the driest twigs. He waited for the flames to gather strength, and then he set about arranging sticks over them. A pair of crows observed his efforts from high in the trees that surrounded the forest glade. Apart from the crackling of wood the only sound was the belated fall of raindrops that had lingered in the branches, for the crows were absolutely still.

At last the sticks began to smoulder, and once they caught fire he added more sticks. In time he was rewarded with a fire that put him in mind of a treasure, considerably smaller than the heap of gold that used to haunt his dreams but just now far more valuable to him. As he held out his hands to it he felt renewed or at least capable of renewal. He was crouching closer when he heard a sound.

Had the fire brought the crows to life as it was restoring vitality to him? The birds seemed not to have stirred, and their unblinking night-black eyes stayed fixed on him. A twig snapped in the heart of the fire, and Kane recognised how similar the stealthy noise had been. It was not the same, and he rose slowly to his feet.

Ahead of him a fallen tree lay along the top of a slope. Kane thought the sound had come from beyond the massive trunk. He was heading for the slope when a footfall snapped another twig. It was behind him, and he had no chance to turn, for a knife was at his throat. "Move and you die," a voice said in his ear.

The blade was already breaking the skin, and it was close to his jugular vein. As he cursed his unwariness – enervation and the task of making the fire must have left him careless – the man with the knife emitted a whistle that caused both crows to flap and felt close to piercing Kane's eardrum. In response the man's companions emerged from behind the fallen trunk.

The pair of them were built like bulls. One was as tattooed as any tribesman. His skin was a chaos of flaming colour, as if, Kane thought, he was dissatisfied with the form God had given him. The other man was adorned with a beard that he must have spent vain hours braiding. He bore a staff much like Kane's, which was resting against a log opposite the slope. As the two men stalked across the glade they brought a smell of decay with them, perhaps from the sodden leaves they were trampling. They halted within arm's length of Kane as if challenging him to defend himself, and peered with a parody of interest at his face. "What's this we've found in the woods?" the tattooed man said.

"Doesn't look at home here," the bearded man remarked.

"Doesn't look like it would be anywhere," said the voice closest to Kane's ear.

Kane smelled breaths like the drains of a tavern – alcohol mixed with stale meat. The men's eyes glittered with anticipation, and it was clear that staying silent would not help him. "I want no trouble," he said.

"That's a pity." The bearded man seemed pleased with Kane's answer. "You've got it," he said and swung his staff with both hands at Kane's midriff.

The handle caught Kane in the stomach, driving all his breath out of him. A wave of nausea surged through him, and he collapsed to his knees. The spectacle appeared to enliven the crows, which flapped as though they were applauding, but it failed to satisfy the tattooed man, who thumped Kane with great force on the back of the neck. This too was audibly appreciated by the crows, and it knocked Kane over. As he lay on the frozen ground with his knees drawn up – he might have been enacting the helplessness of a child yet to be born – the man with the knife stepped into view, sheathing his weapon. He was bald by choice, and his pate looked as raw with the elements as his broad sullen face. He considered Kane's state for some moments before adding a vigorous kick in the ribs.

The breath that Kane had managed to recapture abandoned him, making way for another onslaught of nausea. One of the crows greeted the kick with a caw that could have been mistaken for a mirthless laugh. The three men stood over Kane as if they were pondering how next to cripple him, and Kane could only reflect as he struggled to regain his breath that Christ had suffered worse on his behalf. For the present the trio seemed content with Kane's condition, and they turned away to find what they could steal.

The bearded man grabbed the bag from beside Kane's staff and inverted it. The Bible fell out first, followed by a packet of bread and cheese, and the scrolls Kane had studied at the monastery. A few coins rolled across the leaves, and the tattooed man crouched ape-like to claim them. The bald man tore open the packet of food as his bearded companion shoved a large fist into the bag and groped deep before heaving it wider to stare within. "Nothing," he complained, and his fellows took up the refrain while a crow added a caw. "He's got nothing worth lifting," the bearded man declared, and scowled at the Bible before glowering at Kane. "You a priest?" he said like an accusation.

Kane wished he were entitled to the name, even if it would not save him. He gathered his strength and levered himself to his knees. He might have been at his prayers or awaiting a headsman's axe, but he was simply attempting to feel less ineffectual without appearing to offer a threat. "Just a traveller," he said.

"No traveller's safe in these parts."

"You want to watch out who you make friends with," said the tattooed man.

"Shouldn't ought to have left home," said the man with the raw pate.

Kane was unsure whether they were taunting him as a preamble to worse. "Take what you want," he said.

"Don't worry, pilgrim." The bearded man seemed eager to take Kane's words as an insult. "We will," he said.

His companions were regarding Kane's belongings with disfavour. All at once the tattooed man stooped with an oath. One of the scrolls had partly unfurled, and the man stamped on it as though it were an insect. He used his other foot to spread it out and bent wide-legged to examine it. "Look at these," he urged.

The baldest of them gripped his thick thighs as he squatted to glower at the scroll. "That's no English writing," he objected as if he were challenging anybody to suggest he was unable to read.

The bearded man poked at the scroll with his staff and used the tip to trace the lines of occult symbols Kane had studied in a vain attempt to define the forces ranged against him. The man might have been a child learning to read with a fingertip underlining each word in a primer, except that his lips found no way of shaping the text. Resentment of his inability seemed to stoke his eager rage. "That's magic," he informed his cronies. "That's how witches write."

The three men turned to face Kane as the scroll writhed on the leaves, attempting to regain its secretive shape. It was obvious that they were pleased to find a reason to assault Kane afresh – any reason. The tattooed man tramped at him, pulping leaves underfoot. "What shall we do with you, eh?" he enquired, and a thought seemed to flare in his eyes as he glanced at the fire. "Shall we burn you for a witch?"

A crow cawed, and the other bird flapped like a black flag at a tournament. The man seized Kane by the hair and dragged him staggering to his feet. His grip felt capable of tearing clumps of hair out of Kane's scalp. He manhandled Kane to the fire and forced Kane's head down towards the flames while the shaven-pated man toyed with his knife, testing the point with his thumb, and the bearded man raised his staff as an additional threat. "Burn him," he shouted, and the man with the knife yelled louder "Burn him."

As though it were in league with his adversaries, the fire was blazing now. Kane felt the heat on his face like a reminder of Hell. It seared his cheeks, where he felt stubble begin to smoulder. The fire was stinging his eyeballs by the time he found the power to heave his head back against the grasp in his hair and then to stiffen his whole body against the brute strength of his captor. "Burn him," the others cried like spectators at an execution. "Burn him."

The tattooed man redoubled his grip on Kane's hair and twisted it viciously before shoving with all his brutish might. Perhaps the unjust accusation of witchcraft lent Kane strength. After all his months of meditative retreat on the island – after all that he had done for the church and for himself – surely he was not to be slain as a sorcerer. He tensed every muscle against the assault, and this time his captor was unable to force him down. Eventually the tattooed man gave up the attempt but kept hold of Kane's hair while he moved to peer into Kane's face. His lips drew back from his teeth in a feral grimace. "There's murder in your eyes," he said in delight.

The other men welcomed the development with grunts of pleasure. Kane was silent, and his captor yanked ferociously at his hair. "Would you kill me, pilgrim?" he said.

Kane gritted his teeth while he offered up the painful ignominy to God. "No," he said.

The shaven man brought his face so close that Kane had to breathe in the fellow's raw stale exhalation. "You won't kill the man who steals from you?" he said with disbelief that sounded gleeful.

Kane's time at the monastery was being put to the test, and he did not hesitate. "I will not fight another man."

His interrogator slapped Kane across the face with the back of his hand as hard as he could. His knuckles caught Kane's nose, and blood trickled into Kane's mouth. The crows or the other men – perhaps all of the spectators – uttered hoarse sounds of appreciation. "You worthless coward," the bald man snarled. "Fight me," he urged and punched Kane in the face.

Kane might have fallen except for the grasp in his hair. In a moment his captor released him. He managed not to collapse, though his head swam with the blow and his face throbbed like a wound. He tasted blood, but as his strength ebbed back he refused to let it tempt him to retaliate. "I have renounced violence," he vowed.

The words were not addressed to his tormentors, but the shaven man raised his raw-knuckled hand to cup it behind one misshapen empurpled ear. "What's that you say?" he barked.

The tattooed man put his hands together in a parody of prayer, which the patterns etched into his skin rendered diabolical. "Says he's renounced violence," he intoned like a monk echoing a phrase of holy ritual.

"Well, that's a shame." The bearded man gave Kane a moment to anticipate what kind. "Because we haven't," he said and lifted his staff high. He used both hands to swing it, and the thick handle clubbed Kane on the side of the head. The blow flung Kane to the unyielding earth. In his last moment of consciousness he saw the sneering faces of the robbers, savagely painted by the firelight, and beyond them a crow taking to the air. Then a void as black as the crow swallowed him.

SEVEN

It seemed to Kane that a great voice spoke to him out of a vast darkness, summoning him before the throne of judgment. "You will do as I say, Solomon," it said.

Time and space had no meaning in the dark. Instantly he was back at Axmouth, in the great hall of the castle he had once called his home. The light of many candelabras mellowed the stone of the walls and the columns that supported the high roof, but it could not soften the presence that dominated the hall. He was seated on the massive baronial throne at the end of the room, his powerful hands gripping its arms so hard that every knuckle stood out like a threat of a blow. His sternness might almost have turned him to stone, a statue of a magistrate. He was Josiah, Kane's father.

Not everybody in the room was anxious to face him. The servants busying themselves about the long oaken table in the middle of the hall must be hoping that their activities would lend them anonymity – would let the lord of Axmouth think that they were hardly there at all, as good as invisible, certainly unable to overhear what was being said. The solitary figure who was confronting Josiah, standing defiantly before the throne, was just fourteen years old. What he lacked in age and stature he was making up in spirit, and Kane hardly knew whether to admire or counsel him, for he was Kane's younger self. Josiah's keen grey eyes were regarding him without favour, and the long face etched by harsh experience was set in a decision against which there was no appeal. "Do not forget your place, Solomon," Josiah said for everyone to hear.

The boy drew himself up in mute fury that he should be shamed in front of the servants. Every man must find his place, Kane wanted to assure him; it was ordained by God. He could not speak, and in any case he knew that he would have gone unheard. Before the boy could put his protest into words, Josiah said "You are the second son."

Kane grew aware of the older youth. He stood closer to their father, relishing every nuance of the scene. Marcus had inherited the long face, but his chin was weak, his mouth loose and petulant. He wore his hair luxuriously long, and it was as pale as his eyes, from which it might almost have leached the colour. "Marcus is my heir," Josiah said, but he refrained from glancing at him, so that Kane could have suspected him of loving the idea more than the man. "He will be master of these lands on my death."

"Father, Marcus is a brute." The boy turned to scowl at his brother, who raised a golden goblet of wine in an ironic toast to the truth. "And a bully," the boy insisted.

"You will take holy orders." Perhaps Josiah was determined not to hear anything that would make him regret his decision, rooted as it was in his ancestry, but Kane could have thought he was handing down the boy's fate as a penance for rebelliousness. "You will join the church as I command," Josiah said.

The boy's eyes gleamed with dismayed rage, and Kane could have wished his youthful self to have been as voiceless as he himself was now. "I do not want to be a priest," the boy said.

He was giving voice to all the frustrations of his youth – to being treated as inferior by his father and the traditions of their line and, more maliciously, by Marcus. "What you want is of no importance," Josiah reminded him so fiercely that the words were echoed from every corner of the venerable hall.

Marcus watched his brother's face as if it were a source of delicious amusement and lifted the goblet once more. "Father Simnal is here to take you to the abbey," Josiah said.

Kane grew more conscious of the robed intruders as the boy did. All five men were crowned with black caps that had put his young self in mind of a judge about to pronounce a death sentence – a fivefold sentence that would deny Kane the chance to live as he deserved, to enjoy the world to the full. Father Simnal paced softly forward, stretching out his hands in a gesture of acceptance that might have foretokened a benediction, but the boy turned his back on the contingent from the abbey and faced his father. "I will not go," he said.

Marcus's eyes glittered with wicked delight while Josiah's grew as cold and still as stone. If Kane could have found a means to reach the boy he would have urged him to accept the situation. He was only being sent where he would eventually find a home – in the embrace of religion. He might have found peace all those years ago instead of being driven to seek it as a refuge from all the evil he had committed since. Instead he had to listen to his father pronouncing judgment once again. "If you defy me you will have nothing," Josiah said.

The boy gazed deep into his eyes and saw no hint of mercy. His own face grew stiff with resignation, and he turned away to stride down the long room. Josiah's voice pursued him. "I will cut you off," it thundered.

The servants watched the boy covertly as they performed whatever tasks they could find. Kane thought he discerned sympathy on at least one face. Father Simnal took another pace towards the boy, but the hands that stretched forth from the long sleeves looked ineffectual now. "You will be a landless vagrant," Josiah warned his son, and the priest made to put his hands together in some kind of prayer for Kane if not for obedience. "Is that what you want?" Josiah demanded.

His words seemed to shake the flames of the candelabras. Perhaps the boy's flight did. He was set on his course now, and nothing could stop him. He had the sureness of youth – of knowing he was unappreciated and misunderstood. He strode into the corridor that led to the outer doors, but even here his father's voice was at his back. "Walk out now," it declared, "and you may never return."

Kane knew this was true, and would have grasped his younger self by the shoulder to detain him if he could. The boy seized the rings set in the stout doors and twisted them, and a squeal of metal echoed through the corridor. "Do not defy me, Solomon," Josiah cried.

His voice was overwhelmed by the rumble of timber as the boy flung the doors wide. They might have been the entrance to a furnace, because fire was waiting beyond them – waiting for Kane, who could no longer stay separate from his younger self. The fire streamed along the blade of the molten sword held by the hooded figure he recognised all too well. The sword had been raised high to greet him, and now it swept down. It seemed to part Kane from his consciousness – from everything he had been. For a moment, unless it was an eternity, there was only the absence of light, a void too total even to be described as darkness, and then Kane grew aware of a face hovering above him – an innocent face, a young woman's face. In that first instant he thought that, unworthy though he was, an angel had descended to earth to save him.

EIGHT

The world swayed around Kane as he regained consciousness once more, and at first he thought he was at the mercy of a storm at sea. Light flared above him, but it was not the blazing sword that awaited him at the end of every awful dream. It was weak sunlight, and his eyes flickered open to fasten on it. He was still being rocked from side to side by the vehicle that carried him, but there was no storm. He lay beneath a canvas roof, and above him he saw a young woman's face.

He had seen it before, when he had struggled free of the dream of his banishment from Axmouth. The small delicate face was crowned by a white cap that might have been the garb of a nurse rather than the headgear of a Puritan. "Be calm, sir," she murmured. "You are safe."

Kane saw that they were not alone in the covered wagon. A boy was watching them, and now he parted the flaps at the back and jumped down. "He's awake, father," he called. "That man, he's awake."

The wagon lurched over some unevenness in the road. As it steadied, the young woman leaned closer to Kane, unstoppering a leather flask. "Here," she said softly, "take a drink of water."

Kane found that he was lying on a bed as narrow as the bench on which he had slept in his monastic cell. When he attempted to raise his head from the pillow, he managed just an inch before the effort revived pains all over him – a throbbing of his head, a soreness of the stomach, a dull bruise over his ribs. He remembered the blows that had caused them all, but any rage at his assailants was too distant to grasp. Perhaps he had learned to put such feelings from him. As his head sank to the pillow the young woman murmured "Sir, let me help. Drink if you can."

She slipped a soft cool hand behind Kane's head and lifted it. When she put the flask to his lips Kane sipped and then drank. At last he gasped, and the young woman let his head rest on the pillow. Not just the water seemed to be giving him back some strength; Kane thought her concern for him did. At first glimpse he had taken her for an angel, and it still seemed to Kane that in some way she was capable of redeeming him. "Who are you?" he said and was dismayed to hear how feeble his voice had grown.

The young woman stroked his forehead and then straightened up as if she might have presumed too much. "My name is Meredith," she said.

"Meredith." Kane lingered over the syllables, which sounded almost like a gentle prayer, as she turned away to acknowledge a newcomer. "His fever has broken, father," she said.

In a moment Kane recognised the pockmarked weather-beaten face, the eyes underlain with a trace of humour at odds with the sombre Puritan raiment. "Thank the Lord, sir," the man said and made his way along the swaying wagon. "By His grace you will be well."

He reached for Kane's wrist and found the pulse, which he contemplated for some moments before nodding in approval at his daughter. "My name is William," he said. "William Crowthorn."

"And mine is Solomon." For a breath Kane wondered if his whole name might be renowned for the evils he had perpetrated, but concealing it would be vain and a hindrance to repentance. "Solomon Kane," he said.

Crowthorn gave no sign of recognition, and Kane found he might have hoped the man would know of Axmouth. The wagon had not been travelling from that direction, and realising this reminded Kane "You offered me a ride."

A paternal frown narrowed Crowthorn's eyes, conveying regret rather than rebuke. "I did," he said.

"I should have accepted."

"You should." The frown faded, and Crowthorn's eyes grew reminiscent. "The good Lord must be watching over you," he said. "He guided us to your rescue."

"Master Crowthorn..." As much as the drink of water, the sense of being in the bosom of a family seemed to be restoring Kane's vigour. "Perhaps you have set me back on the road to my destiny," he said.

"It shall be as God wills."

Kane's words had fallen short of expressing what he felt – that the Crowthorns were somehow bound up with his fate. They must have turned back to find him, unless they had been led astray by the tracks through the forest – in fact, led true. And had Meredith not seemed to stand between Kane and the reaper in his dream? It would hardly be proper to speak of this, and he held his peace as Crowthorn raised his voice. "Edward, pull over now," he called. "We'll make camp for the night."

"I see the place that has been provided for us, father."

The response sounded more elderly than the speaker, whom Kane guessed to be in his twenties. He heard the driver urge the horses onwards with an impatient clicking of the tongue that Kane could have taken for a sound of disapproval. Soon the wagon rumbled to a halt. "Pray excuse us, Master Kane," Crowthorn said and set about unloading the wagon. "Rest now and regain your strength."

Meredith gave Kane an encouraging smile as she picked up utensils before following her father. In the calm after the incessant thunder of the wheels Kane heard a horse snort, the soughing of a wind in trees, the placid rippling of water. He lay and listened until the rattle of cooking utensils and the thuds of poles driven into earth made him feel idle. He raised his head without wavering, and found that he was capable of sitting up and swinging his legs off the bed. His various pains came with him, but he had suffered worse in battle, and they should be no excuse for indolence. With barely a stumble he made his way to the back of the wagon.

It stood in a glade beside a river. Despite the muffling of the sun, he could tell that the muted light denoted late afternoon. Traces of frost outlined the bark of the trees, but for the moment there was no sign of snow in the air. At the edge of the river the water raced over stones, stretching weeds away from them as if the ripples were combing drowned hair. Meredith and her mother had set up a cooking pot on a stand beside the river. Crowthorn and his elder son were building a rough shelter for the night while the boy Kane had seen in the wagon was stooping to the river, collecting stones to keep or to skim across the water. "Samuel, water the horses," his brother called to him.

The boy stayed in his crouch. "Why me?" he protested.

"Samuel," his father called more sternly than Kane would have expected of him. "Edward has given you a task. See you set to it at once."

Kane saw the elder son fix a disapproving look on

Samuel. Unlike the boy, he had inherited their father's features, though not all the strength of his mouth. Kane thought his lips seemed secretly a little petulant, hence more determined to wield power. Or was he interpreting the young man's face in terms of his own troubled memories? Samuel opened his hands, and the stones clattered into the river. As the boy trudged to unhitch the horses, Kane stepped down from the wagon.

Crowthorn's wife hurried over to him, stretching out her hands. They must once have been delicate, but they were worn with toil. "Master Kane," she protested. "You should be resting."

"I can hardly repay your hospitality with idleness." Kane flexed his muscles and experienced no immediate loss of strength. "Give me a few minutes to clean up," he said, "and then I'll come and help you as I can."

Concern gave way to resignation in her eyes. Perhaps she was used to the stubbornness of a husband and two sons. She laid a hand on Kane's and then turned back to her family. Kane's bag was in the wagon, and proved to contain the few belongings the robbers had left him. He found a cloth and made his way across the ground strewn with leaves to the river.

He came to the edge not far from Samuel, who was waiting to lead the horses away once they had drunk their fill. He was aware of Kane but did not glance at him. "You tend them well," Kane said. "No task is unimportant if it does good."

He stopped short of assuring the boy that his father and his brother would be proud of his attentiveness. They might well take it for granted, Edward in particular, and in any event it was hardly Kane's place to offer the opinion. "What is your name, boy?" he said.

He wanted to prevent him from realising that Kane had

heard Edward say it like a rebuke. Samuel affected not to hear, gazing hard at the endless transformations of the ripples on the stones. "You need not fear me," Kane said. "Tell me your name."

The boy only lowered his head as if he meant to emulate the horses at the water. Kane heard soft footsteps on the leafy earth, and saw that Meredith had interrupted her task to come over to him. She had brought colour into the wintry glade with a red shawl draped over her shoulders. Kane remembered the glimpse of red the wagon had afforded him as it left him behind, how many days ago? The shawl put him in mind of a favour given at a tournament – an offer of a lady's colours that he had failed to accept – although it was rather a token of rebelliousness, a hint of resistance to her austere Puritan life. "Your younger brother has lost his tongue, I think," Kane said.

"He's just shy of strangers." Meredith shook her head in mock reproof, dislodging a lock of glossy black hair from beneath the white cap. "Remember your manners, Samuel."

As Samuel raised his head and risked a sidelong glance at their companion, Meredith offered Kane a bunch of herbs that she had picked. "Marjoram for your bruises," she murmured.

"You are skilled in the ancient ways, then," said Kane.

"My father says that every natural thing has been put into the world for us. It is our task to learn the ways God means us to use them."

Kane had not meant to accuse her of practicing magic, but he could not know how strict the prohibitions against the old arts had become during his time at the monastery. "Thank you," he said and accepted the herbs. "For all your care."

He was conscious that Samuel was watching him and Meredith. The boy's attention seemed to hold them in an awkward tableau. "Well," Kane said, "perhaps you have other... I mean to say, I need..."

"Of course, you came to wash." For a moment a tinge of the colour of the shawl showed in Meredith's cheeks. "I should be at my tasks," she said.

As she started back to her mother Kane wondered how intimately she might have had to minister to him in his fever. He laid the bunch of herbs on the grass beside the river and pulled his shirt over his head. The garment was torn and stained brown with dried blood. He plunged his hands into the racing water and splashed handfuls over himself. The river was carrying the essence of an even colder place, but after the first violent shiver the icy chill began to invigorate him. He was bathing his face when he noticed the boy staring at him. "Speak to me, Samuel," he said.

"What are those?" Samuel said with a bluntness characteristic of his age, and pointed at him.

"The marks of a robbery. I would not bear them," Kane said, "if I had accepted Master Crowthorn's invitation. Your family is a protection to you, Samuel."

"Not those," the boy said impatiently and pointed harder. "All that."

Kane finished wiping himself dry and set about rubbing the herb on his bruises. The marjoram felt cool on them yet spread a warmth through them. "Some of these are of my own making," he said. "No, all of them must be. I made them by the life I chose to lead."

Samuel was gazing at Kane's back. "But you're carrying a cross."

"It is a comfort to me, and it wards off evil." Kane pulled on his shirt, hiding the tattoo as well as the occult symbols that had begun to suggest his confusion more than any power. "Just like the crosses you and your family wear," Kane said, reflecting that the crosses showed the Crowthorns were not fanatically Puritan.

Samuel seemed frustrated not to have more time to read Kane's history from his flesh. "There were scars," he protested.

Kane's hand strayed towards the mark that his cheek still bore. He left it untouched, wishing that the memory it roused could be ignored too, and was glad when the boy indicated his shoulder. "What was that one?"

"An African tribesman made it with a spear."

"In Africa?" Samuel's eyes widened as if they were greedy to take in more of the world. "You were at sea," he said.

"I was a captain," Kane admitted.

"A sea captain!" The boy seemed almost breathless with awe. "We are to sail for the New World," he said. "My father had to sell everything to pay for our passage."

"Then you should admire him more than me, Samuel." Kane had heard a hint of disappointment in the boy's voice. "I have been many kinds of man," he said, "and most of them do not deserve your respect. Let me try and make amends now. We both have our tasks to perform."

He gripped the boy's shoulder to hearten him and then tramped across the glade, where water had begun to bubble in a pot over a fire. "Tell me how I may help, Mistress Crowthorn," he said.

"Everything is done that must be, Katherine," Crowthorn told her. "You can best repay us by regaining the strength God means you to enjoy, Master Kane. You will dine with us and become yourself once more."

"As God wills," said Kane.

NINE

"Holy Lord, I have sinned times without number, and been guilty of pride and unbelief..."

Apart from the eternal murmur of water and the crackle of the fire, Edward's voice was the only sound in the glade. Like the rest of the family and Kane, he sat on the cold earth, his hands folded in prayer. Despite the open Bible on his lap his eyes were closed as if, Kane thought, he meant to demonstrate that the entire text was contained within him. No head was bowed lower than Kane's, and yet he was alert to everything around him: Crowthorn's satisfaction with his elder son, Katherine's pride in him, a hint of suppressed resentment on Samuel's part, a glimpse of red at the edge of Kane's vision, denoting Meredith's shawl. A twig snapped in the heart of the fire, but Kane did not look up. He was vigilant for signs of danger – too vigilant to misinterpret any sounds he heard. It was no longer just himself that his fate charged him to keep safe.

"...of failure to find Thy mind in Thy word, of neglect to seek Thee in my daily life..."

There was a great deal more to Edward's prayer, so that Kane wondered if the austere commitment to Puritanism might conceal or even betray a hint of the young man's pride in his own Godliness. He heard Samuel shift his position on the ground and observed how Edward stiffened his stance, whether to set an example or with disapproval. In the course of the prayer dusk gave way to nightfall, thickening the dimness between the trees. At last the silent listeners were able to respond, and Kane's "Amen" was the loudest of all. "Thank you, Edward," Crowthorn said. "You have kept our souls on the path to God."

As Edward inclined his head, a submissive gesture that might equally have taken the thanks as his due, Samuel said "When shall I be allowed to say the prayer, father?"

Crowthorn scrutinised the boy's face in the firelight, and his gaze softened. "Continue with your Bible studies and you shall lead us in prayer soon," he said. "We remember when Edward asked the same of us, do we not, Katherine?"

"I am sure you remember too, Edward," Katherine said.

"If I have shown Samuel the way to honour God I am content," said Edward.

He frowned at Meredith, who had raised her eyes heavenwards with a less than devoted look before shaking her head in frustration. "Well," William said, "let us honour God by eating what He has provided for us."

Katherine dipped a ladle in the steaming pot above the fire and filled a dish with a generous portion of stew. "Master Kane," said William, "you are our guest. You must sit in judgment on my Katherine's skills as a cook."

Kane thanked her for the dish she handed him. The Crowthorns must have bought the mutton in some village they had passed through. There was little enough of it, but Katherine had cooked it tender and seasoned it with herbs. As Kane swallowed the first mouthful, warmth and energy coursed through him. "Mistress Crowthorn," he said, "I believe this is as fine a meal as I have ever had."

Katherine's appreciative smile revealed a dimple in her cheek, and only Edward looked suspicious of a fib. Kane waited while the family was served, and then he ate hungrily. "I see you have found your appetite, Master Kane," Katherine said.

"My Katherine's cooking could bring a man back from the dead." Perhaps William felt this strayed too close to impiety, because he was quick to add "She can make a feast from anything. One time I do believe she served us leather shoes and nettles."

"I certainly did not," Katherine protested, but with a laugh.

"Tasted like it," Samuel said.

His mother cuffed the air well short of his head while the family joined in his mirth. Edward contributed a grunt more dutiful than humorous. Kane felt he should not presume to be included, and bent his head to his dish. The laughter dwindled to a giggle from Samuel, and as it petered out Katherine said "Samuel tells us you were a ship's captain, Master Kane."

Kane looked up to see all the firelit faces watching him. They might have reverted to ancient times, when listeners clustered around a fire to listen to a storyteller. Eagerness glinted in Meredith's eyes and Samuel's. "He spoke the truth," said Kane.

Samuel gulped down a hasty mouthful so as to be able to ask "Did you fight the Spanish?"

Kane recalled himself at Samuel's age, impatient to see a world of which he knew so little and to set his mark on it. While there might be glory in discovering far lands, he had found no glory in battle. Worse, he had been deluded that he had, by himself or by the Devil. "I have fought men of every nation," he confessed. "I have served many masters, even the French."

"A man should have only one master," Edward declared, "and He does not reward our service with earthly wealth."

Samuel was too hungry for Kane's tales to be inhibited by his brother. "Did you find treasure, Solomon?" he urged.

"Such as I found I gave to the church. Your soul is worth far more than any booty, Samuel. Perhaps your treasure is your life with your family." Kane saw William and Katherine appreciate the suggestion, but Edward seemed to feel that Kane was intruding, while both Meredith and Samuel looked disappointed by the turn Kane's reminiscences had taken. "I once voyaged with Admiral Drake," he told them.

Meredith's eyes grew brighter, and Samuel cried "Admiral Drake!"

"You speak of him as if he were a saint," Edward said.

Kane was unsure whether the reproof was aimed at him or Samuel if not both. He had meant only to restore a little of Samuel's fancies and Meredith's, which were surely harmless enough, but now he was beset by memories of carnage, of the light he had extinguished in the eyes of every man he slew, so many of them that he could call just a solitary face to mind – the one that haunted his worst dreams. "It did not end well," he said.

Meredith seemed determined not to hear this, and he thought she spoke for Samuel as well. "It must have been so exciting," she said. "Seeing the world, learning new things…"

"Has Master Kane not conveyed his lesson?" Edward said. "How can you admire a life devoted to bloodshed and violence?"

"That is not what I meant, and you know it." Meredith's eyes flashed for an instant. "Edward, why do you always argue with everything I say?"

"Because I have seen more years than you and Samuel." As Meredith looked ready to scoff at him, a shadow of petulance seemed to flicker around Edward's lips before they grew firm. "It is my duty to set you back on your path when you stray from it," he said.

To Kane's surprise, it was Katherine who intervened. "Now," she said without looking at Edward or his sister, "that's enough."

Meredith showed no reaction, but Edward's mouth grew almost childishly small. Kane sensed that their father meant to placate every one of his listeners if he could. "You know," William said, "I fought in the Queen's army for a time before I found my faith."

Samuel's interest was roused at once, but before the boy could blurt out a question, William added "The taking of another man's life is not an easy thing to do. Is that not so, Master Kane?"

"For many, yes." Kane wished he were speaking to a priest – one who could offer him absolution – rather than simply to a good man. "But I confess killing came easily to me," he said. "I was never more at home than I was in battle."

"Then how did those robbers best you so thoroughly?" Edward objected.

"Edward, your manners set a poor example," Meredith said.

"The question was a fair one," said Kane without knowing whether Edward had thought to catch him in a lie or to challenge his valour. "It was by choice, Edward. I have learned the evil of my ways, and I swore an oath never to harm another man. I will not fight again."

"Never?" Samuel said with the incredulity of youth. "Not at all?"

Kane gave him a tolerant smile. "Not at all, Samuel," he said. "You have my word."

"Let that be today's lesson," William said and rose to his feet. "Let us cleave to our vows and strive to keep God's peace." He turned sharply at a sound somewhere deep in the forest and crossed himself. Kane wondered if Crowthorn had thought, as he had, that a raucous laugh had greeted his pronouncement. It had only been the call of a crow in the dark.

TEN

As the boy tramped along the path above the bay he heard shouts beyond the cliff. A wind streamed through the grass all around him and ruffled his hair as he hitched up the straps of the bags that burdened him and went to the edge of the cliff. The wind had made the shouts sound closer than they were. They came from the crew of a three-masted ship that was tacking across the mouth of the bay towards the sea as wide as the horizon. While the boy could not name the style of vessel or the way it was rigged or the methods the crewmen were using to bring it into the wind, he vowed that one day he would learn all those skills and, by voyaging, master himself and the world. The thought gave him strength as he turned for a last sight of Axmouth.

His old home seemed to frown at him, the outcast. The massive stones of the castle were as gloomy as the sunless sky. It had no more life than a monument, he tried to tell himself. Life and all its possibilities were out there in the world. He rubbed his eyes fiercely to clear them as he turned away from the castle and strode with renewed determination along the path.

If Kane could have sent him back he would have. He imagined how Josiah might have welcomed him – might even have been so relieved by the prodigal's return that he would have rescinded his command to join the priesthood. There were many ways to God, and perhaps Kane might have found his own sooner. But even prayer could not alter the past, and so Kane could only watch as his younger self halted once more on the cliff.

The boy had heard voices again. He glanced at the ship that was performing its stately manoeuvre on the ocean. The wind was no longer carrying sounds from shipboard, and in any case, had one voice not been too high for a man's? In a moment the boy heard it again, higher than ever – a cry this time, a scream. It was beyond a rise ahead of him.

As he ran up the slope he saw the cross beyond it, a Celtic relic that his father had left intact, believing that it helped to sanctify the environs of Axmouth. It was witnessing no sanctity now. Among the grassy rocks a man was grappling with a girl, one arm holding her close to him while he tore at the fastening of her dress. "Stop," the boy shouted, but the attacker ignored him. The girl was a servant from Axmouth, he saw – Sarah. "Stop, I say," the young Kane yelled with all the authority his parentage might have lent him.

For a moment he thought his disinheritance was already common gossip, since his words were answered by a jeering laugh. Sarah was gazing at him, but there was pity in her eyes as much as pleading, whether because of his youth or because she feared he no longer had the power to intervene. The man ripped the fabric of her dress, exposing one small breast, and seized her wrists with his other hand as she struggled to cover herself. The torn flap of her dress fluttered in the wind that sent a shiver through the grass on top of the cliff. The boy ran to drag the attacker away from her, and then he faltered as he saw what he had not wanted to believe. The attacker was his own brother. "Marcus, what are you doing?" he cried.

The question sounded childish to him even before
Marcus met it with a sneer. "Have you not run away yet,
little brother?" he enquired, twisting Sarah's wrists as she
tried to pull away from him. "I thought you were fleeing
the priesthood as fast as your legs would carry you."

The boy had no time to respond to the gibe, although it
made his face hot. "Sarah, are you hurt?" he said.

This was naïve too, but she seemed pathetically grateful
to be addressed. "Solomon," she pleaded, "he wants to
– "

"Quiet!" Her words had enraged Marcus, though the
boy suspected that he was delighting in his rage. "I gave
you no leave to speak, girl," Marcus shouted and thrust
her away from him.

The boy was so untutored in the ways of the world that
he thought his brother might have been about to let her
go. Marcus was simply giving himself more room to strike
her across the face. His grip must have slackened for an
instant, because Sarah stumbled almost out of reach, and
the back of his hand caught her only a glancing blow. She
staggered but managed not to fall, a result that plainly
dissatisfied Marcus. "This is none of your concern, little
brother," he said with renewed fury. "Be on your way
before you come to harm."

As he lurched to recapture Sarah the boy stepped in
front of him. "Run, Sarah," the boy urged. "Run to my
father."

The girl hesitated and then dodged past them towards
Axmouth. Marcus whirled around to grab her, but the
boy blocked his way and pulled out a knife. He had
brought it with him more as a tool than a weapon. The
nearest it had ever come to violence was being embedded
in the trunks of ancient oaks in the forest beyond the
castle, where the boy used to practice his throwing skills

when he was allowed time to wander by himself. The sight of the knife seemed to amuse Marcus, so that he lingered rather than immediately pursue Sarah – perhaps he knew that Josiah could never take a servant's word against his. "Would you come between a master and his sport?" he said.

"Sport?" The word in the boy's mouth tasted as if it had been poisoned. "Is that how it will be when you are the lord of this land?" he protested. "Our father meant this to be a holy place."

"You no longer have the right to call my father yours." Petulance distorted Marcus's lips, and then he raised his chin as though to counteract its weakness. "You should have joined the priesthood if you are so concerned for my soul," he said. "You could pray for all my sins. You would pray for the rest of your miserable life."

"I pray that our father will see you at last for what you are."

"You were warned never to speak of him again." Marcus was no longer relishing his anger as he glowered at the knife. "Do you dare to threaten your own brother with that puny weapon?"

With a lunge he seized the boy's wrist. For all his inner weakness, Marcus was powerfully built, and his brother was no match for him. He bent the boy's arm until it felt close to snapping like a twig. A convulsion opened the boy's fist, and Marcus caught hold of the knife. "Take this in memory of me. Bear my mark wherever you may wander," he said and slashed the boy's cheek.

Kane felt the cold blade part his skin, and a chill salt wind probing the wound. Marcus dragged him to a high place on the cliff beside the cross. "Enjoy your last look," he said, holding the boy by the scruff of the neck. "All this will be mine," he said, sweeping an open hand at the castle and the land as far as the eye could see, "and you will have nothing."

He gave the boy a final contemptuous glance and shoved him in the chest hard enough to bruise him. The boy staggered back, but not far. Kane's entire being yearned to hold him still, to keep him from retaliating. Perhaps it was the pain of the cut in his face, or the disdain in his brother's eyes, that sent the boy forward. While his shove might not have been as forceful as his brother's, it took Marcus unawares. He floundered backwards, and his foot caught on a stone that might have been a fragment of the cross. His arms flailed the air, and the knife gleamed in his fist as he toppled over the edge of the cliff.

His scream was echoed by a chorus that seemed to mock him. Kane could have fancied that they were the gleeful cries of demons as they flew to claim Marcus, though he knew they were seagulls disturbed by the fall. As the boy rushed to the edge of the cliff and saw his brother lying raw and broken on the rocks below, the gulls flocked away towards the ocean and the ship that was retreating into the distance. Whatever the colour of the birds, just then they looked as black as eternal night to him, and so did the world.

ELEVEN

Kane's eyes sprang open and could fasten on nothing except blackness. He might have thought the dark of his dream had not merely seized his soul but closed over the world. In a moment it flickered, and by the faint uncertain light he was able to discern a canvas roof above him. He was lying in the wagon, which had come to rest. No, the canvas was too sharply slanted, and he was lying on little more than earth. He was in the lean-to that William and his elder son had constructed while Kane was regaining his strength.

Kane pushed the rough blanket aside and peered out of the shelter. It and three tents surrounded the fire in the middle of the clearing. All the tents were as silent as deep sleep, and so was the solitary figure on the opposite side of the fire from Kane, reading a Bible by the firelight while he kept watch. He was smoking a pipe, the smell of which Kane savoured as he rose quietly to his feet and approached the watcher.

He had almost reached him before William became aware of him. Crowthorn hugged the Bible with one arm and groped for a cudgel beside him. "Friend," Kane murmured as the fire cleared the shadows from his face.

"I'd be little use if you were not," William admitted with a rueful laugh and laid the cudgel down. "My fighting days are long gone," he said and scrutinised

Kane's face. "You have learned to be stealthy, Master Kane."

"I meant only to leave your family undisturbed."

"And you." Crowthorn's gaze grew keener. "Could you not sleep?" he said.

"Bad dreams," said Kane.

"I thought I heard you try to call a name." William clasped the Bible with both hands as he said "Are you plagued by mere fancies, or have you troubles you would share?"

"I believe such dreams are best not spoken of."

"Should they not be brought into the light, as God means us all to be?" Crowthorn left the question to be pondered while he used his cudgel to poke the fire, stirring it into renewed life. "Come, join me," he said.

Kane squatted close to the fire. It failed to relieve the chill that the dream had left at the core of him, and he had to stiffen so as not to shiver. "How are you feeling?" William said.

"Just aches and bruises." Kane could have ignored them by now, but they made him more alert for any danger. "Your daughter has a healer's gift," he said.

"She does indeed. Just like her mother." Crowthorn reached inside his shirt to find an object that hung on a cord around his neck. Kane expected him to produce a cross, but the religious symbol was not the only pendant he wore. He lifted a locket over his head and opened the small oval to show Kane. "The two most beautiful women in the world," he said softly.

The left half contained an image of Meredith's face, and the other one framed Katherine's. They were skilfully rendered, and the glow of the fire lent them more life. Kane wondered if Edward might disapprove of this hint of pride on his father's part. "My family is all and everything to me," William said.

"You are blessed," Kane told him.

William gave the portraits a last look and closed the locket gently before returning it to its place next to his cross. "Do you have kin?" he said.

"I had a brother once." For a moment Kane was close to confessing. The fire flared up like a reminder of the molten sword, and he knew he must remain alone with his action and its consequences. "That was a lifetime ago," he said.

"I have lost loved ones." There was sympathy in William's eyes and resignation, which it was plain he hoped to communicate. "To plague, to persecution and bigotry," he said and took a breath. "Edward," he said more quietly still, "he had a wife and child, but the Lord saw fit to embrace them."

The revelation silenced Kane but not his thoughts. He saw Edward in a new light – saw him clinging to his faith as the most constant element in a perilous world. Even his inflexibility with Samuel and Meredith could be an aspect of his determination to protect them as he had been unable to protect those he had lost. Kane stared into the flames and said "So you sail for the New World?"

"Sometimes we all need to start again." Crowthorn paused to fix Kane's gaze with his. "You might consider joining us, Solomon," he said.

"That is a kind offer. Thank you." Kane was tempted to say nothing further, but he could no longer afford to yield to temptation, nor would it be fair to his rescuers. "Let me be honest with you," he said. "You must know what kind of man you are taking in."

"I think perhaps I know, Solomon."

Kane could have thought that even the kindness was a form of temptation. "I have done terrible things," he said.

"Cruel things beyond description. I am – " As he lifted his hands to indicate himself he wakened traces of the pains his refusal to defend himself against the robbers had left him. "I was," he dared to say instead, "an evil man."

"The Lord speaks of redemption and forgiveness, Solomon."

Kane yearned to feel protected, safe in the firelight surrounded by the family and by their faith. "But my soul is damned," he said as the fire flared up. It failed to relieve the vast darkness around him; it only suggested what might await him there. "Satan's creatures will take me," he said, "should I stray from the path of peace."

"Then do not stray, Master Kane." Crowthorn's eyes seemed to fasten on the light and render it as steady as his gaze. "Do not stray," he repeated, and for that moment Kane was sure that the Crowthorns could keep him on his chosen path.

TWELVE

"Captain Kane."

It was a form of address that he might have hoped never again to hear. The last man to use it Kane had shot in the back, and every other memory it awakened seemed to be tainted with blood. The voice was not a man's, however. It was Meredith's, and perhaps it was even capable of purging the words of their taint of evil.

She was riding in the front of the wagon beside Edward while Kane walked ahead with the horses. The exercise invigorated him, and the open fields on either side showed him no danger. The last few hours had felt like a promise of peace. A few snowflakes were abroad under the pale sky, and one touched the fading bruise on his forehead, a hint of chill that instantly melted away. Kane let the horses overtake him and turned to look up at Meredith. "Yes, miss," he said.

She had been sewing, and looked suddenly embarrassed as she displayed the results. "I made these clothes for you," she said and hesitated until Edward glanced at her. "As your others are so…" she said, and nothing else.

"So what, miss?" Kane said.

"I thought…" Perhaps she was abashed by his attention and Edward's. "As your others were so worn," she said with an effort that turned her cheeks prettily colourful, "I thought you might like these."

Edward watched her hand Kane the bundle, and Kane thought he saw approval in the young man's eyes. Perhaps it was just for the Puritan clothes, a dark tunic and shirt. "Thank you, miss," he said.

"Let us find a sheltered place to take our repast, Edward," William called from pacing behind the wagon, "and then Solomon may don his new attire."

"We are coming to a river," Edward said.

Kane saw only a line of trees in the distance ahead. Edward had the better vantage, and Kane had to hope that he was vigilant – surely he would be alert for danger when he had lost two people dear to him. Nevertheless Kane redoubled his watchfulness as the landscape grew less open. Snow had begun to fly across the fields, but not so thickly that it interfered with his view. Soon he saw water glinting between the trees. He strode ahead of the wagon, and the river seemed to raise its breathless voice to greet him.

Both banks were thinly forested, and he made sure they were deserted. As soon as the wagon trundled to a halt beside the water Katherine and her younger son climbed down from the back. "Here is your dressing-chamber, Master Kane," Katherine said.

Kane hoisted himself into the wagon as Meredith and Edward left it. He dragged his torn shirt over his head with scarcely a twinge from his bruises. The one that had empurpled his chest was barely visible now among the symbols that covered his skin. He took a moment to imagine that eventually those might fade too, if there came a time when he no longer needed their protection, but he could not afford to feel safe. However comforting it was to be surrounded by the family, he had to remember that he might bring peril upon them. He dressed quickly and stepped down from the wagon.

Meredith smiled at him, but mostly to herself. "Now there's a fine figure of a man," Katherine said. "Don't you think so, William?"

"Better than those rags you were wearing, Master Kane. There's no doubt of that."

Kane saw Meredith permit herself another smile and knew that William had conveyed more praise than his words seemed to contain. "So I meet with your approval?" Kane said.

"Finally you are respectable," Katherine told him.

Kane did his best to match her humour, but his words defeated him. "It has been a long time since anyone said that of me."

He bowed his gratitude to Meredith and for the first time heard her laugh. The sound was as liquid and spontaneous as the ripples of the water. He was bowing again to revive it when Edward intervened. "Enough of this vanity," he said. "Let us eat and press on. We still have far to go."

Snow had begun to sift between the trees on a rising wind. Kane joined the family as they gathered in the shelter of the wagon while Katherine handed out portions of bread and cheese. As soon as all were served William said "Edward, grace if you will."

"Please, allow me." Besides his need for prayer, Kane's sense of belonging among the family prompted him to speak. William extended a hand in agreement, but when Edward said nothing Kane spoke only to him. "With your permission?"

"As you will," Edward said.

Kane seemed to have won his approval, however grudging and conditional, and Samuel appeared to be content for Kane to lead the prayer. Perhaps he was secretly glad that Kane was ousting his brother. Kane bowed his head and put his hands together, gestures that brought many words to the brink of his lips. He had undertaken to pray, not to confess or to petition for his soul, and so he uttered the simplest prayer he could. "Lord," he said, "we offer thanks for the blessing you give us in these ill-favoured times. And I offer you my thanks for delivering me from my own darkness and into the arms of this family. Amen."

"Amen," the family responded, and everyone looked up. Meredith's and Katherine's eyes were moist, and there was puzzlement in Samuel's. William's had grown sombre with sympathy, but it was impossible to tell what thoughts had darkened Edward's. "Thank you, Master Kane," William said.

The wind dropped as they finished the simple meal. A few unhurried snowflakes met Kane as he made his way back to the road, followed by the wagon. A crow that he had failed to notice in the trees gave a harsh cry that he could have taken for a signal, but there was no audible response. His having overlooked the presence of the crow made Kane glad to return to the open, even beneath the sunless sky. The sun seemed no more than a memory, and he could have thought the land was in the grip of some force more deathly than winter.

Edward was driving the wagon, but the rest of the family had elected to walk. William and Katherine followed the wagon while Samuel and Meredith stayed close to Kane. He heard the boy murmuring to his sister before Samuel caught up with him. For some paces they walked in silence, and then Samuel said "Are you going to come to America with us?"

"I'm not sure, Samuel."

The boy almost managed to hide his disappointment. "Why?" he said.

"Because you and your family are beginning a new life," said Kane, "and I need to undo my old one."

"You could be captain of the ship we sail on," Samuel urged him. "You voyaged with Admiral Drake."

"I am sure it will already have a captain, Samuel."

"You could give him your advice," Samuel said stubbornly. "He may not have been at sea as long as you have."

"I am certain he will deliver all of you safely to your destination." As the boy seemed about to protest afresh Kane said "Just as you are guided by your family, Samuel."

For whatever reason, this silenced the boy. The only sounds were hoofbeats on the packed earth of the road and the creaks of the axles and the constant muffled rumble of the wheels. As Kane glimpsed a thin dark cloud beyond the frostbound fields, Samuel rediscovered his voice. "Those men who hurt you..."

"What of them, Samuel?"

"You could have killed them if you wanted, couldn't you?"

"If I had wanted." Kane might have let Samuel believe that, but the truth would not be quelled. "There was a time," he said, "when I would have cut their hearts out of their chests while they still beat with life."

This was plainly more than the boy had expected to hear, and he fell back a pace. Kane hoped he had conveyed a lesson, but he was glad that most of the family had been out of earshot. Having regained his pluck, Samuel overtook him once more. "Would you fight me?" he said.

"If you persist in your questions I might," Kane replied with a laugh.

He was striding onwards towards the dark cloud, which

he thought he had identified as smoke from a chimney, when the boy dodged to the hedgerow alongside a field and disentangled a stick from the twigs. "Fight me now," he said, poking Kane with the stick.

It found the bruise on Kane's chest, but the ache no longer troubled him. "I have no reason to fight you, young man," he said.

The boy ran to Meredith and grabbed her around the waist, flourishing his stick. "Stop it, Samuel," she said, but with an indulgent smile.

"Now you have a reason, Solomon," the boy called. "You must help save this beautiful maiden from me."

"Help, Solomon," Meredith cried. "Save me or I shall be lost forever."

A horse snorted and whinnied. "Don't scare the horses," Edward objected.

It was only play, thought Kane, and strode ahead to find a stick on the verge of the road. He lifted it with the toe of his boot and kicked it deftly into his hand, spinning it several times before he turned to Samuel and parried his thrust. He could have snatched the stick from the boy's grasp with a flick of the wrist, but he was careful just to deflect Samuel's attempts to prod him. "I knew you'd fight if you had to," Samuel told him.

Meredith clapped her hands at the spectacle, and her parents watched in amusement. Even Edward seemed to find no cause for disapproval. He leaned forward in his seat, and then his gaze rose beyond the combatants. "Dear Lord," he said, and "Father."

He reined the horses to a stop as Crowthorn hurried past them to stare ahead. "Samuel, get back to the cart," he said. "Go on." The boy retreated unwillingly to the wagon, and Kane saw a black shape flutter up above the road. The way led to a village, where the shape swooped purposefully down and was lost to sight. Kane preferred not to speculate on its purpose. The cloud he had seen was indeed smoke, but not from any chimney. Even at that distance he could see that the village was a blackened shell.

THIRTEEN

As the men came abreast of the outermost cottages a fragment of oily blackness rose into the air as though to greet them. It drifted towards the wagon, which was halted several hundred yards beyond the remains of the village. Samuel waited beside the horses, murmuring to them as one gave an uneasy snort and pawed the bare earth of the road. His mother and Meredith stood together in front of him, and Kane thought they hoped to block his view. He would have liked to think they saw as little as Samuel did.

The village had consisted of a handful of buildings gathered around a green, but every one had been destroyed. Nothing remained on either side of the uneven road except blackened skeletons of cottages – timber remnants gnawed by flames and scaly with charring. Even the earth around the ruins had been seared black. Might the village have been plundered and then burned to the ground? Kane had heard no rumours of marauders, but he was about to question his companions when he saw an object in the remains of a doorway. It had been a villager, and the sight filled Kane's mouth with a sour taste of evil. Far worse had befallen the village than a raid.

The man was sprawled across the threshold with his legs still in the road. The heat that seized him had been so fierce that it was impossible to distinguish his peeling skin from the shreds of his garments. Kane wondered if the corpse had been distorted by the heat, given the awkwardness of its position, but then he saw that the man had twisted his torso around in a desperate attempt to fend off whatever was pursuing him. The arms were still outstretched, and the fingers were charred to the bone. Might an agonised spasm have contorted the body as well? The mouth was gaping in a grimace, however nearly lipless, and the eyes must have expressed outrage too. But the eyes had been seared from the head.

Now that Kane had noticed one corpse he saw them everywhere. Some of the villagers had sought refuge in their cottages, where they were almost indistinguishable from the rubble. Some had died in the street as they fled. One man's hands had gouged furrows in the hard earth before his fingers were reduced to blackened bones. Another had perished clutching at his face, with which the heat had melded the remains of his hands as his body clenched itself. Kane could identify the bodies of women only by the children they had died trying to protect, because the women's skulls were charred as bald as any man's. The children were the worst, their small shrivelled bodies not merely clasped in their mothers' arms but literally inseparable from them. Every child was eyeless. "Who could have done this?" Edward muttered almost too low to be heard.

The question seemed to release the men from a silence that the devastation had imposed on them. "The Devil has been here," William said in a voice quiet enough for church.

Kane thought it did indeed resemble a vision of Hell: the tortured bodies, the stenches of charred wood and rubble and worse, the heat that still lurked on every side, parching his breaths and turning his throat raw.

William's remark sent Edward to his knees in the road, to raise his voice in prayer. "Holy Father…"

As though in response to his entreaty, a crow flapped up from the heart of the village. Kane preferred not to wonder how it might have been busy until it had been disturbed. He heard more wings fluttering ahead, and strode towards them, only to halt. "No," he said, "not the Devil."

In the middle of the green, surrounded by a patch of blackened grass, a stake protruded from the top of a pyre. While the lower section of the heap of fuel had been partly consumed, the stake was undamaged. "There was a witch," Kane said.

William advanced to stand by him. Not for the first time since entering the village, he made a sign of the cross. "There was a burning," Kane told him, "but the creature must have broken loose."

A dull glint drew his attention to the top of the pyre. A heavy chain was coiled like a serpent around the foot of the stake. So the intended victim's bonds had not burned through. "We should leave," said Kane.

Edward abandoned his prayer and stumbled to his feet, hurrying to join his father. "We cannot leave these people to the crows," he protested.

Kane disliked the prospect, but had Edward forgotten his young brother and the women? "We can do nothing for them, Edward," Kane said. "The witch may still be here."

Edward folded his arms and faced him. "They must be given a Christian burial," he said, and his mouth had grown firm.

"My son," William said, "you are a constant reminder of our duties."

"It must be done by nightfall," said Kane. Given the

state of the bodies, it seemed a daunting task. He was staring about at the ruins, to make sure if he could that the creature responsible was not concealed among them, when Meredith called "Is someone there?"

Her voice was closer than it ought to be. Kane turned to find that she had ventured as far as the edge of the village while Samuel and their mother lingered near the wagon. Meredith was peering into the remains of one of the outermost cottages. As Kane and his companions hurried to her, she stepped through the charred doorframe and picked her way across the rubble. "What is it, Meredith?" said Edward.

She was stooping in the middle of the ruin. She had found a woman's body, Kane saw. It appeared to be less affected by the fire than the others he had seen; even the clothes were largely intact. In a moment he realised that the corpse was not alone. A child clung to it, her face against the dead breast, and she had just stirred, however slightly. Meredith murmured words too soft for Kane to hear and touched the child's shoulder.

The girl raised her face, which was rounded and plump, grubby with soot and gap-toothed. She appeared to be about eight years old. She wore a cap like Meredith's, but it was discoloured with smoke. For a moment she gazed up at Meredith as if she hardly knew where they were or who she was herself. Then awareness seemed to flood her eyes, and she screamed at the top of her voice, sending crows flapping into the air all around the village. "The witch is here!" she cried. "The witch!"

FOURTEEN

"Keep the fire well stoked, Edward," his father said. "We must keep the shadows at bay tonight."

Kane wondered if he meant to speak of evil or just to reassure. They had left the ruined village as far behind as they had been able to travel before the night overtook them. Even Edward had despaired of the task of burying the villagers in the hours of daylight that remained, but he had insisted that each corpse should be protected by a cross composed of sticks taken from the pyre. Now the family and their companions were camped in a glade within a natural grove at some distance from the road. No doubt William had chosen the location because it gave them cover, but Kane doubted that it would conceal them from the destroyer of the village if it should come to find them.

He felt as though some aspect of the blackness that had overwhelmed the village had already followed them. Perhaps it was observing them from beyond the trees, where he heard the occasional flutter as if the night were a nest. He stayed close to the trees, alert for any hint of an approach out of the darkness, while the Crowthorns gathered about the child. She was seated between Meredith and Katherine, wrapped in a blanket and drinking from a bowl of broth. The women were intent on her needs, while Samuel watched her with all the curiosity of youth, but it was William who uttered the question that concern for her state had left unspoken till now. "Can you tell us what happened, child?" he said.

The firelight trembled, and a swarm of shadows blurred the child's face. "Let the poor girl be, William," his wife said.

The girl took a last sip and lowered the bowl. Wiping her mouth with the back of her hand, she gazed up at William. She looked like a child in the bosom of her own family now that Katherine had bathed away the soot and grime. "They tried to burn a witch," she said.

The flames in the midst of the clearing seemed to leap up at her words. As the light flickered over the edge of the glade, the trees appeared to inch stealthily forward, closing in. Though the girl's voice was stronger and steadier than Kane would have expected, Katherine and Meredith moved closer to support her. "People came to watch her die," she said.

Kane heard a twig snap. It was in the fire, but it sounded too much like a hint of the presence of an intruder. He felt as if the girl's words were attracting what they named, and he wished that William had refrained from questioning her while it was dark. For herself, she seemed untroubled by the darkness. "The flames didn't hurt her," she said, and the fire touched off a reminiscence of them in her eyes. "She came down from the stake and said now all the Devil's children were free to walk the earth."

Shadows shifted restlessly among the trees, where Kane could have thought the diabolical army she had conjured up was massing. Even if he was able to master his fancies, he still had a sense of evil looming somewhere close by in the dark. "Then she killed everyone who came to watch," the girl said. "She burned out all their eyes because they did."

As Meredith and Katherine each put an arm around her, Samuel said "Didn't you?"

"Hush, Samuel," his mother urged.

The boy looked abashed, and Edward said "We should pray."

Samuel shuffled onto his knees at once, setting an example to someone younger than himself. Meredith and Katherine let go of the child to fold their hands. Katherine nodded at the child's idle ones, but the girl let them sprawl apart. "I'm tired," she complained.

"Take just a few moments to pray," Katherine said.

"I don't want to pray!" The child's voice was suddenly close to a screech. "I'm so tired," she whined, and her face sagged until it seemed in danger of losing its shape with exhaustion.

"Prayer will bring you peace, child," Edward insisted, "and then you will sleep."

"Please," the girl cried, and appealed to Meredith. "You can see I'm tired, can't you?"

"Of course you must be," Meredith said and made to stand up. "Let's find a place for you to sleep, you poor thing."

As the girl smiled and hugged her tight, the flames sprang high and then crouched low. They awakened prancing shadows among the trees before they drew the darkness closer all around the people in the glade. Kane ignored it, because he was in no doubt where the blackest darkness lay. "Edward," he said, "I think the child should wear your cross for protection tonight. Would you mind?"

"Of course not." Edward had seemed defeated by the girl's refusal to pray, but now he was certain again. He lifted the plain wooden cross on its cord from around his neck. "Here," he said.

Kane took the cord in his fist and paced over to the girl, who peered up at him and huddled against Meredith. "Here, child," he said. "Wear this tonight."

The flames leapt, and shadows dodged among the trees before growing very still. The silhouette of the cross swelled up and shrank as it settled on Meredith. The girl was gripping Meredith's left hand in both of hers. "I don't want to," she said.

Kane stooped towards her, dangling the cross. Its shadow almost found her before she sidled away, still clutching Meredith's hand. "It will help to keep you safe," Kane said.

"No," the child whined and turned to Meredith. "I don't want to," she pleaded.

"Solomon, stop it," Meredith protested. "Can't you see she's frightened?"

Kane glimpsed doubt in Edward's eyes – perhaps in his father's too. "Who would fear a cross?" Kane said.

Without warning, the girl moved. She snatched one hand away from Meredith's, and for that instant Kane could have thought he was mistaken – that the child was about to take the cross. Instead she turned Meredith's hand palm upwards and swiftly traced a sign on it with her fingertips. Meredith flinched and pulled her hand free. "What did you do?" she cried in shock and pain.

The girl reared up and hissed like a snake in her ear. "It's you he wants," she whispered so shrilly that the sound seemed to reach the edge of the glade.

As Meredith recoiled, Kane dropped the cross into the child's open hand. A convulsion seized the small body, and the girl writhed away from him with a snarl. Her eyes glared wildly, no longer just with the reflection from the fire. As she tried to dart past Kane he grabbed her, still holding the cross by its cord. "This is her!" he shouted.

"This is the witch!"

His captive squirmed like a reptile in his grasp, and in moments he was no longer holding a child. The plump face lengthened and relinquished its colour, turning grey and rough as ancient stone. The eyes grew large and red-rimmed, and the nose sharpened to a cruel beak above a widened sneering mouth. The body he was struggling to restrain seemed to be composed mostly of muscle and bone. Its long nails clawed at Kane's neck and were reaching for his eyes before he managed to pinion the arms. Even then he could not match its inhuman strength. It tore itself free and leapt away from him, into the air. "The Devil is waiting for you, Solomon Kane!" it screamed in glee.

It sailed above him like a monstrous predator, its wild hair streaming, tattered clothes flapping. In a moment the flapping separated into fragments, because the body had. The black silhouette broke apart into a flock of crows that swooped into the night – thirteen of them. Their triumphant cawing faded into the distance, and then Kane was alone with the family that had accepted him.

FIFTEEN

The day was not long – just a few hours of dull sunless light between one darkness and the next. Kane and the Crowthorns had been travelling throughout most of it with very little rest, and yet he felt as if they might as well have stayed in the ruined village. More than once they saw the smoke of burning houses far away across the fields, and Kane could not have said how many times he had been troubled by the harsh calls of crows, although perhaps he was alone in hearing them. Worse than the notion that the witch and creatures like her might be lurking anywhere around him in some altered form, no matter how open the landscape, was his sense of having brought down evil on the family that had rescued him. They had heard the witch name him, and yet none of them had questioned him. Perhaps their faith would not allow them to believe that evil could triumph, and Kane could only pray that it would keep them safe.

He was trudging behind the wagon, having stood guard for most of the night. Meredith and Samuel were seated at the back. Meredith glanced at her brother to see that he was intent on the flat whitened landscape they were leaving behind, and then she sneaked a quick look at the palm of her left hand. The mark that the witch had left there might have been a stain of soot, but its blackness seemed somehow to resist the muffled daylight. Meredith frowned at it and closed her hand as if she found it somehow shameful. When she raised her eyes to find Kane watching her he did his best to appear reassuring. He was wondering what he could say that might ease her fears when he heard voices ahead.

They did not belong to the Crowthorns, and they were strident with panic. Kane overtook the wagon, which William was driving while Katherine sat beside him, and joined Edward alongside the horses. As William reined the horses in, a band of peasants came into view around a bend in the hedged road – about a dozen in all. Most of them were bruised or bleeding, and one had a child in his arms. Her eyes were big with the terror that Kane saw on every face. "What has happened?" William called as he climbed down from the wagon.

Some of them peered fearfully at him, but they all ignored the question. As the foremost of them crowded past the wagon William appealed to their companions. "What is wrong? What lies ahead?"

The child the man was carrying gave a dismayed cry and hid her face against his shoulder. The man grimaced at William and stumbled onwards at a run, followed by a few stragglers. One was a priest, his hair dishevelled, his collar torn and bloodstained. It was clear that he wanted only to flee, but William caught at his arm. "You must tell me, father," he pleaded. "What has befallen your people? Was it the witch?"

"A witch?" The priest's eyes trembled at a memory. "Dear God," he whispered, "I almost wish it had been."

Unease made Kane's voice harsh. "What, then?"

"The raiders." The priest glanced apprehensively behind him and around him. "They once were men," he muttered.

"And now?" Edward demanded. "Speak, man."

"No human soul looks out through their eyes. No man could revel in such cruelty." The priest's hand shook as he made a sign of the cross, so hastily that it seemed to vanish almost before it was drawn in the air. "They will ravage the land," he cried. "Perhaps they are claiming it for Satan."

"Can no man stand against them?" Edward challenged him.

"The men of the village tried to fight them. These few escaped. Some of their fellows were slain, and some…" The priest raised his hand again but seemed to have no use for it. "They have joined the monstrous horde," he said.

"How can that be?" William protested.

"The leader of the raiders has them in his power. A devil's power." The priest's mouth worked as if it was struggling to find words, unless he was attempting to hold them back. "He hides his face behind a mask, and he is in every one of his followers," he whispered. "He uses their eyes and their voices."

A shudder passed through him from head to foot, and he floundered onwards as though the spasm were compelling him. As he passed the wagon he shouted to Katherine "Turn back while you can."

He stumbled after the remnants of his flock, and Kane heard him attempt to lead them in prayer. As they fled into the distance, darkness seemed to loom over the fields. The air had grown colder, flecked with vicious windblown snow. Meredith and Samuel came forward in the wagon as their mother said "What must we do, William? Can we go on?"

Edward frowned in concern at his sister and their brother. "We must turn back."

"I believe this is the only road that will take us to the

ship," William told him.

"You would never lead us into danger," Katherine said.

"You know I would not. I would lead us to the New World, where all our futures await us."

"But William..." Katherine glanced at Samuel as if she wished he could not hear. "There is evil abroad," she said. "The witch and now these raiders. Might it not be evil that is waiting for us?"

"Then more than ever we need to leave this land." Perhaps William had failed to grasp her meaning, unless he preferred to leave it unremarked. "Solomon," he said. "Can you help us?"

Kane gazed ahead to see that the road forked in the distance. The left branch led westwards. "I will do everything I can. I believe we should turn west," he said and felt as though his destiny was speaking through him.

SIXTEEN

"Solomon," Edward murmured and leaned forward from the wagon in order to keep his voice low. "Are you sure this is the safest way?"

"There is no safe way, Edward." Kane had already been alert, but now he narrowed his eyes against the racing flakes of snow to stare around him. Beyond the trees between which he was leading the horses along a narrow track, the extent of the forest was veiled by windblown snow. At least the storm had laid an icy quiet on the woods, where the only sounds were the creaks of the wagon and the monotonous clopping of hooves on the frozen track. "You must know the Devil is abroad in many forms," Kane said.

He glanced back to find agreement in Edward's eyes but no satisfaction. Beside her son Katherine said "He is speaking of the raiders, Solomon."

"I hope we may slip past them unseen," said Kane. "I believe they may travel from village to village." Too much reassurance was unwise, and he had to say "Be wary all the same. These forests are not without their dangers."

The wagon emitted a sharp creak, which the snowfall ought to muffle before the noise travelled far. Samuel had climbed forward to peer between Edward and their mother. "What kind of dangers?" he said in a bid to sound adventurous.

"None that will harm us, Samuel," his father said behind him.

"Solomon will keep us safe," his mother assured him.

As Kane stared along the track, where the pallor of the snow was holding back the winter dusk, the boy said "Oughtn't we to stop?"

His mother tried to look no more than puzzled. "Why, Samuel?"

"If we stop while it's snowing it will cover our tracks."

"Well thought, Samuel," Edward said. "Would you not say so, Master Kane?"

"Indeed I would," Kane said, pleased not just for the boy but that his brother had praised him. He pointed ahead, where a gentle slope led down to a hollow sheltered by evergreen foliage. "Would that serve, Edward, do you think?"

"It is the choice I would have made myself," Edward told him.

Kane led the horses down the slope and across the hollow, where a stream trickled through the mossy roots of trees outlined by snow. While Samuel unhitched the horses and led them to the water, the rest of the family began to set up camp. Kane went to Meredith as she applied herself to erecting one of the tents. He knew she was proficient at the task, but she seemed untypically awkward now. She was favouring her right hand, and he took hold of the other.

Meredith resisted for a moment and then let him open her hand. Her palm was raw with scrubbing, which had been unable to erase the mark the witch had made. The shapeless blackness had spread, extending twisted tendrils almost to the edge of her small palm. The blotch and its filaments appeared to be embedded in the hand. "Does it hurt?" Kane murmured.

Meredith gazed at the hand as if she hardly recognised it. "I don't feel anything," she said.

A snowflake settled on the blotch, and Kane was dismayed to observe how long it lay there before it began to melt. Meredith shivered and brushed it off her hand. "Why did that creature mark me?" she whispered.

"Evil has its own reasons, Meredith, and only evil knows them." This was hardly reassuring, Kane saw. "Believe me," he said, "there is no evil in you."

"Father says so often there is evil in the world, but I had never seen it before."

She was still gazing at her defaced hand. Kane grew aware that William and Edward had paused in their tasks to watch him and Meredith. "It is my fault you have encountered it now," he said. "It followed me."

Meredith raised her eyes to him. Whatever feelings they contained, pity was uppermost. She might have spoken, but William did. "It may have followed you, Solomon," he said, "but I do not believe it is within you. You should not blame yourself."

"Evil does not hunt evil down," said Edward. "It is all of us who honour God that it is impatient to claim."

Kane wanted to accept this for himself, and saw that Meredith wished to embrace it too. As he kept his peace she asked him "Are we safe?"

"You are as safe as any family can be in this world." This seemed too guarded, and so he vowed "I will do everything within my power to make sure you are." With a surge of energy he set about rigging the tent. "That'll hold a mains'l in a Nor'easter," he declared.

Samuel left the horses to drink while he found wood for the fire. "Bring the biggest pieces if you want soup," William called after him.

Kane stole over to William and took him by the arm,

murmuring "Perhaps you should set only a small fire tonight."

William glanced at the snow that came whirling out of the twilight. "It will be colder by dawn."

"We do not want to attract unwanted attention." Even more quietly Kane said "Yet while I am with you, perhaps you will."

"Then we shall confront it together," William said and grasped Kane's arm.

SEVENTEEN

Even after William took over his watch in the depths of the night, Kane did his best not to sleep. He lay beneath the canvas shelter and listened to the noises of the forest and the camp. Underlying every sound was the constant murmur of the stream. Now and then a horse would snort, its breath steaming like a geyser in the icy air, and more than once Meredith murmured uneasily in her sleep. Sometimes branches creaked, but the sound was always followed by a soft rush and a loose thud as foliage shed its pelt of snow. There were no signs of life outside the camp, not even the fluttering of birds, so that eventually Kane gave up his attempt to watch the pallid dimness through the trees beyond the firelight. He closed his eyes, and for a while he was aware of nothing until a figure loomed over him.

His eyes sprang open as he twisted onto his back. He seized the hand that was reaching for him, and then he saw that the figure silhouetted against the greyish glow of dawn was Samuel. "Solomon," the boy whispered.

He had been eager to take his turn on watch, and his father must have agreed at last. "What is it?" Kane said low.

There was a tinge of excitement in the boy's eyes, but apprehension too. "I heard something," he said.

Kane rose into a crouch beneath the awning. "Where?"

"Beyond the trees," Samuel whispered and pointed past the ashen remains of the fire. "Somewhere over there."

Kane grasped the boy's shoulder to stay him and to communicate his approval. "Wait here, Samuel," he said.

In a very few moments he was out of the camp and swiftly climbing a slope on the far side from the woodland track. By the time he reached the summit he could hear the sounds the slope had concealed – a muffled rumble of wheels, a guttural clamour that might have been of voices. They were several hundred yards away, beyond another rise. He picked his way quickly over the frozen snow to the foot of the ridge and ran as fast as stealth would let him to the further slope. He could hear cries now and, in response to them, shouts that seemed close to bestial. He had almost reached the crest of the ridge when he heard someone behind him.

Samuel was halfway to him. Kane gestured him back, but the boy advanced. As he climbed the icy slope there was nothing in his eyes but determination. "Keep down," Kane murmured urgently, "keep quiet," and fell into a crouch as he gained the top of the ridge.

Even if Kane's warning failed to silence the boy, the spectacle must have robbed him of words. Below the ridge was a track wider than the one the Crowthorns' wagon had taken. Two horse-drawn vehicles were trundling along it – metal cages on wheels. They were full of prisoners packed together so cruelly that some were crushed against the bars. A third prison cart had been halted beside the track while more captives were herded in. Their cries were piteous, but their captors paid no heed, and Kane knew them for the raiders that plagued the land.

They were hulking and brutish, and bald to a man. They were garbed in discoloured leather that only made them look more nearly animal. Their raw lips were drawn back in ferocious grimaces that seemed far too much like the expression of one solitary face, while their eyes were as black as the moon's hidden side – as the eyes of any creatures that might lurk in that unearthly region. Their faces were covered with symbols that Kane recognised as the language of the blackest magic, and the signs were not merely inscribed or even tattooed on the skin. Perhaps they were branded, but he had the unpleasant impression that the livid sigils had overgrown the flesh like some diabolical species of parasite. He crouched lower and grabbed Samuel's shoulder. "Listen to me," he whispered. "Go back to the camp and tell your father we must move out with all speed. And go quietly for all our sakes."

Samuel met his gaze like a man twice the boy's age. In a moment he was sliding down from the ridge, and Kane turned to watch the raiders. The door of the third cage had been slammed and locked, and a raider was slashing with a whip at any hand or arm that protruded through the bars. Some of his fellows snarled hideous threats at the captives or jeered at them as the cart began to rumble along the track. Kane was pacing along the ridge in case the raiders turned towards the Crowthorns when he heard Samuel cry "Solomon!"

Kane whirled around and saw smoke above the glade where the family was camped. He ran down the slope so fast that he was barely able to maintain his balance on the icy earth. He heard cries and brutish shouts, but they were not behind him. The smoke rose to meet him as he sprinted up the further bank. The Crowthorns' wagon was ablaze, and he could have thought the flames were prancing in grim triumph.

At least a dozen raiders had invaded the camp. Two

of them were dragging Meredith backwards to fling her down at the edge of the glade. Her mother threw herself at them, but a thickset raider felled her with a punch to the back of the head and slung her like a sack next to Meredith. William had found a sword and was slashing at several attackers, but they evaded him with mocking ease. Two seized his arms and wrenched them back until the sword dropped from his fist, and a third seized it by the blade to club William to his knees with the hilt. Edward was being punched almost insensible by a raider while two others held the victim's arms. Both men were thrown down beside the women while Samuel watched in dismay from behind a tree halfway down the slope. Kane shouted a warning, but it was too late; a raider whose lividly blemished face was additionally decorated with an eye-patch had captured the boy with a forearm around his throat. "Stop," Kane shouted.

The raiders became still, but not in response to him. Something was approaching through the mist that had risen with the dawn. Kane heard a sound like a victorious drum, which resolved itself into hoofbeats as a shape appeared between the trees. The horse was as black as the eyes of the raiders, and so was the garb of its rider. His hands were hidden by leather gloves, and his face by a mask. Stitches reminiscent of raw flesh crisscrossed the mask, whose mouth was an implacable slit devoid of emotion. While the eyes that peered out of the mask might belong to a man, Kane saw no soul in them; they seemed inhumanly indifferent to the victims of the raid. They gazed at Kane as if he were hardly worth noticing, and then they turned to Samuel as the raider who had captured him flung him down beside his family. "Leave them alone," Kane shouted.

The masked rider spurred his horse forward and reined

it to a halt near the blazing wagon. He merely nodded at the man with the eye-patch, but his minion understood, and Kane had the awful notion that the raiders had just a single evil soul between them. The man hauled Samuel to his feet and dragged him away from his family, into the middle of the glade. The raider's one eye glinted like a snake's at Kane, and so did the eyes within the mask. "Leave him be," Kane yelled and started down the slope.

Nobody else could rescue Samuel. Several raiders stood over the Crowthorns, swords poised to cut them down if they should move. Katherine and Meredith cried out, and William groaned from the depths of his soul while Edward mumbled some prayer, because Samuel's captor had drawn a knife from his belt. The blade was the length of the boy's forearm and serrated along one edge. The other looked sharp as a razor, and that was the edge the man put to Samuel's throat. "Don't you hurt him," Kane shouted.

"Solomon," Meredith pleaded, "help him."

It seemed to Kane that the horseman and his minion were issuing some kind of challenge to him, perhaps for daring to confront them. Otherwise, why had he not been overpowered or slain? He took a pace towards Samuel, but the boy's captor pressed the blade against Samuel's throat, and Kane saw it was close to breaking the skin. He held his ground and strove to fix the horseman's gaze with his. "Listen to me," he said as evenly as he could. "These people are no threat to you. You can see they're Christians. They want only to leave this land."

The eyes in the mask seemed to gleam with malicious amusement, and Kane saw the identical expression in the raider's one eye. Perhaps Kane should not have mentioned Christianity, and he was searching for words when Samuel, inflamed by the bite of the knife or by the treatment of his family, called out "Kill them, Solomon. Kill them all."

Kane thought he glimpsed anticipation in the horseman's eyes, and fancied that the look had appeared in the eyes of every raider. "Don't struggle, Samuel," he urged. "He knows you can do him no harm. I am certain he will let you go."

"Listen to him, Samuel, listen," William cried.

Katherine and Edward and Meredith exhorted him too, but perhaps the boy's plight made him deaf to their advice. "I know you can do it, Solomon," he pleaded. "Kill him!"

"Just be quiet, Samuel," Kane said with a savagery born of desperation, and turned to the rider. "You," he said and glimpsed some kind of response deep in the eyes of the unseen face. "Are you their master? What is it you want?"

The eyes considered him and then found Samuel. The horseman lifted one gloved hand, and Kane was afraid what the gesture might be about to convey. "I'll do anything," he vowed.

The hand closed into a fist with a creak of leather. The raider who held Samuel moved, and Kane grew fearful for the boy, but the man was only lifting his disfigured head. The face overgrown with symbols twisted as if it was straining to adopt a different shape. The man's throat worked convulsively while the solitary ebon eyeball bulged in its socket. The thick greyish lips were distorted by a violent grimace, and blood trickled from one corner. The eye focused on Kane, and the mouth spoke. "Kill me," it said. "Can you?"

The voice was scarcely human. It was deep and harsh and resonant, and seemed to reverberate through the forest. Kane understood at once that it belonged less to the speaker than to the man behind the mask, who had commandeered his minion's body to speak on his behalf. Kane hardly knew which of them to address, but he appealed to the leader. "I cannot," he said. "I am a man of peace."

The rider's eyes were as unresponsive as his mask. Kane heard Samuel attempt to suppress a cry, and turned to see that his captor had pulled the boy's head back by the hair. The family cried out, and Meredith's plea was loudest. "Solomon, stop him!"

Kane dug his fingernails into his palms in an agony of powerlessness. "Don't you hurt that boy," he snarled as though his words might have the force of prayer.

"This boy..." For a grotesque moment the hand that gripped Samuel's hair might almost have been laying a benediction on his head. "This child has more heart than any of you," the voice that had borrowed the distorted mouth declared. "He is the only man here."

Kane saw the horseman lift his gloved hand. The eyes in the mask were blank with indifference, and all at once Kane was filled with dread. "Listen to me," he begged. "A child can be no use to you. Take me instead."

Before he had finished speaking, the emotionless gaze abandoned him. It fastened on Samuel, and the raised fist fell like a hammer. The gesture was weighty enough to drive a nail into a coffin, but its effect was deadlier. In less time than it took Kane to draw a breath, the one-eyed man cut Samuel's throat from ear to ear.

The boy's eyes widened in disbelief that looked very much like betrayal. They were gazing straight at Kane as they dimmed and misted over. The man with the eye-patch held up Samuel's body as if to display it for his master's approval. Once it had twitched its last he let it fall to the frozen earth, where it turned the leaves around it red.

Kane heard cries of horror that fell short of expressing his own. "Oh God," Katherine wept, "my son…" Grief seemed to have separated her from William, who moaned "My boy, oh Samuel…" Edward attempted to pronounce a prayer while Meredith found nothing to say except, in worse than despair, Kane's name. As Kane struggled to find some response, the one-eyed raider spared Samuel's body a glance. "This was the only man here," said the voice that occupied his mouth.

He turned to stare at the Crowthorns with the same detachment that he had applied to cutting Samuel's throat. "Take the marked one," the unnatural voice said. "Kill the rest."

As the raiders guarding the family moved to obey, Katherine cried out to Kane. "Do something," she pleaded. "Help us."

The raiders grew as still as puppets while their masked leader observed him. When Kane took a pace towards the Crowthorns, the one-eyed man stepped into his path and raised the blade stained with Samuel's blood. Kane halted beside the ashes of the dead fire and lifted his eyes heavenwards, stretching his arms wide. He might have been offering himself up as a sacrifice, which was how he felt. "What is it you want of me?" he said, so quietly that only God would have heard him. "Is this all I am to you?"

The sky was hidden by the mist that had overwhelmed the forest, and there might as well have been nothingness above him. The blank expanse at which all the topmost branches appeared to be pointing offered not the least sign of a response. Everyone in the glade might have been holding their breath – everyone but Samuel, who had none to hold. The masked rider's horse snorted and pawed the earth, and the impatient sound seemed to be the nearest to an answer Kane could hope for. "Then so be it," he said.

He lowered his gaze to the man with the knife, who cocked his head as much in mockery as threat. "If I kill you," Kane said, "I am bound for Hell."

The one eye glinted in derision, and the thick lips curled in a sneer. Kane heard one of the Crowthorns whisper what might have been a prayer. "It is a price I will gladly pay," Kane said and advanced on the man with the knife.

The man lumbered to meet him, slashing almost negligently at him. He seemed to view Kane as sport rather than as any kind of danger, and looked ready to linger over despatching his unarmed adversary. Kane sidestepped and, grabbing the man's sword-arm by the wrist, twisted it over his own shoulder and threw all his weight against it. Brawny though the arm was, it snapped at the elbow like a branch. As the man's fingers writhed Kane seized the knife and drove it backwards. He felt it slice deep into flesh and puncture a kidney. He turned the knife in the wound and dragged the serrated edge upwards, sawing open the man's back.

As Kane wrenched the blade free the man toppled to his knees and then fell prone. The nearest of the raiders rushed at Kane, roaring like beasts and brandishing their swords. Their ferocity was feeble by comparison with his. Once again he was the man he had been, but he was no longer impelled by the lust for wealth; he was driven by pure rage. When the first man cut at him with a sword Kane blocked it with the knife, which he drove deep into his assailant's heart. The man staggered backwards, and Kane snatched the sword from him.

He was unstoppable now. A wide sweep of the sword met two men as they ran at him from either side, and cut them both down like a scythe. He parried their companion's sword and dashed it from the man's grasp before chopping into his neck. He hacked at it and hacked again, and the headless corpse fell away from him, gushing blood. More raiders hurled themselves at him, and Kane stepped aside to let the impetus carry one past him, then sliced through the tendon behind the man's left knee. As the man crumpled to the earth Kane slashed open a raider's throat, and the man tottered away, gurgling like a crimson fountain. Another man jabbed viciously at Kane, but Kane avoided the lunge and lopped off the man's hand, which fell to the ground with the sword still in its clutch.

Kane was fighting his way towards the Crowthorns, but not swiftly enough. Two raiders had seized Meredith and, despite her struggles, were hoisting her into the rough embrace of one of their number on horseback. As William made a grab for her, a sword was thrust clean through him, and he collapsed with a despairing groan. Edward cried out with grief and rage, throwing himself on the attacker, but two raiders seized him and flung him on his back so that one of them could plunge a knife into his heart. The sight inflamed Kane's fury, and as more raiders came at him he spilled one man's entrails with his sword and drove the point deep into the chest of another. The blade snagged between the ribs, and he was striving to heave it loose when two men with axes rushed at him.

One of them clubbed him in the stomach with the handle of an axe. The blow doubled him up and sent him backwards to fetch up against a rock at the edge of the glade. He saw the raider on the horse spur it past the remains of the wagon, Meredith sprawling across the animal's back, one brutal hand pinning her down. Kane straightened up with a painful effort, only for his attackers to pinion him against the rock with his arms stretched wide. One man swung his axe up single-handed to split him open.

Kane pressed his spine against the rock and kicked out with all his strength. His boot caught the man in the groin. As the grip on his wrist slackened Kane broke free of it and grabbed the axe before the man could stagger out of reach. He slammed it against the haft of the second raider's weapon with such force that the axe sprang out of the man's hand. Without pausing Kane swung the blade and sliced the raider's belly open. The man floundered away, spilling blood and innards, and Kane sprinted after Meredith's captor.

It seemed that he might overtake the raiders. While the horses that had drawn the Crowthorns' wagon were nowhere to be seen, and all the remaining men were on horseback, they had waited on the track for their master. The masked rider gave Kane a dismissive glance before spurring his horse out of the glade. He might have been inviting Kane to pursue them and, equally wordlessly, deriding the proposal. As Kane dashed past the blazing wagon, the rider urged his steed into a trot – a canter – a gallop.

The other horsemen matched his speed, and the foremost was Meredith's captor. Kane sucked in an icy breath and put his soul into a dash along the track. He was gaining on the riders; in moments he might be close enough to bring the hindmost rider down and take his steed. He saw Meredith struggling helplessly across the back of her captor's horse, and the sight lent him a swiftness that he would never have believed he had in him. The last horseman was almost within reach of a sweep of Kane's sword, and the horse stumbled on a fallen branch that was frozen to the track. It regained its balance, and the rider spurred it faster to keep up with his companions. As Kane managed not to slow down while he filled his lungs with a great breath, the riders drew ahead.

They had reached the mist, which seemed eager to embrace them. Kane's entire body felt like a single ache that had its source in his raw lungs, but he did not slacken his speed. In seconds the horsemen and their steeds were no more than fading silhouettes, and then there was only a receding thunder of hoofbeats. Kane heard Meredith utter a cry that seemed muffled by the murk before the sounds of hooves retreated out of earshot like the last rumble of a storm.

At last Kane stumbled to a halt and stood panting as the mist gathered among the trees around him. The only sounds in the forest might have been the thudding of his heart and his harsh efforts to recapture his breath. His body burned as though it were in the grip of a fever, the taste of which was in his mouth. As he came near to shivering with exhaustion and the chill of the mist he trudged back to the camp.

His first glimpse of the glow of the smouldering wagon put him in mind of a corpse light hovering over a grave. The mist retreated, unveiling the glade strewn with corpses. Samuel's chest was stained with his own blood like an infant's with food, and his face looked almost as youthful. Edward lay near him, hands clenched on the dagger in his chest as if he had died in the act of a last prayer. They were surrounded by the bodies of raiders, a sight that made Kane's gorge rise – and then he saw that more had departed from the raiders than their lives. Their flesh no longer bore the signs of magical subjugation. One man was still alive, but he died as Kane watched. The livid marks disappeared, sinking into his flesh, and his eyes grew blank but human – clear as an empty sky after a storm.

William was resting in Katherine's arms against a tree at the far side of the glade. He was alive, but only just. Although he was scarcely able to raise his head as Kane picked his way through the carnage, his eyes fought off their dimness to focus on him. "Solomon," he said in a low but fierce voice that might have been reaching up from the depths of his soul. "Get her back."

Kane made to take the hand that was not in both of Katherine's. "I will," he said.

"No." Perhaps William had failed to hear, unless he found Kane's words insufficiently fervent. "You get her back," he exhorted, seizing Kane by the arm. "Swear this to me now."

The last of his strength was enough to pull Kane towards him. Kane sank to his knees on the frozen leaves, which felt cold and hard as a mosaic. The plea that gleamed in William's eyes filled Katherine's as well. "I swear," said Kane.

"Deliver her from this evil. It will be – " William clutched harder at Kane's arm as if he were clinging to a raft in the midst of a flood. "It will be your redemption," he said.

"Listen to him, Solomon," Katherine whispered.

"These are my last words. I know God in Heaven hears them." William's gaze was fixed on Kane, and yet he appeared to be seeing far more – a vision that included Kane. "If you save our child," he said, "if you do this…"

He coughed, and blood trickled from his mouth. He redoubled his grip on Kane's arm, anchoring himself in another few moments of life. "If you do it," he managed to pronounce, "your soul will be saved. I know it to be true."

Kane yearned to believe him, and it seemed to him that William was experiencing a vision he had earned with his life. "Now swear to me that you will find her," William said, though he scarcely had the breath to speak. "Swear it, Solomon."

"I swear I will find her," Kane said with all his soul.

He never knew if William had heard. As the grasp relaxed on his arm and fell away, Kane laid a gentle hand on William's face to close the sightless eyes. The gesture seemed to waken Katherine from her grieving trance. She lifted the chain of the locket from around William's neck and handed it to Kane. "Go now. Find her," she said.

Kane could tell it was as passionate a prayer as Katherine had ever uttered. He strode from corpse to raider's corpse, gathering weapons – swords, knives, a brace of pistols, a pouch of gunpowder. He found shot for the pistols and loaded them before thrusting them into his belt. His search had brought him close to the entrance of one of the tents, and he glanced back at Katherine, who nodded as she cradled her husband's body. "Whatever you need is yours," she said almost too softly to be heard.

Kane stooped into the tent to retrieve William's cloak. He swung it about himself and then clapped Edward's conical buckled hat on his head. He was uniformed as a Puritan at last, and his weapons made him an avenger. A splash of crimson on the blanched ground caught his eye. It was Meredith's shawl, cast down like a challenge. As he tied it about his waist, he could have fancied that he was wearing her colours to a tournament. All he required was a steed, and in a moment he heard a muted whinny and the sound of hooves. A saddled horse, which must have been ridden by one of the raiders, had appeared out of the mist on the track.

Kane mounted it and wheeled it to face Katherine. Her arms were around William, her cheek pressed against his.

For a moment her gaze found Kane. "God go with you," she whispered and turned her eyes back to William. She was as motionless as her husband when Kane glanced at them from the track, and the mist swallowed them as Kane rode to meet his fate.

EIGHTEEN

Before Kane had ridden far along the track he heard hoofbeats ahead. He urged the horse faster and peered into the mist, from which tree after dripping tree advanced to meet him. While there was no sign of the riders, the sound of hooves was growing louder. He was not overtaking his quarry. More than one of the horsemen had turned back to deal with him.

As they rode out of the mist they spurred their horses to either side of the track, drawing swords to cut Kane down. He drummed his heels against his horse's ribs and sent it galloping between the riders. He had a pistol in each hand. The moment he came abreast of the riders he discharged both weapons, and the men were dashed to the ground in a flurry of leaves. Kane did not even glance at them as he rode at all speed down the track. Although he strained his ears and held his breath, he could no longer hear any hoofbeats ahead.

Had the riders turned aside to lose him? He cursed the mist that might be hiding them. He could only follow the track for want of any other. Was that a distant sound of hooves or just the pounding of his heart? Surely the noise was ahead of him, where the mist appeared to be thinning. So were the trees, and seconds later he was in the open.

The forest had given way to moorland. The greater part

of the mist stayed among the trees. Enormous slabs of mossy rock and expanses of heather sparkling dully with frost stretched to the horizon. The moor was a labyrinth of paths, but Kane did not hesitate. A horseman was riding westwards, carrying a girl who lay across the back of his steed.

He did not look around until Kane began to narrow the distance between them. His horse must be exhausted; it was unable to outrun Kane's, even when the rider drove his spurs into its sides and then raked them through the flesh. In minutes Kane had halved the distance, and in another he was closer still. The horseman jerked the reins cruelly to direct his steed towards a stone circle that stood in the midst of the heath. Perhaps he thought the ancient weathered stones might retain some pagan magic that would protect him from vengeance, unless he was so desperate to take refuge that the incomplete circle looked like cover. He rode onto the patch of frozen grass encircled by the stones and reined the horse around to face Kane, who stayed at the edge of the circle. "Give me the girl," Kane told him.

The black eyes flickered like a lizard's, and the livid symbols around the raider's mouth seemed to twist it into a grimace. Kane thought the man might attempt to flee or, worse, to injure Meredith. He began to ride around the perimeter of the circle, so fast that the raider could not turn to keep him in sight. "Give her to me," Kane said so harshly that it was clear he would use no more words.

Perhaps the rider was as fatigued as his steed, which stood panting and dribbling foam. He raised the hand that was planted in the small of the girl's back and shoved her off the horse. She fell to the earth with a gasp and drew in all her limbs, covering her face with her hands. Kane dismounted and hurried to her. "Meredith," he murmured, brandishing his sword to keep the horseman well away. "If she has been harmed…"

She flinched when he took her gently by the shoulder. He had to hold her more firmly and start to help her to her feet before she would take her hands away from her face. He had after all not recognised her long dark dishevelled hair and sombre clothes. The girl was not Meredith.

She recoiled as Kane strode away from her to seize the rider by the throat. Before the man could find a weapon Kane dragged him out of the saddle and flung him to the ground, knocking all the breath out of him. "Where is she?" Kane demanded.

"There," the man panted, jabbing a thick finger towards the girl. "You have her."

Kane let him stumble to his feet before he hit him. The man's face felt swollen and misshapen, and put Kane in mind of fungus. "That is not her," Kane said through his teeth. "Where is the girl you took from our camp?"

The man wiped blood from his split lip and turned a coaly glare on Kane. "I don't know."

Kane punched him in the mouth once more and felt rotten teeth yield in their sockets. "Tell me where she is, or I swear by the living God – "

"I don't know," the man protested doggedly and spat blood on the pallid grass. "I don't know you. I was never at your camp."

"I am Solomon Kane." He struck the man a third time. "You know who took her," he said. "They are of your kind. They must have ridden this way."

"We are legion," the raider said, spitting out a tooth as brown and porous as old bone. "We are everywhere in this land."

The girl cried out and hid her face anew as Kane took

his knife from his belt and held the point against the man's cheek beneath the left eyeball. He had a sickened notion that the flesh might split like a toadstool, releasing some substance he would rather not envision. "Tell me what you know," he said under his breath, "or you will never see again. Where will they take her?"

"To our master's castle," the man said as if he were speaking of his god, and licked his bloody lips. "For sacrifice. He needs the blood of such as her."

"Who is your master?" Kane demanded. "The creature who must hide his face behind a mask?"

"Not the Overlord." Fear glimmered in the black depths of the raider's eyes. "The sorcerer," he whispered. "Malachi."

Kane sensed that dread was close to silencing his informant. He pressed the point of the knife against the skin beneath the eye. "Where is this sorcerer's domain?"

"Ride west," the man muttered and struggled to regain his voice. "Ride – "

He choked as though his tongue had withdrawn into his throat like a worm into the earth. His eyes bulged, filling with a deeper blackness. His lips twisted as if the symbols embedded in the flesh were strings that were tugging at them. "Where?" Kane said urgently.

The ebon gaze stayed fixed on him, but all at once he knew that someone else was using the eyes to observe him. The mocking laugh that emerged from the mouth could have been no more unnatural if it had been uttered by a statue. It was followed by the voice of the creature that had slain Samuel. "Solomon Kane," the enormous thick voice said, and the swollen lips writhed into a mirthless grin. "Will you play the torturer?"

"I will do what I must to find the girl," vowed Kane.

"You may carve the flesh from this worthless body."

The raider spread his arms wide as though to parody a crucifixion. "But it will not tell you what you want to know. I will not let it," the voice said.

The eyes seemed delighted not just at his predicament but with the helplessness of the raider. "What in God's name are you?" Kane demanded.

"I am nothing in your God's name," the man declared and grinned viciously at him.

A movement in the sky distracted Kane. More than a dozen crows were circling against the sullen clouds that hid the sun. They might have been hovering to form an unholy halo for the figure below them – a horseman watching from the crest of a rise on the moor. Though it was hundreds of yards distant, Kane knew that its face was concealed by a mask. Its voice was directly in front of him. "Your quest for the girl will only lead you into darkness," it said.

Kane saw that darkness eyeing him. "I will find her," he said like an oath.

"Not before her life is taken." As Kane held back from slashing the man's face in response, the eyes gleamed in anticipation. "To free the demon sent to claim you," the voice relished telling him.

Kane snatched the blade away and turned towards the distant horseman. "I will hunt you down," he shouted, "and send your black heart back to Hell!"

"I have no heart." It was still the man within arm's length who spoke. He gave a laugh that spilled blood from his mouth. "Nor do you," he said.

The Overlord wheeled his horse around and rode westwards at a gallop, accompanied by the crows, which cawed as they flocked above him. As though invisible strings that bound him to the puppeteer had snapped, the man in the stone circle jerked and twitched like a victim of a fit before crumpling to the earth. A final spasm doubled up his body and released it, and then the blackness drained from his eyes, leaving them dead but human. As the skin absorbed the symbols that marked it, Kane heard a muffled sob. The girl had watched the transformation, covering her mouth to stifle her dismay. Kane took a pace towards her, but she scrambled backwards. "I mean you no harm, child," he murmured. "You are safe."

He faltered for a moment as he recalled assuring Meredith that he would keep her and her family safe. Meredith would be; that was his destiny now. "The beast is gone," he told the girl.

She risked a doubtful glance at the prone body. "Is it dead?" she whispered.

"I promise you it is." Kane removed his cloak and offered it to her, and she allowed him to drape it around her shoulders. "Are you injured?" he said.

She rose to her feet, wincing a little. "No," she said with a touch of defiance.

Kane smiled at her bravery but desisted when she frowned at him. "What is your name?" he said.

"Elizabeth Bracewell," said the girl, defiantly still.

"I am Solomon Kane, Elizabeth."

She seemed scarcely to hear him. She limped to the edge of the stone circle, staying well clear of the body on the grass, and gazed across the empty moor. "I want to go home," she said.

Kane saw that her bravado was a way of fending off the truth of her situation. He stood next to her between the broken stones and made to take her arm. "You should rest," he said.

Elizabeth moved beyond his reach and peered about at the moorland paths as if she imagined that her way might reveal itself somehow. A chill wind came to greet her, shivering the crystallised heather. "No, I want to go home," she said, sounding younger than her years.

"Child…" Kane put a gentle arm around her shoulders. "They leave none alive," he murmured. "There is no home for you to return to."

For a moment she struggled against his support and the knowledge. Then a great sob shuddered through her, and she was overwhelmed by tears. Kane held her for a long time before her sobs grew intermittent and she began to gulp for breath. He was seeing Meredith's family slaughtered once more, and his own failure to protect them. When he sensed that Elizabeth was trembling with cold as well as grief he led her into the shelter of the largest standing stone. "You must have something to sustain you," he said.

The horses had already found a nearby stream. Kane laid the body of the raider out of the girl's sight in a hollow on the moor some way from the stones. He spoke a brief prayer and then set about collecting fuel to build a small fire. Before long Elizabeth came to help him. Among the contents of his saddlebag were the makings of a broth, which was lukewarm by the time he served it to Elizabeth. He waited until she appeared to have recovered some of her stubborn courage, because he had to question her. "Tell me what you know of the raiders," he said.

"They came from the west." Elizabeth's gaze ranged nervously about the moor, but she must be unable to orient herself beneath the concealed sun. "There were just a few at first," she whispered, "but more and more came. It was like a plague."

It seemed to Kane that the land might indeed be cursed as Egypt once had been – rendered barren by the implacable winter, robbed of sunlight and infested by the raiders. "Go on, child," he said.

"They came to our village. That masked one brought them." She glanced uneasily towards the distant cawing of a crow. "Some of our men chose to join them. If they didn't," she said as though she felt bound to defend people whom she must have known all her life, "they were killed or taken away."

Her eyes grew blank, attempting to shut out the memory, unless they were trapping it within her. "It is over now," Kane murmured. "Put your trust in God."

He saw a plea in her eyes before she voiced it. "Can anyone fight this evil?"

Kane felt as if he were renewing his vow, on her behalf as well as Meredith's. "I can," he said.

He left Elizabeth to finish her broth while he led the horses back from grazing, and was unsurprised to find her asleep beside the remains of the fire. He distributed the provisions between the saddlebags of the horses, and then he loaded a pistol and laid it on the ground next to Elizabeth together with shot and a bag of powder. He straightened up, only to stand protectively over her. Every moment he lingered might be endangering Meredith, but he turned away burdened by doubt. He was leading his horse out of the stone circle when Elizabeth stirred and awoke. She struggled to her knees, throwing off Kane's cloak that she had wrapped around herself. "What are you doing?" she pleaded.

"I have left you half the provisions," Kane said. "Do you know how to use a pistol?"

"Why?" Elizabeth said before her eyes filled with awareness that looked painfully close to renewed grief. "Are you leaving me?"

"I must, Elizabeth." Kane returned to her and went down on one knee before her. "You cannot come where I am going," he said. "I am bound westwards."

Defiance reawakened in her eyes, and a yearning for protection too. "When you have rested take the horse and ride east," he said, pointing in the direction opposite to that the Overlord had taken. "Find a church and beg sanctuary."

He saw Elizabeth discover some resolve within herself. The sight both heartened him and made him feel shamefully inadequate. "May God protect you," he said and touched a sign of the cross to her forehead.

As he stood up, Elizabeth rose too and held out the cloak to him. "You will need this more than me," she said.

Kane accepted it wordlessly, moved by her determination. When he mounted his horse Elizabeth stayed within the stone circle, as though on some atavistic level she felt that it might help to keep her safe. "What are you going to do?" she asked him.

Kane gave her a grim smile that he hoped would add to her fortitude. "I'm going hunting," he said.

NINETEEN

When the man beside Meredith lolled against her yet again she knew he was dead. She risked a glance at him and saw that his bruised and bloody head had fallen back, raising his empty gaze heavenwards. God had taken him, she thought. All the same, she pushed the corpse away, lodging it in one corner of the cage. Its left hand dangled through the bars, and one of the raiders cut at the fingers with a whip before seeing they were lifeless. He emitted a grunt that might have expressed brutish amusement or dissatisfaction, and his blackened eyeballs turned towards Meredith. For a moment she was both afraid and hopeful that he meant to open the cage and drag her forth. If he did, she vowed, she would elude him – elude all of them and run wherever she could hide. But the discoloured gaze strayed away from her as though there was very little of a brain behind it, and the hulking creature recommended trudging beside the cart as it lurched over the uneven track through the forest. Meredith could only bide her time and put her trust in God.

Her father used to say that they would never fully understand God's purpose for them until they were granted a sight of Him. She prayed her father and the rest of her family had that now – the knowledge and the reward of being in God's presence. She wanted to believe that they might be interceding on her behalf, but was she not setting herself above her fellow captives in the cage? Every human being was meant to be equal in the eyes of God, which seemed to imply that even the raiders must be, if they were still human. She found this hard to grasp, and she had to struggle to remember that until His children were summoned to Him, they should devote their lives to those things that would please Him. She could see nothing anywhere around her that would give pleasure to God – not the bestial men disfigured by occult symbols, not the victims crammed into the cage and moaning with despair or whimpering in pain as the cart jolted over the road, except for those who had been reduced to hopeless silence. Meredith could have imagined that she had been cast into Hell if someone had not been attempting to pray on the far side of the cage. The low voice was silenced by a crack of a whip, but Meredith seized upon the prayer and kept it within herself. Perhaps that was the purpose of their plight – to encourage the devout to immerse themselves in supplication, to concentrate on secret prayers that would bring them closer to God.

In that case, perhaps it was not wrong of Meredith to pray for deliverance. Captain Kane had said that he would do everything in his power to make sure that she and the family were safe. Even if he had failed to protect them, surely God would not prevent him from keeping such a solemn word to her, and might even help him. She peered through the bars at the track. Aside from the raiders who were following the prison cart the road was deserted, and there was no sign of a rider among the trees. A raider grinned evilly at Meredith as he saw that she was hoping to be rescued, unless he had some fouler thought in mind. She raised her eyes beyond the black inhuman gaze and strove to hold on to her faith, in God and in

Captain Kane as well. Then she wondered if her prayers had been answered in some unexpected way, because the cart was slowing down.

She heard shouts and cries ahead. The road was emerging from the forest, beyond which it led into a small village. Most of the raiders marched into the single lane. While they resembled a rabble more than an army, they were united in brutal purpose. As they began to smash their way into the cottages and hunt down villagers in the street, the driver of the prison cart assumed authority over his fellows. "Clear out the dead," he barked.

One raider unlocked the barred door at the back of the cart, and his companion crouched into the cage to drag out the corpse beside Meredith. As he flung it sprawling onto the track she made her bid for freedom. She had reached the doorway before the raider with the key planted a large simian hand between her breasts and shoved her so hard that she fell helplessly against a woman. He prodded Meredith with the handle of his whip to keep her there while his confederate hauled two more corpses from among the prisoners, and then he slammed the heavy door with a clang that reverberated through every bar and set the horses snorting. As he thrust the key into the lock Meredith demanded "Where are you taking us?"

The raiders gazed at her, and the symbols around their mouths seemed to twist them into identical grimaces of contemptuous indifference. As they turned their hulking backs on her she raised her voice. "What do you want of us? What is going to happen to us?"

"Be still, child." The woman into whose arms she had been thrown touched her shoulder. "Make your peace with God," she murmured as she might have comforted a daughter. "It is over for us."

"God does not wish this fate for us," Meredith said fiercely. "He would never leave us in the clutches of the Devil and his creatures. There must be a way out. I know there is."

Their fellow captives looked as if they feared her words would bring the raiders' wrath upon them. "Slavery or sacrifice," the woman whispered, "those are our only ways out. God has abandoned us. He will not deliver us from this."

"He will not abandon anyone who puts faith in Him." Meredith felt her words renewing her own belief. "We mustn't give up," she said. "Take my hand. We shall find the strength to survive this."

A clangour shook the bars against which she was forced to lean, and the vibrations shivered through her spine into her skull. A raider was dragging the flat of his sword across the bars. "Shut your row," he snarled at her.

As the other captives mutely urged her to obey, Meredith heard a woman in the village street. "Please don't," the woman cried and then screamed "No!"

Meredith turned to see the raiders at their evil work. In the irregular space that did duty as a village square, a dozen gibbets had been raised. Men and even boys hung in mid-air, jerking voicelessly as stranded fish while women cried out on their behalf. Raiders were emerging from the cottages with their arms full of provisions, but none of them acknowledged the hanged with so much as a glance. Another dozen victims were lined up on their knees in the square. Women and children and old men had been herded into a corner, some of them burying their faces in their hands. One man bolder than his companions found his voice. "Don't do it," he called to the kneeling men. "Don't join them."

His intervention emboldened a youth in the line, who

shouted along it "Don't, father."

Several raiders were advancing to subdue the protest until another of the men who had been forced to kneel turned to his fellows and then to the other villagers. "What choice is there?" he said, his voice small and alone in the open space beneath the low dull sky. "If we join them they will let the village stand."

He stiffened with his head turned, and the raiders grew as still. A horseman had ridden into the square. Meredith recognised him and clenched her fists fiercely, but only the right one ached. As though in a grotesque demonstration of his power, his great harsh voice emerged from two of his minions at once. "Will you serve the Master?" it said.

More than one of the men on their knees shuddered at the sound, and the man at the right-hand end of the line seemed to feel compelled to speak. "Yes," he stammered.

"Father," his son protested afresh.

The man did not look at him, but lifted his head as the masked rider dismounted and approached him, hands outstretched. Perhaps he imagined that he was about to be raised to his feet, but the hands clamped themselves to his skull. "What are you doing?" he cried in a voice that seemed to be struggling to hold onto its shape.

"To serve us," the monstrous duo chorused, "you have to join us."

"No," the man pleaded, but the hands held him fast. Meredith did not see what overtook him, because the youth who had called to him sprang to his feet. He could have been no older than fourteen. He dashed at the masked figure, snatching out a short blade that had been concealed inside his shirt. "Father," he shouted in an agony of grief.

The figure observed him as he might have watched an insect run towards him. As the boy came within reach, his adversary met him with a great blow of a sword, cleaving his skull open. His father was standing now. His face was a mass of livid symbols, and his eyes had filled with blackness. They betrayed not a flicker of emotion as he watched his son twitch on the cold earth and grow still.

Meredith's soul revolted at the spectacle, and there was something even worse. Three men had apparently been attracted to the village by the sounds of grief and looting: a tattooed man, a deliberately bald one, a third with a braided beard. Tramping past the prison cart, they halted in the square. The masked leader of the raiders turned to scrutinise them and seemed pleased by what he saw – their bulk and their affinity with him. "Will you join us?" his doubled voice said.

The tattooed man strode forward, and the masked figure held out his hands. They closed around the man's head, and Meredith saw tendrils swarm from the fingertips to burrow under the man's skin, forming arcane symbols in the flesh. The man's eyes bulged, flooding with blackness, and his head reared up. He was not struggling to free himself; he was celebrating the transfiguration, thrusting his head against the hands like a pet against its master's. "It's good," he bellowed in a thick transformed voice, and Meredith saw that she was witnessing a kind of blasphemous baptism. In that moment she vowed afresh that she would do whatever was necessary to escape.

TWENTY

As Kane rode across the moor the sky grew prematurely black, and a veil descended to the horizon as though whatever lay beyond it ought not to be seen. The veil was rain, advancing inexorably to meet him. The downpour was so savage that Kane saw rank after rank of shrubs bow down beneath the onslaught while exposed rocks glistened and began to stream. He kept his head high and received the first gust of rain full in the face. He dashed water from his eyes and urged the horse doggedly onwards as shrubs around them creaked with the burden of rain. For minutes he might as well have been blind, and only the instincts of his steed kept horse and rider on the track that the storm was walling off from them. The rain started to relent as they approached the edge of the moor, and by the time they reached it the downpour had slackened to a persistent chilly drizzle. Below him on the sloping land, a prison cart was lumbering along the muddy track.

Kane spurred his horse over the edge and rode fast along the verge of the road. Half a dozen raiders were accompanying the cart, and soon one of them caught sight of him. He and another brute wheeled their horses around and galloped in an explosion of mud to deal with Kane, who warded off their concerted attack and chopped them down without breaking his pace. Three more converged on him, but their assault was haphazard. He ran the first of them through with his sword, and slashed the second raider's neck wide open, and laid the last man's sword-arm bare to the muscle. The guard who had stayed by the cart advanced with brutish stubbornness, but Kane shot him and rode on to cut down the driver of the cart. As the body toppled to the earth Kane seized the reins of the horses and guided the cart to a halt. He dismounted and tramped through the mud to remove the key from the guard's belt and unlock the cage.

It was packed with captives, but he could not see the face he sought. As soon as he heaved the barred door open they began to struggle out, shivering in the drizzle that misted the heath. The first of them clambered down into the mud and stared fearfully about as though expecting their captors to reappear out of the murk. "You are free," Kane told them, but they only blinked at him, afraid to take his word. "Run," he urged, "go now." Their reluctance was frustrating him, and he shouted "Meredith!"

The name brought no response. As Kane helped the prisoners out of the cage he saw all too soon that Meredith was not among them. He reached inside his cloak for the locket that hung around his neck. He remembered William's pride in what it symbolised – remembered the mute plea in Katherine's eyes as she had entrusted the locket to Kane. He showed the portrait of Meredith to the prisoner who was venturing gingerly down from the cart, an old man with rheumy eyes. "Have you seen this girl?" Kane asked him.

The old man rubbed his eyes with thin arthritic fingers, but barely glanced at the locket. He seemed nervous of speaking, and stumbled away from Kane, almost falling in the mud. Kane seized him by one bony shoulder.

"Look at it," he urged.

The man peered uneasily at the miniature portrait of Meredith. A raindrop trickled down his forehead like a thread of sweat. "No, sir," he mumbled.

Perhaps he was frightened of his rescuer – of any man with weapons – but the denial brought Kane close to rage. "What do you mean?"

"No, sir," the old man blurted before managing to find more words. "I've never seen her."

Kane scrutinised his face before letting him go. As the old man and his fellows retreated past the fallen guard Kane turned to stay a girl who was climbing down from the cart. "Where were they taking you?" he said. "Where were you going?"

Even the thought of the prospect appeared to dismay her. "I don't know," she confessed.

Kane tried not to hear this simply as an echo of the old man's denial. "Help me," he said as she attempted to step around him. "I have to find this girl."

As he held up the locket, a raindrop blurred Meredith's face. He dabbed at it with a thumb and cupped the locket in one protective hand. The girl bent her head towards it, rain dripping from her bedraggled hair. She wiped her eyes clear, and then she shook her head. "Are you certain of it?" Kane said in some desperation.

"She was never with us. There are raiders everywhere." Perhaps the girl meant that Meredith might be anywhere with them, but she had reminded herself of the threat, and her eyes grew big with fear. "Please don't hurt me," she said.

Whatever the purity of Kane's intentions, he was terrorising her when she had already suffered terrors. "Go in peace, child," he said. "I pray you find refuge from this evil."

He helped the last of the captives down from the cart and unhitched the horses for them. Some led the animals to the most injured and enfeebled members of the party and assisted them in mounting the horses, which emboldened others of the fugitives to round up the remaining steeds. As Kane rode away he saw the motley band disappear into the misty drizzle. He had done all he could for them, and at least they were heading into any safety that was left in the land. He breathed a prayer as he spurred his horse westwards. The encounter had left him more anxious for Meredith, and he closed a fist around the locket at his throat as if it were a talisman that would guide him.

TWENTY-ONE

When the last of the cages clanged shut Meredith thought she was safe. She held her breath and clenched her fists to keep her body still. Wheels began to rumble away along the track, and more wheels trundled after them, bearing the groans and whimpers of those captives who still lived. The sounds receded among the trees, and Meredith was about to risk trying to move when she heard voices far too close to her. At once she was as motionless as any of the other bodies in the heap, although they had an advantage when it came to stillness. They did not need to pretend to be dead.

The voices closed in on her, and she recognised them. They belonged to the trio she had seen transformed in the village square: the tattooed man, the bearded one, the man with the savagely shaven pate. They were less distinguishable now that they bore the elaborate marks of possession, but they had stayed close to her cage on the road. "Plenty of blood in these," one said.

"No use to him. He likes them alive."

"No use to us neither," the third raider complained with what might have been a lingering remnant of his personality. "Nothing worth lifting."

"Wait, though," the first said, and his voice descended towards Meredith. "Here's a girl."

She was struggling not to betray the smallest hint of

movement when another voice came close. "She's dead."

Meredith was resisting the temptation to relax, even if it might not be apparent when she did, but she stiffened in dread as she heard the response. "Won't have much to say for herself, then."

"That's the way I like them too."

"Makes three of us for it, then," said their companion, and it was plain to Meredith that the power of the masked rider had not just overcome them; it had rooted itself in the blackest parts of their souls and seized on their corruption. She squeezed her eyes shut and kept so still that she was afraid of trembling with the effort. The men would have to drag aside the corpse that was pinning her down, and the moment they did she would run. Surely surprise would give her a start, and could she not outdistance men like these? She was attempting to be ready for the exact moment when she heard another cart move off. "Leave the dead," a brutish voice yelled.

The vibration of the wheels revived the cries of prisoners, and Meredith heard heavy boots tramping to rejoin the cart. She had to breathe, but she did not relax until the sounds were minutes distant. By the time they grew inaudible she was all too aware of being pinned down and hemmed in by dead flesh. She braced her hands against the muddy earth and attempted to crawl from beneath the corpse that lay on her shoulders like a cross. It failed to shift even an inch, and its weight held her down. She had prayed for immobility, and now she had her wish.

She made herself reach up and touch the body. It was a woman's; the breasts were flattened against Meredith's back. One of Meredith's reluctant hands found the dead face, and the loose lips seemed to respond with a kiss. Her other hand pressed against the flabby stomach.

Meredith was caught between revulsion and dismay that the woman had been denied a Christian burial. The last vestiges of respect deserted her as she imagined being trapped among the cadavers until she succumbed to their state, and she heaved at the corpse with all her strength. She was afraid that before she could struggle free it would subside on her, burying her face in the mud. She dug her elbows into the earth and gave a final desperate shove, and the body sprawled ahead of her with a large slack thud.

She was distressed to recognise the woman who had tried to comfort her in the prison cart. Meredith was still walled in by corpses, ravaged faces staring sightlessly at her, mouths gaping in their last grimace, bodies so drenched by the insistent rain that she was unable to distinguish sodden clothes from softened flesh. As she made to clamber over the dead woman, a raindrop trickled across one unresponsive eyeball. The sight appalled Meredith, and she scrabbled backwards, only for her hand to sink into a muddy burrow inhabited by an enormous slimy worm.

It was an open mouth, full of rain that kept the dead tongue wet. Meredith snatched her hand out and lurched away from the corpse. Her panic threw her against a pile of cadavers, and for an awful moment she thought they were going to collapse on top of her. She felt the pile totter, and planted a hand against an old man's scrawny ribcage. She had no time to spare for respect now. As the heaped corpses tumbled away from her she staggered to her feet and tottered forward, almost trampling on the woman's body. In moments she was in the open and crying aloud with relief.

Otherwise the forest was silent except for the hiss of rain on the track and the plops of raindrops on the leaves beneath the trees. The tree-trunks were blackened by rain, while the further reaches of the woods were grey with mist and distance. Apart from the twitching of branches overhead, Meredith could see no movement anywhere. None of the corpses was stirring, even if they looked restless with the rain that swarmed over them, but the sight was another reason why she fled along the track.

She had no idea where she was going other than away from the raiders she had escaped. Rain streamed down her face and veiled her eyes, rain plastered her clothes to her body. She could hardly have been colder, except for her left hand, which felt no sensation at all. When she risked a glance at it she saw that the mark had grown. The irregular blotch was half the size of her palm now, and the tendrils that blackened the skin had reached her fingers and thumb. Surely the mark did not bar her from God's protection – Captain Kane had assured her she was free of evil. Nevertheless the blemish made her feel as though something too dreadful to be named had taken her by the hand – as though however far she fled she would never elude its grasp. Her eyes were drawn back to it as she stumbled fast along the rutted muddy track, and it claimed so much of her attention that she did not immediately hear someone riding through the woods.

Which direction were the hoofbeats coming from? If they were ahead of her, could the rider be Captain Kane? No, they were at her back, and there was more than one horse. She dodged off the track and ran between the trees, desperate to find one that would hide her, but the trunks were no thicker than the masts of a ship. The only cover she could reach in time was a low bush. She fell to her knees on the waterlogged leaves behind it as the horsemen appeared on the track.

They were raiders – three of them. Through the

dripping leaves she saw them rein their horses to a halt. She thought they had seen her, and she crouched lower before realising that they had stopped beside the heap of corpses. One rider dismounted and poked at the bodies with the toe of his boot, turning over those that lay face down and favouring some with a kick. "Not here," he eventually grunted.

"Can't be far."

"We'll find her," the third raider said loudest of all.

Did they intend Meredith to hear? Were they hoping to frighten her into the open? Even if she had not been kneeling she would have offered up a silent prayer. The first man remounted his horse, which snorted as if it were adding to the threats to Meredith. The riders turned their horses and glared into the trees. One man's gaze passed across Meredith's hiding-place, and then another's found it and lingered. She had to struggle not to adopt more of a crouch in case they glimpsed the movement, and at last – perhaps in no more than a second – the black gaze veered away. Then the riders stared at one another, and a thought passed between them, unless it was the same in all their brutish skulls. One spurred his horse along the track in the direction Meredith had been following, and the second rode into the woods on the far side of the track. The last rider came straight towards Meredith.

She took a breath that she prayed only she could hear, and saw the rider hesitate. The breath caught in her throat, and she was in danger of coughing uncontrollably until she realised that the horse had simply missed its footing on the treacherous ground. The rider jerked the reins to urge his steed aside. For the moment he was looking well away from Meredith, and she glanced back. A few yards behind her was a hollow strewn with leaves and deep enough to hide her if she lay at full length. She peered through the bush at the rider, who was scowling at a clump of trees. She backed away as swiftly as she could without making any noise that was louder than the incessant sibilance of the rain. Even if the rider looked towards her, surely the bush would block his view. She felt her toes fumble over the edge of the hollow, and found the downwards slope with them. Then a cold thick finger tapped her on the shoulder.

She did not cry out. She twisted around to face the raider who had sneaked behind her, and at the same time she threw herself aside on the slippery earth. But there was no raider, only a weighty raindrop that a tree had let fall. For an instant she was overwhelmed by a surge of relief so fierce it drove away all thought, and then the rider shouted "Here! She's here!"

She heard hooves galloping towards her and sprang to her feet. The rider was hauling viciously at the reins to send the horse around a fallen tree – the tangled branches reached too high to jump – while his fellows rode to head Meredith off. She dashed past the hollow and ran between the trees, slithering over drenched leaves, slipping on a muddy slope, almost sprawling headlong. For the moment she had no thought other than somehow to leave her pursuers behind, and then she heard a liquid sound that was more than rain. She was coming to a river.

It was the nearest to a hope she had. She put on a speed that she would never have believed she had in her. Her lungs were heaving and her breaths felt harsh as fire by the time she reached the line of trees that marked the river's edge. She swept rain from her eyes with the back of her hand, and then she faltered. It was not just the prospect of plunging into the icy torrent that made her waver. She was not on the bank of a river. She was on top of a cliff.

At the foot of a sheer drop of perhaps a hundred feet, a river quite as wide rushed foaming over rocks. As Meredith retreated a step before dizziness could send her over the brink, she heard hoofbeats converging on her, and swung around to find the riders at her back. Every face bared yellowed teeth in the same bestial grin of triumph. "You're going nowhere, girl," the rider closest to her said.

"You belong to the Master," said the horseman to his left.

"He has a special purpose for you," their fellow exulted.

Their grins widened, and their blackened eyeballs glared at her without a blink, despite the gusts of rain that assailed their faces. They held the horses where they stood and waited for Meredith to try to dodge between them. She would never elude them that way, and so she turned her back on them. She took a breath that tasted tearful with the rain, and breathed a prayer, and then she paced forward and stepped off the edge of the cliff.

TWENTY-TWO

Night was falling when Kane found the lake. The clouds on the horizon were tinged red by the last of the sinking light; the sun was more apparent in its extinction than it had been all day. The raw sky lent its colour to the water as though the lake were stained with blood, and indeed it had been a day of bloodshed. After releasing the captives on the road Kane had chanced upon a second band of raiders, encamped in the ruins of a castle on a hill. They appeared to believe themselves invulnerable, unless they thought none would dare attack them, for they had not even troubled to set a guard. Kane had ridden into their midst and slain them without mercy, interrogating more than one as they lay dying. They told him nothing – they barely spoke, and he was sure that he saw the same eyes glaring out of every face at him. They had no prisoners, and so Kane stood among the dead as they resumed whatever humanity they had surrendered, and murmured a brief prayer for them. The prayer he uttered as he rode away was not on their behalf. While he had released them from the evil that held the land in thrall, he was no closer to rescuing Meredith.

The lake was some hundreds of yards from the road, across a meadow starved of life by the vicious winter and bedraggled by the day's rain. A copse occupied the far bank, where the foremost trees fingered the depths with their roots and with the reflections of their leafless branches. As Kane guided his horse through the dead grass, which was so tall it stooped, the glow dulled and drained out of the sky. He dismounted on the ragged border of the lake, and scarcely had time to examine the horse for cuts and scratches, finding none that would require treatment, before the land grew dark.

He led the horse to a gap in the reeds that fringed the lake and stroked its neck as it lowered its head to drink. A mist was seeping between the trees to drift across the lake, obscuring several rounded overgrown rocks that protruded just above the surface of the water. Kane squatted on the margin and cupped his hands as the horse dipped its muzzle in. Ripples spread through the water, slapping playfully against the rocks, uncovering a submerged inch of the nearest. Kane peered towards the rounded shape in the gloom, and then he narrowed his eyes and crouched over the water's edge. Another ripple let him glimpse the topmost section of the object, where he distinguished two waterlogged tufts above a pair of bulging lumps. Those were staring although sightless, and now he discerned more beneath the surface of the water: dim arms outstretched on either side, a torso sunk too deep to be wholly visible, unless it ended above the waist. Kane sprang to his feet and tugged at the horse's reins. "Don't drink," he cried. "It's foul."

The horse showed little inclination to obey. Kane might have wondered if it had been tainted by the evil that possessed the raiders, except that it had no soul to possess. "Can you not taste it, animal?" he raged, hauling at the reins until it lifted its reluctant head. In truth he was angry with himself, having made out that all the shapes he had taken for rocks belonged to bodies, drowned and rotting. He should never have allowed himself to be so unwary, and he was coaxing the horse away from the polluted water when he stiffened. Something had moved somewhere near him.

The horse snorted and shook its head uneasily, so that Kane had to stroke its muzzle to quiet it. As it subsided with a final whinny he heard the other sound again – a surreptitious restlessness of the grass. He might have assumed it was a stray breeze, but the night was as stagnant as the lake. He turned to face the meadow, one hand on the hilt of his sword. The grass and weeds were a smudged mass of blackness, which appeared to be utterly still. Here and there the drooping tips of grass-blades or the downcast heads of weeds were dimly outlined against the night sky, but they betrayed no movement. Then a withered flower twitched to his left, and another one swayed yards away to his right. Without further warning, the creatures that must have been lying low in the meadow rushed at him.

They came on all fours, scuttling faster than a horse could gallop. They were naked as babies and smaller than a man. The pallor of their flesh suggested that they had never seen the sun and never should. The eyes were too large for the avid bony faces, and so pale that they appeared to glow with an unholy lurid light. The mouths were unnaturally huge, gaping to display the fangs of predators, and further enlarged by blood smeared like an infant's food around the lips. So much Kane saw before the leader of the pack leapt at him.

He barely had the chance to draw a sword, and none to brace himself. He swung the blade up just in time to meet the creature in mid-air. The sword impaled it through the guts, but Kane had not judged the force of the leap. It sent him staggering backwards into the lake as a second creature sprang at the horse, jaws wide.

The horse gave a whinny that was close to a scream. As the creature seized its neck with all four scrawny limbs, it reared up and lost its footing on the slippery grass. Before the attacker could sink in its fangs, the horse crashed to the ground. As the thing at its throat tried to scrabble out of danger, it was crushed by the horse. Kane heard ribs snap like a bunch of twigs, and a dying snarl that sounded uncannily close to a word.

He was up to his thighs in the water. Another of the creatures was ranging back and forth along the margin, apparently uncertain whether to spring at Kane or to assail the horse. The creature that had attacked Kane was still skewered on the sword. Kane plunged the blade into the lake and trod on the thing's chest while he pulled the sword free. Water surged away from him, and the nearest of the drowned bodies wallowed in response, waving its bloated arms and nodding its decayed head so vigorously that it seemed on the point of raising whatever remained of its face out of the lake. As Kane lifted the sword, the horse struggled to its knees before it succeeded in standing up. This might have been the signal for the third of the pack to spring on Kane. He brought the sword down with all his strength and hacked the monstrosity in half.

The severed halves continued to twitch as they sank to the bottom of the lake. The sword was deep in the water too, and a fourth creature was poised on the edge. Kane dragged at the sword – dragged harder, but it was entangled in a mass of weeds. As the thing on the margin of the lake prepared to leap at him, he snatched a pistol from his belt and pulled the trigger. The weapon was aimed straight at the monstrous head, but it was useless. Kane's fall into the lake must have dampened the powder, and the pistol failed to go off.

He flung it at the creature, which dodged and

immediately sprang at him. As the pistol landed on the bank Kane let go of the trapped sword. Throwing out his hands, he seized the creature by the throat as it reached to fasten its clawed hands and feet on him. He twisted it around and bowed forward to hold the head underwater. The thing flailed the water with its limbs, struggling to find Kane with its lethal claws, but he pinned its arms between his knees and forced the head deeper. At last the body jerked into stillness, and a final unclean bubble swelled up from the water and burst. Kane lifted the limp body and peered at it, seeing what he feared he would. Despite its size, which suggested that its frame had withered around the evil it contained, it was clear that the creature had once been human.

Kane let it sink into the lake and retrieved his sword. He floundered to the bank and climbed out of the water to recover the pistol. For minutes he stood absolutely still, listening for any hint that more of the creatures were abroad. When he was sure there were none he stroked the horse's neck until the animal ceased trembling. It shied when he attempted to mount it, and he had to murmur to it as though he were saying a prayer. Eventually it suffered him to remount, and he ventured to ride it across the meadow – there was no other way back to the road. Once they were clear of the grass he did not permit himself to imagine they were safe. He was painfully alert now, knowing that any part of the land could be the lair of some unimaginable evil. Worse, the thought made him wonder what might be happening to Meredith.

TWENTY-THREE

The fall from the cliff snatched away Meredith's breath and the last of the muffled daylight as well. She might have thought that the abyss had already swallowed her, robbing her of every sense, if it had not been for a gust of rain that found her face. It kept her breathless and stung her blinded eyes throughout the endless fall. She had time to imagine being caught up by angels and borne back into the midst of her family, however vain and arrogant the hope was, before her plunge came to an end.

She had been most afraid that she would hit the rocks. Instead she struck open water, which was vicious enough. The thump it dealt her was hard enough for earth. Her left arm took most of the impact, but she had no chance to recover before the river closed over her head. A relentless current dragged her down, and she thought she was drowned. Thick weeds stretched out to entangle her, but the rocks where they were rooted slowed the torrent and turned it aside. For the moment it was tamed, and Meredith was able to struggle gasping to the surface.

Perhaps her prayer had been answered more thoroughly than she would have dared to hope. Even if you should not pray for salvation in this world, surely she had encountered so much evil that God would never leave her at its mercy. While the banks of the river were too steep to offer her a refuge, even supposing that she could have reached one and held on, that meant the raiders had no way down to her that she could see. The torrent was rushing her onwards, deafening her with its roar and dashing foam into her face, but she might not be helpless for long. She was being swept towards a pair of jagged rocks, and a fallen sapling was wedged between them.

As the tree came within reach she clutched at the trunk. The impact bruised her right hand – the left was devoid of sensation – and shuddered through her arms. The current was so strong that it sent her cannoning against the trunk. The collision knocked the breath out of her and loosened her grasp on the slippery wood. It dislodged the sapling from between the rocks, and Meredith wrapped her arms around it as it raced downriver.

At least it was heading eastwards, where any safety ought to be. The river was clear of rocks now, and she wanted to believe that the headlong speed at which she was being borne was only to her good. It might even be faster than anyone could ride along the cliff. Had the raiders seen her reach the surface? Perhaps they assumed the fall must have killed her, or that she had drowned. As she composed a silent prayer – the torrent left her no breath for even a whisper – those were among the entreaties she made. Her eyes were so blurred by spray, and the course of the river had grown so dark, that she did not immediately observe that the nearer bank was no longer a cliff.

Soon it was no taller than she would be if she could stand. She blinked at it through the spray as the torrent rushed her onwards, and saw nobody in the gloom among the trees. The land sloped down until it was level with the river, which sprouted reeds along its margin. Meredith grappled with the tree and the implacable current, and eventually managed to steer the tree towards the bank.

The branches snagged the reeds and became entangled in them, and the trunk swung landwards. As it bumped against the bank Meredith scrambled over the supine tree and sprawled face down on the muddy grass.

She lay there, panting and drenched and utterly spent, until she realised that the tumult of the river would prevent her from hearing anyone who approached. She pushed herself up on her unsteady arms and blinked hard at the dark. Tall dim silhouettes and hulking ones gathered around her, and their companions appeared behind them in the gloom, but all of them were trees and bushes. As far as she could make out, none of them hid anything more human or once human. All the same, anybody searching for her would look for her close to the river.

She lurched to her feet and stumbled away. The rain had stopped, but she could not be any more soaked. Her saturated clothes clung to her like an icy second skin, and her hair dangled like drowned weeds against her face. Stealth was impossible; once she left the sounds of the river behind she heard the mud suck at every footstep. The treacherous ground slowed her down until her body felt like a burden too ponderous for her exhausted legs to support. When she lost her footing in the mud she no longer had the strength to save herself from falling. She grabbed at a bush but succeeded only in snapping a handful of twigs before she hit the sodden earth.

She was almost too weakened to gasp. Her bruised hand and the insensible one spread slackly open on the drenched grass. At least she was away from the river and surrounded by bushes. Surely they would hide her, even from any searchers. Surely she ought to be safe there while she regained just a little of her strength – and then she heard a muffled footstep, and another.

Had her pursuers left their horses for the sake of stealth? She made to pray not to be found, and then as her hands moved to join together she felt how the left one was tainted. Perhaps that was one function of the mark – to prevent her from praying as she had prayed ever since she had words. She could only inch her right hand forward to keep her face out of the mud. She closed her eyes and clung to an idea no less childish than desperate – that so long as she was unable to see, she could not be seen either. But the inexorable footsteps came on, halting just a few yards away. Meredith released a breath that felt as though she were giving up more than air, and then she raised her head.

A solitary figure was just visible against the thick night sky. It was smaller and slighter than a man. As Meredith peered at the face it began to take shape. She could hardly believe she recognised him, but it seemed she did. "Samuel," she whispered. "Am I dead?"

"Dead, miss?" The boy gave a laugh so nervous it was barely audible. "You ain't dead. You can't be. You're speaking to me."

He was not Samuel. His accent reminded her of Captain Kane's. Meredith managed to sit back on her haunches and brushed ineffectually at the muddy front of her soaked dress. "I thought I was," she said, not without wistfulness.

"We may be," the boy muttered, "if we wait round here much longer."

He started as a black shape flapped out of a tree – a crow. It flew towards the ill-defined horizon, and the boy glanced apprehensively about. "What is it?" Meredith whispered.

"There's terrible things in the dark, miss."

He spoke as if he was afraid his very words would bring

them. Meredith wanted to believe he was just beset by night fears – he seemed more timid than Samuel – but she was too aware of the evils that were abroad. She tried to stand, only to discover that her legs were incapable of the task. "Please help me," she said.

The boy hesitated until Meredith held out her shaky hands, and then he trudged forward to grab her arms, so that she felt he was avoiding the touch of her infected palm. Having hauled her unceremoniously to her feet, he let go at once. She caught at his arm as her legs wavered. "May I lean on you?" she pleaded.

"I'm meant to be finding the ewe. She's wandered." When Meredith staggered against him the boy relented. "I'll help you a bit of the way," he said. "Where do you want to go?"

"I don't know." Even if it had not been so dark Meredith would have had to confess "I don't know where I am."

The boy peered into her face and reached a decision. "You can come home," he said. "You'll be safe there for the night."

"Thank you." The words seemed not just inadequate but impersonal. "What is your name?" Meredith said.

"Thomas." With a hint of defiant familial pride the boy said "Thomas Woolman."

"Thank you, Thomas. I'm Meredith," she said and found she was unable to go on.

As soon as they took a step she stumbled. "You can put your arm round me if you like, Mistress Meredith," he said.

She draped her right arm across his shoulders, and he matched his pace to hers. Their slowness gave her time to imagine an attacker behind every bush, especially since Thomas had begun to peer nervously at them. She would have searched for conversation, but she sensed he would be nervous of that as well. She tried to silence her thoughts too until the bushes thinned out and the trees gave way to bare fields. "There," Thomas murmured.

He was pointing across the nearest field at a group of small buildings huddled against the featureless dark. A rush-light flickered beyond a cottage window, but the other buildings were unlit. "That's my father's farm," Thomas said. "Don't make any noise now. They mustn't know you're here."

Meredith had an uneasy notion that he did not mean his family. "Who?" she whispered.

"Anyone," Thomas said and supported her to the hedge around the field. Now that they were in the open he seemed more anxious. As he guided Meredith along a rough path that followed the perimeter of the field, she sensed his impatience with her tardiness. The night was silent apart from the bleating of sheep, with no sign of life from the farmhouse. Thomas steered her off the path well before they reached the building and ushered her around the edge of the farmyard. A hen clucked in its sleep, but it was a man's cough that made the boy start. When nobody appeared at the lit window he hurried Meredith to the barn.

The door opened with a faint creak, and Thomas glanced nervously towards the house. As soon as Meredith was through the meagre opening he offered her, the boy dodged in and shut the door. The darkness felt like some undefined threat rendered tangible until Meredith heard the striking of a flint, and a rush-light flared up to illuminate the interior. Shadows fluttered bat-like above the rafters and performed a ponderous dance behind bales of hay, but the large room seemed empty of actual danger. Thomas watched Meredith sink onto a heap of straw, and then he cleared the floor in front of her and set the rush-light down. He took off his heavy woollen coat and settled it around Meredith's shoulders, then stepped quickly back. "Nobody but me will come in here," he said. "You can sleep."

"Thank you. God bless you, Thomas," Meredith said.

"I'll get you when it's safe," Thomas said and frowned. "Where will you go?"

"I don't know." The admission seemed to isolate her with all that it summoned up. "I managed to escape from – I can't say what they are," she whispered. "The raiders. Servants of evil, some terrible evil."

Thomas glanced towards the door as if he wanted to escape what she was saying. "They – " Meredith blurted, and her words did their best to desert her, but they were all that remained in her mind. "They killed my family," she said.

The boy watched unhappily as she was overwhelmed by tears. "There's nothing you could have done," he mumbled.

Meredith sobbed and gulped and eventually recaptured her voice. "How do you know that, Thomas?"

"The raiders came here too." As Meredith shivered, not just with the chill of her drenched clothes, he said "To our village. We gave them food. We gave them whatever they wanted. That's how everyone survives here. My father says we might as well be slaves."

He must have seen that Meredith felt vulnerable again. His words had brought the raiders and the threat of their return too close. "This place is safe," he said. "It'll be warm. I'll try and bring you some food and clothes when I can."

He retreated to the door and stood with one hand on the latch. "Don't go outside," he said. "Don't go near the door." He snatched it ajar and slipped through the gap. In a moment it was shut as if the boy had vanished like a will-o'-the-wisp. Shadows pranced behind the bales and veered about under the roof, and then the flame steadied. As Meredith gazed at it her eyelids seemed to gain an unbearable weight – to take on all the exhaustion she had been fighting off. In another breath she was asleep, and there was no peril where she found herself, nor any cold or loss.

TWENTY-FOUR

As Kane rode through the low hills he was aware that a change had invaded the late afternoon. Was there a sound besides the incessant hiss of rain, which had begun to seem as constant as the sunless sky? His horse had sensed something ahead, and gave an uneasy snort. Kane stroked its wet head and guided the horse up a hill. Before they reached the top of the gradual slope he thought he heard an unfamiliar noise – a murmur too low to be defined, or perhaps just an unidentifiable vibration. He came to the brow of the hill and was scarcely aware of reining the horse to a standstill. "Dear God in Heaven," he breathed.

Beyond the hills the landscape flattened out, and it was thronged with people fleeing eastwards. A few couples supported each other, but most of the fugitives were alone. Every head was downcast as a penitent's, lashed by the rain. Even at that distance the spectacle exuded despair. It was plain that the refugees believed their world had been brought to an end. The exodus might have been mistaken for a pilgrimage, but Kane thought they were advancing as hopelessly as a beast goes to the slaughterhouse. The notion enraged him, and he rode downhill.

No doubt some if not all of the throng took him for a raider. Many kept their heads down, and even those who glanced up in fear or beaten resignation seemed to find no reassurance in the sight of him. He rode back and forth among them, but none of the solitary girls was Meredith. He might have shown the fugitives the locket, except that his instincts told him that they were too immured in their own misery to identify a stranger, unless their despondency had infected him as well. He could almost have imagined that they were trudging without souls, in a devilish parody of the Day of Judgment. When at last the parade of defeated faces came to an end, Kane rode fast until he found a westward track.

The rain fell behind as though it were pursuing the refugees. A dull glow took hold of the sky ahead, but the sun was still hiding its face from the land. The track meandered between unfenced fields overgrown with weeds, and Kane could see for miles. The way was deserted, which only made him feel as though he no longer knew where he was bound or what drove him – as though even his adversary had abandoned him, finding him too insignificant and powerless to be worthy of attention. He had vowed to save Meredith, but was he simply clinging to an illusion that she was still alive? If indeed she had survived, might she have succeeded in escaping? In that case she would surely have fled eastwards. His doubts weighed his mind down, and he was continuing along the track only because the horse had been given no reason to halt when he heard a bell ahead.

The note was low and intermittent. Kane could have thought it was tolling for the fate that had overtaken the land. Above the horizon the sky grew red, and flakes of snow began to sparkle dully in the air. When Kane made out the tower silhouetted against the muffled sunset he thanked God that the church still stood. Its bell rang across the fields like the note of a buoy in the midst of an open sea, and Kane wondered if he dared to feel reassured that he was on the right path after all. He was scant minutes away from the church when he saw the sky through the roof.

Perhaps the church was only derelict with age. Kane dismounted at the lich-gate and tethered the horse to a gatepost before stepping into the graveyard. Monuments towered over him, their inscriptions blurred by moss. A solitary splintered tree stood among the neglected graves. The bell had fallen silent, hanging inert in the tower above the exposed beams that were almost all that survived of the roof. The thick stones of the walls were piebald with lichen and rough with centuries of weathering. Kane climbed the steps to the door beneath a rounded arch and removed his hat as he twisted the heavy ring to lift the latch.

The door creaked inwards, and he heard wings fluttering among the rafters. He passed beneath the arch and then, as if in deference to some obsolete ritual, closed the door of the ruin behind him. A chill wind and a dance of snowflakes came along the nave to meet him, and he wondered if a wind could have rung the bell. The grey tiled floor was stained and scattered with debris. Rotting leaves had gathered around the bases of the stout pillars on either side of the nave as if the shafts were tree-trunks. A hole gaped in the left-hand wall, where a statue depicting a saint or some benefactor of the church had fallen supine, its face shattered to powder. It seemed to Kane that none of this dereliction mattered, for one thing had remained intact: a stone crucifix in a niche to the left of the altar. Falling to his knees in front of it, he bowed his head. "Dear God, I beg you to listen to me now," he said.

Did he sense a response? He gripped his hands together

until the knuckles ached. "I have failed you," he said, words that made his mouth taste as raw as an open wound. "I cannot find her."

There was indeed a response. Perhaps it had been attracted by his supplication or simply by his presence. Was he not even to be allowed to pray in peace? He loosened his hands but kept them clasped. "I am lost and I need your light to help me find my way," he said, which was all he had time to pronounce. Snatching his hands apart, he drew his sword as he spun around. In a moment the edge of the blade was at the throat of the man who had crept up behind him.

The man had raised a cudgel to strike Kane down. His red-rimmed eyes stared wildly out of a thin pallid face. His long ragged locks were several shades of paleness, some of them almost white. However discoloured his round collar and black robes might have grown, he was a priest, and Kane laid his sword on the tiles so as to display his empty hands. "Such times we live in," he said.

The priest's eyes jerked in their sockets, but he did not speak or change his stance. "Forgive me, Father," Kane murmured. "I wished only for a little refuge and a moment for prayer."

The priest stared about him as if he were remembering the church, and then he let the cudgel drop. He caught it within inches of striking the floor and clutched it with both hands to his chest like a relic of the Cross while he lifted his eyes heavenwards. "Praise God in His sanctuary," he cried. "Praise Him in the firmament of His power."

Perhaps he was seeing more than Kane could – more than the reddened clouds like raw flesh exposed by the wounds in the roof. His wild gaze stayed fixed on the sky until the clouds grew black as though rot had crept into the wounds, and then his stare sank into the church. "I have seen such terrible things," he declared.

"I too," Kane said and felt compelled to reassure him if he could. "I left few of them alive."

"Night has come." The priest seemed unable to keep his eyes still, and his gaze jerked away from Kane. "Will you find sanctuary in my church?" he said.

Kane wanted to refuse. The night should not daunt him from searching for Meredith. Then the priest shuffled to a corner of the ruin to gather an armful of kindling, and Kane saw a cooking-pot there too. He would make better progress if he were dry and fed, and he could regain the time lost. Perhaps in some sense the priest might prove to be an answer to his prayer. "God bless you, Father," he said.

He was disconcerted to see the priest start to build the fire in the middle of the nave. Why were there no pews? Had they been used for fuel? The priest's hands shook as he struck a flint, but eventually a spark set a bunch of twigs alight. The fire spread to the wood heaped above them, and Kane was reminded of the stone circle on the moor – of that primitive instinct to use a fire to ward off the darkness and whatever lurked there, and the refuge that the girl Elizabeth had seemed to find in the pagan place. The thoughts were less than welcome – they seemed capable of rousing doubts that he could not afford to entertain – and he spoke in the hope of banishing them. "This is your home?"

The priest was hanging the pot full of rain on a metal stand over the fire. "I have nowhere else," he said and stared at Kane across the flames. "Have you come far?"

"Three days' hard ride brought me here," Kane said and crouched towards the fire. "But where here is, I know not."

"These are the borders of Somerset and Devonshire."

Kane felt as if some aspect of his destiny had overtaken him by stealth. "My home too," he muttered.

The priest leaned closer, and shadows worked his face. "This, your home?"

"I grew up – " Since this was hardly the case, Kane said "I spent my childhood not so very far from here."

"A sad homecoming for you." Kane thought the priest might offer solace, but the man's thoughts appeared to have settled elsewhere. "What is your name?" the priest said.

"Solomon Kane."

He saw no recognition in the priest's eyes; indeed, it was impossible to fix their expression. "I am Michael," the priest said.

He must be named for the angel who had fought the hordes of Lucifer, and Kane could only wonder what dread confrontation had reduced him to his present fearful state. "What is your mission?" Father Michael said.

"Like you, I am pledged to fight evil. I must rescue a girl who was taken by the raiders," Kane said. "They killed her family. Have they been here?"

"Those black-eyed jackals of Malachi?" Father Michael's eyes grew unnaturally bright, as though to demonstrate they were free of blackness. "Aye, they passed through here," he said and glared about at the ruined church. "What malice they must have to desecrate the house of God."

Kane gazed past him at the crucifix. However the shadows tugged at it and played mockingly around it, the cross and the figure nailed to it stood steadfast. "They may cast down the house," he said, "but they cannot cast down God. He is eternal."

Father Michael seemed not to hear. "And now they hold sway over all the lands west of here," he said.

Once more Kane had a sense that his fate was upon him – had perhaps never left him. "Then I shall be riding westward."

The priest clasped his hands together in prayer or the memory of one. "You shall ride to your death, my son."

"Better destruction than cowardice," said Kane.

"They say no man may stand against Malachi." The priest had rediscovered some vestige of nerve – enough to resent Kane's retort. "I heard you at your prayers," he said. "It seems you have despaired of your mission."

"Not while I live." Kane did his best to turn his rage away from the priest. "Who is this Malachi?" he demanded. "Why should any who fear God fear him?"

"A servant of the Devil." Father Michael lowered his voice as if in fear of being overheard. "A sorcerer," he said.

"I was told this," Kane said impatiently. "Where has he found such power?"

"No-one ever sees him." Perhaps the priest meant this for some kind of an answer, unless he had begun to mutter with no thought of his listener. "He hides away in his castle and sends forth that masked warrior to do his bidding," he said. "His army makes slaves of the weak and soldiers of the strong."

It seemed that the question Kane needed to ask was apparent on his face, because the priest declared "God will save the faithful."

"He has saved you. That is your meaning." Kane could not suppress his anger. "I have seen the faithful slain without mercy," he said. "I have seen a boy slaughtered in front of his parents' eyes."

"I speak of their souls," Father Michael rebuked him.

"This is the end of days."

A chill wind glittering with snow snatched at the flames, which hissed, and shadows capered around the church. "Do you truly believe that?" Kane protested.

"I have read it." The priest darted away from the fire, and his prancing shadow grew gigantic on the tiled floor. It seemed to be absorbed by the ravaged wall as he climbed the steps to the pulpit and brought down a heavy volume. "I have read it," he repeated like a prayer.

He carried the Bible to the fire and squatted to turn the pages. The light plucked at them, and his nervous fingers did. "It is here," he insisted.

Kane stood up and wandered towards the altar rather than observe the priest's agitated search. He had a sense that Father Michael was driven by some force that the priest scarcely understood. Now that Kane was so close to the altar he saw little evidence of desecration; it seemed disused rather than defiled. How secure was Father Michael's grasp of what was real? He was still clawing at the pages with his fingernails, but his eyes were flickering so wildly that Kane doubted he saw the words. "Such things are here that never should be," the priest muttered. "Every foul thing that the light of Christ kept at bay is crawling out of the pit to curse the land."

He glared about the church as though he saw worse than the restless shadows. "God is testing my faith," he said.

The submissive piety was more than Kane could bear. "I think Christ and all His angels are asleep whilst we are left to suffer."

"You mind your blasphemy!" Father Michael clapped the Bible shut, and the echoes of the dull sound were swallowed by the eager darkness. "It can only be as God wills it," he proclaimed.

Kane felt as if he were the solitary worshipper at the mercy of a sermon. While he wanted to believe, he had seen too much suffering. "How can it be as God ordains?"

The priest hugged the Bible and raised a pious hand. "My son..."

Kane began to pace like a beast in a cage. "How can it be right that this evil walks among us when all we have to protect us is – what? Simple faith?"

Father Michael clutched the Bible to himself as if that were sufficient answer. Kane saw the priest clinging to his faith beside the fire dwarfed by the vast darkness, and the sight aggravated his rage. "Tell me, priest," he said. "Where are the men to fight this power?"

The priest gazed at him and then fumbled to open the Bible. "It is written in the Scriptures – "

Kane jerked up a hand. Even if the gesture seemed close to profane, he had to silence Father Michael. "What was that?" he breathed.

Until it was repeated he might almost have taken the noise for a wind in a crevice of the church. If it was a voice, it belonged to nothing human. It was not solely a low moan, nor quite a snarl. He peered towards the windows, but the blackness that the narrow arches framed was impenetrably thick. The priest seemed confused by Kane's behaviour, and blinked rapidly at him. "I heard something outside," Kane said.

All at once the priest's gaze steadied. "No, my son," he said. "There is nothing evil out there."

Kane could only think that the priest's mind had proved unequal to the threat they faced. "Father, if you listen – "

Father Michael shook his head so ponderously that his thoughts might have been weighing it down. "The evil is already here," he said.

He laid the Bible on the tiles beside the fire and

beckoned to Kane, who watched him trudge along the nave and stoop to a section of the floor beyond the reach of the firelight. The priest prised up a metal ring and hauled a trapdoor open, then let it drop on the tiles. The impact seemed to call forth an inhuman chorus of hungry snarling. "See," Father Michael said with a kind of defiant pride.

Kane stepped forward, but to the fire. He found a stick that had only just caught the flames and dragged it forth. Holding the brand high, he paced along the nave. He was yards short of the trapdoor when a stench came to meet him. It put him in mind of the foetor of a cave that was the lair of many reptiles, and there was the reek of raw meat and the stink of droppings too. An outburst of snarling greeted the torchlight as it flickered into the depths. The voices sounded worse than bestial – far too close to human. Kane made himself venture to the opening as Father Michael stepped back to leave him more room. He thrust the torch into the opening and had to steel himself not to recoil as the things beneath the floor turned up their faces and stretched out their clawed hands in a vain attempt to drag him into the crypt. "My God," Kane whispered.

The words were no longer a prayer. Perhaps no prayer could encompass what he saw below him. The night had veiled some details of the creatures that he had encountered by the poisoned lake, but the torchlight spared him nothing. The faces that were straining up towards him like a brood in an evil nest were almost as fleshless as skulls – the skulls of a link between humanity and some diabolical species. They looked starved not just of nourishment but of their souls. In their eyes there was only savage hunger, which appeared to have forced their jaws forward, stretching their mouths unnaturally wide.

Every head was balding, patched with tufts and strands of hair, and what remained of their flesh was pale as the undersides of slugs. As a score of discoloured scrawny arms reached up in a horrid parody of yearning for the light, Kane cried "What deviltry is this?"

"Satan hath desired to have them, that he may sift them as wheat." While he intoned the words from the Bible the priest seemed to recall his vocation, but then he giggled like a child unable to contain his mirth. "What was I to do?" he said.

He was answered by the snarls of many wordless voices under the church. "Destroy them, man," Kane told him.

"I cannot destroy them." Father Michael's eyes glistened with compassion. "They were men and women once," he said. "They were people I knew."

"They are no longer," Kane said over the inhuman clamour. "Release their souls. If God has any purpose for them now, that must be His will."

"There is Janet. There is Winifred." Father Michael was peering at the malformed faces, but Kane was unconvinced that the priest recognised them. "It was Malachi's curse that changed them," Father Michael said with some defiance. "It was no fault of theirs."

"Then cleanse them of this evil," Kane urged, lifting the torch like a sword.

"They are my test of faith." Father Michael fumbled at his throat, where he seemed to expect to find a cross. "I am to love even the foulest creatures," he insisted, and turned an uncertain smile on the horde below him.

"But do not love their foulness," Kane said, and had to swallow as a wave of the inhuman stench overwhelmed him. "Deliver them from it. That must be our task."

"They are my flock and I am their shepherd," Father Michael said, and his voice swelled with a distorted pride.

"I pray with them each night," he assured Kane, "and hear them raise their voices to God."

In that moment Kane saw that the priest was far worse than stubborn – that he had lost his mind. "I keep them," Father Michael said. "I care for them." He reached out his hands as though in benediction, but the gesture might have been emulating the talons that reached up from the crypt. His proud smile grew lopsided, and he giggled again. Barely audibly he said "I feed them."

"Feed them?" Kane's soul revolted at the thought. He leaned forward to thrust the torch lower and search the crowded gloom. The hands clawed at the light as if they sought to tear it to shreds, the gaping mouths snarled and bared their bloodstained fangs. He could see nothing of their food – nothing but the pallid bodies pressed together close as maggots in a container of bait. "What do you feed them?" he demanded.

"Flesh," Father Michael said, and rushed at him.

Before Kane could retreat from the opening, the priest's hands slammed against his back. There was more strength in his wiry frame than Kane would have expected, and he must have been husbanding it for that moment. Kane teetered on the edge and almost regained his balance. Then his foot skidded on a slippery tile, and he fell into the midst of the creatures that were slavering for him.

He was still gripping the torch. At the last moment the inhuman throng backed away from the light, tumbling over one another in their haste. Kane struck the earth floor with an impact that hammered all the breath out of him and jarred the torch from his grasp. As he glared about him at the ghoulish horde, Father Michael called down to him. He was still secure in his priesthood; he might almost have been preaching a sermon. "I deliver you unto Satan's creatures for the destruction of your flesh, that your spirit may be saved. May God have mercy on your soul," he intoned and shut the trapdoor with a slam that laid low the flame of the torch.

TWENTY-FIVE

It was harvest time, and Meredith had never seen the like. The sun was huge and golden, exactly the colour of the haystacks that stood all about the fields. They resembled monuments to fruitfulness, and their scent filled the mellow air, making her head swim. Her senses felt renewed, and she was a child again, playing hide and seek with a girl whose delighted laughter she could hear somewhere among the stacks. Meredith would have liked to stand inhaling the autumnal scent while the gentle colours of the landscape settled like balm on her eyes, but she was not alone, and so she ran to find her playmate.

The bales receded into mist and distance. There seemed to be no end to them, and no sign of the other girl. The fields were unfenced, and so Meredith had no idea what boundaries she might be crossing, unless there was just a single field so vast that she would never find its limit before nightfall. Only the laughter of her unseen playmate led her onwards, past rank after rank of hulking bales that had begun to darken and drip with mist. The stubbled earth had grown dank too, and toadstools sprouted where the hay had been cut down. Had a mocking note crept into the girlish laughter? Meredith ran in the direction where it seemed to be, but was rewarded only by the harsh call of a crow that flapped up from behind a haystack. The bird must have been pecking at a mass of fungus, which looked unpleasantly suggestive of a supine body discoloured by corruption. Meredith hurried past the prone shape and then had to swing around, because the shrill laughter was now at her back. She saw a figure dodge behind a shaggy bale, but when she ran to pounce on it she found that it was another crow, which pranced away from her with an arrogant nonchalance suggesting that it and its fellows owned the land. Then it turned its cruel beak towards Meredith and fixed her with its utterly black gaze, and emitted its call. But the sound that emerged from the gaping beak was not the harsh cry of its species. It was a little girl's laughter.

In a moment it was answered from all around Meredith, and the members of the chorus strutted from behind the haystacks. They were crows, a dozen of them. Their black eyes were as emotionless as bits of coal, and yet their childish laughter sounded gleeful. They hopped forward, flapping their wings as though to drive Meredith to her fate, and she whirled around in search of a way of escape. Just one avenue was unguarded by any of the monstrous flock. She dashed along it, between the towering hulks of vegetation that looked grey with rot as well as with the mist that was closing in. The mist had engulfed the sun and blurred the haystacks ahead; the massive squarish shapes might have been composed of grey stone. She glanced fearfully about, and saw that she was indeed surrounded by the ancient stones of a pagan site, unless the place was devoted to some older magic. As the megaliths loomed above her, black shapes hopped and flapped between them, and she heard hoofbeats galloping to encircle her. In a moment the rider emerged from the mist. At the sight of his mask she cried out and awoke.

The smell of hay was still in her nostrils. She was lying in the barn, covered with a ragged mass of straw.

However feverish her dream might have been, she was no longer shivering, even if her limbs ached with a reminiscence of the chill. The rush-light was almost spent, but it showed her that she was alone on the floor of the barn. She had no means of judging how much time had passed since the boy Thomas had brought her food and a change of clothes. She was fighting off the dread that the nightmare had left behind, and wondering how soon Thomas might be able to sneak her away from the farm, when she heard a little girl's muffled laughter.

For a dreadful moment Meredith thought the dream was real, and then she grasped that the sound of laughter had been the germ of the dream. Was the girl Thomas's sister? She might come into the barn, and Meredith was looking for a place to hide when she heard a man's voice just outside the door. "Is she in here?"

The voice sounded rough with anxiety. The man must be searching for the little girl, and the nightmare had left Meredith so dazed that she only just refrained from calling out that the child was not in the barn. In any case he was bound to look in there, and Meredith was burrowing under the straw when Thomas spoke. "Father, why do we need to do this?"

"Why do you think, boy?" Even now Meredith thought they were talking about the boy's sister until the man said harshly "If Malachi's soldiers find we've been sheltering her they'll burn us out." Emotion weighed his voice down, so that Meredith barely heard him add "Or worse."

"She lost her family," Thomas pleaded.

"So did we," his father said.

The words reawakened Meredith's grief, but she had no time to yield to it. She rose swiftly to her feet, wavering a little as her head swam, and stared about the barn. Could she hide in the hayloft? She was making for the ladder that led up to it when she froze like an animal that has sighted the hunter. The little girl whose gleeful laughter she had heard was seated on the edge of the hayloft, swinging her legs. She was the witch who had marked Meredith's palm.

She gave Meredith a grin that seemed almost conspiratorial. Grotesquely, she looked no worse than childishly mischievous. Her eyes gleamed at Meredith and then turned towards the ladder, and Meredith knew there was no refuge up above. She glanced desperately about and saw a pitchfork leaning against a wall. Outside the man was saying "I'll not lose anything more just to save a stranger. Show her to me."

Meredith darted to grab the pitchfork. She was afraid that the witch would be effortlessly swifter, but the shaft was not snatched from her grasp. She swung it in front of her with both hands as she turned to confront the witch. But the loft was deserted, and the only movement to be seen was a solitary wisp of straw floating down from the loft. Meredith might have wondered if the apparition had been a last trace of her dream, but she had no more time for thoughts, because the latch of the barn door had been lifted with a clank like the fall of a trap. "Find her for me, boy, or I will," the man said.

As the left half of the door creaked open Meredith dodged behind a ragged bale of hay. The flame of the rush-light was flattened by a draught, and all the shadows bowed low as if deferring to the man in the doorway. Meredith did her utmost to keep herself and the pitchfork still. "Go on, boy. Do what you must," his father said under his breath.

There was a stubborn silence before Thomas lurched into view, obviously having been pushed. He trudged to the straw where Meredith had slept and began to spread it apart with both hands. Though he must have been able to see at once that she was no longer there, he continued to sift the straw. He might have been playing a joyless game, delaying the moment when he would be forced to find her. His antics gave her time to steal around the bale of hay, but it was no use; if she retreated his father would see her, and if she stayed where she was the boy would. Eventually he stood up, and she thought he meant to tell his father that she was nowhere to be found, but he could not avoid seeing her now. As he met her eyes his mouth worked, and he muttered a phrase low enough for a private prayer. "What are you saying, boy?" his father urged.

Thomas gave her a stricken look, but she could not find an expression in response. "She's here," he said with a defiance that might have been aimed at Meredith as much as at his father.

His father tramped to scowl at her. He was a brawny red-faced man with thinning hair and too many wrinkles around his eyes. He looked haunted by memories and starved of sleep, but grimly determined. As he paced towards Meredith she backed away, raising the pitchfork, and glanced accusingly at Thomas. "You betrayed me," she told him.

The boy's lip trembled. "I'm sorry," he whispered.

"Leave him be, girl," the man said, "and put that down. There's nowhere you can hide."

"Just let me go," Meredith said and gripped the pitchfork harder. "Nobody will know I hid here. Let me go now and nobody will see."

"I cannot." The farmer shook his slow head as though her suggestion were a burden he had to dislodge. "Malachi's creatures are everywhere now," he said. "Anybody who denies them will be killed. We have to show our loyalty."

Perhaps Meredith glimpsed regret in his eyes, but it was quickly suppressed. "By sacrificing me?" she protested in rage that felt close to grief.

"If need be," the man said and lunged heavily at her.

Meredith stood her ground, because there was no way out other than the door beyond him. She jabbed the pitchfork at him, and he made to knock it aside with one muscular arm. He seemed almost amused by the sight of her presuming to take him on. His reaction enraged her, and she darted forward, thrusting the pitchfork at him with all her strength. The tines penetrated his shoulder, and she felt them dig deep into flesh until he recoiled, yelling as much in outraged surprise as pain. Meredith held onto the pitchfork, and his retreat pulled it out of his shoulder. As he stood in the middle of the barn, recovering from the assault or from the shock of it, Meredith sprinted to the door.

It was not just capture that she was desperate to escape; it was Thomas's reaction. His cry of dismay had been louder than his father's yell, and she had glimpsed the boy's distraught look. Meredith had become indistinguishable in his eyes from the evil that had invaded his life – that had snatched away his family. Captain Kane had assured her that there was no evil in her, but he and his faith had deserted her. As she clutched at the latch she might have been seeking to flee her own self. She threw the door wide, to be confronted by the figure that was waiting in the dark.

His gaze was as cold as the expression of his lipless mask. His minions were massed behind him in the farmyard, cutting off even the slimmest chance of escape. All the same, Meredith jerked up the pitchfork and drove it with the last of her strength into his chest. She felt the tines pierce leather and flesh, but the only response he granted her was a thin chill laugh, hardly more than a mocking whisper. He dragged the pitchfork out of his body and wrenched the shaft from Meredith's hand.

For a moment she thought he was about to turn the weapon against her. A quick death seemed almost welcome; it would return her to her family, at any rate. Instead he flung the pitchfork in the mud and fastened his gaze on her like a predator inspecting a victim. As she attacked him she had heard Thomas cry out once more, and his father's groan of pain or apprehension. Perhaps at least she could save them as she had been unable to save Samuel and her family. "They did not know I was here," she said as steadily as she could. She was praying that the masked figure would believe her as its head leaned down towards her. For another moment the eyes held her with their unreadable gaze, and then a black-gloved hand came down like a mallet on her skull.

TWENTY-SIX

As Kane took a breath that smelled worse than any tomb, it seemed to draw the scrawny figures closer all round him. The light of the torch on the floor of the crypt glistened on the teeth in the snarling mouths and flickered in the feral eyes as if it was taking the place of every lost soul. He was struggling to regain the strength that the fall had knocked out of him when one of the creatures, braver or more famished than the rest, darted to fasten its teeth on his leg.

Kane kicked out, driving the creature backwards before it could savage him, and snatched a pistol from his belt. In the enclosed space the shot was deafening. It splintered the ghoul's ribs, flinging the creature into the arms of several of its fellows. They fell on it at once, rending it apart with their claws and tearing mouthfuls out of it with their teeth.

As more of the pack turned on the fallen victim, Kane lunged to retrieve the torch. It was not the only object like a stick on the floor of the crypt. There were bones gnawed by fangs, and they had once been human. Kane had scarcely closed his fist around the gnarled shaft of the torch when two of the ghouls sprang on him, clawing at his legs. Perhaps they sought to disable him, if they had anything in their minds besides hunger. Kane roared in pain and fury, twisting on the floor to thrust the torch

into their faces. They cowered back with screams of
bestial fear, but they did not retreat far. They were poised
for a renewed attack as Kane rose to his feet and glared
about the crypt.

While the ceiling was low, the trapdoor was out of
reach. Beyond the pack of ghouls he saw passages on
every side, leading into darkness. A narrow corridor
should be more defensible than the space in which he was
presently trapped, but he had no means of judging where
any of the passages might lead. As a ghoul sprang at him,
baring its teeth like a rabid animal and reaching its claws
for his throat, Kane smashed its skull with his pistol butt
and dodged towards the corridor beyond. Before he could
gain it, several ghouls were on him.

Though their strength was not considerable, the
combined force of the attack almost sent Kane sprawling.
He felt claws tearing at his garments in search of his flesh
and teeth attempting to close on his back. He whirled
around in a rage, jabbing at the soulless possessed faces
with the torch, and blew a ghoul's scalp open with a shot
from his second pistol. A pair of ghouls began to fight
over the contents of their fellow's skull, but most of the
pack converged on Kane. Alternately slashing at them
with his sword and thrusting the torch at them, Kane
retreated into the corridor.

It was lined with sarcophagi. Some had been broken
open, and the torch revealed the incompleteness of their
contents, which Kane glimpsed as the ghouls swarmed
into the corridor. There was room for three abreast, and
Kane sliced open the whitish belly of one with his sword,
and slit another's throat, and cleaved the head of the third
ghoul half off its shoulders with a downward stroke. This
did little to hinder their fellows, who trampled over the
bodies without lingering to ravage them. They were too

eager for fresh meat now – Kane's flesh.

How many of the ghouls were there? How large had the village been? More of the creatures than he had seen in the central room were crowding hungrily into the passage. He was suddenly afraid that he might be backing towards a dead end. He thrust the torch at the foremost ghoul and set its ragged clothes on fire.

The creature staggered away, prancing like a hellish puppet and clawing at itself. In seconds its flailing arms were ablaze. It backed into its companions, which filled the passage like worms in a cadaver. Its torso was aflame now, and the flames spread to several of the ghouls as they scrabbled at it to fend them off. Their claws only dislodged burning chunks of the victim. As the way was blocked by a press of blazing flesh that snarled and shrieked and rent itself with its overgrown nails, Kane turned sickened from the spectacle and ran along the corridor.

It ended at a wall. Kane was about to voice his frustration and rage when the flames at his back and streaming from the torch showed him that there was a junction ahead. A few strides brought him to the transverse passage. He could see no light in either direction, and he was holding the torch high in the hope that it would show him the right way when a louder outburst of snarling made him glance back. The mindless hunger of the pack had overcome the obstruction. The impetus of those behind had thrown the burning bodies to the floor and sent several of their kind sprawling on top of them. As more of the ghouls clambered over the bodies, heedless of their dying struggles, Kane dodged into the right-hand stretch of corridor.

He heard the ghouls swarm snarling after him. He had no chance of reaching wherever the corridor led before they could see him. A nervous shadow drew his eye to a niche in the wall ahead of him, and he was taking cover there when the ghouls reached the junction. His sword was ready in his right hand while his left held the torch in a corner of the alcove as he used his body to hide its light. His pursuers crowded out of the passage, and the inhuman wordless chorus rose in pitch and volume. Then it turned away from Kane and receded along the left-hand corridor.

He was about to step into the open when he thought he heard another sound – a muted snarl. It was not repeated, and in a few seconds he ventured into the corridor. He came face to face with a ghoul that was creeping towards the light Kane had not entirely concealed. As it sprang at him Kane impaled its throat with the sword, and it lurched backwards, choking on its tainted blood. Then it gave a gurgling cry, and the last of the pack swung around to glare along the corridor.

It saw Kane and emitted a shriek of hideous triumph. The sound could well have been the call of its unnatural species, because the rest of the pack turned as one in response. With a chorus of snarls that resembled the voice of a single rudimentary mind they rushed at Kane like maggots spilling out of a rotted carcass, and he ran down the corridor.

The flames of the torch fluttered like a flag without an emblem. The light danced mockingly ahead of him, feigning to discover exits that were only shadows. The sarcophagi in this section were intact, which made him feel more trapped. Then the light came up against a wall directly ahead, and showed him darkness leading away on both sides of the junction. As he dashed towards it the darkness drew into itself and lost its false perspective before vanishing into either corner of the wall. There was no junction. He had reached a dead end.

He was about to turn and make a last stand, if he could not fight his way past the abominable horde, when the torchlight steadied, allowing him to see that it had blinded him to another light. It was the merest sliver, visible through a crack in the roof at the end of the passage. It was moonlight, which had found the gap between the halves of a trapdoor.

The door was reached by a ladder. It must be, since it was so high overhead, but there was no ladder in the passage. Kane gripped the shaft of the torch with both hands and prayed that the door would not be locked as he thrust at it with the blazing end. The left half gave and then reared up, tottering erect for a moment before it fell open with a thud on stone or packed earth. He shoved at the other half, and it fell away too. He was about to hurl the torch at his pursuers, to gain himself precious moments while he attempted a desperate leap, when several of the pack seized him from behind.

Claws wrenched at his hair as one ghoul attempted to haul Kane's head back and tear out his throat. More talons raked at his arms, and jaws chewed at his shoulder, determined to rip through the cloak to his flesh and bone. The sensations filled him with loathing, and he thrust the torch into the faces behind him. He heard and felt it dig with a moist hiss into an eye or a mouth, and the claws let go of his hair. This let him twist around and beat off the attackers, first with the torch and then with the sword, chopping indiscriminately at the pack. He felt as if he were hacking at meat – certainly at nothing human. A belly shed its innards, and a scrawny limb was cleaved from a shoulder. A throat was laid open, exposing the windpipe, and a snarling head was almost parted from its body, tilting back so far that it might have been

parodying a martyr's heavenward gaze. Soon a mass of
bodies blocked the corridor, and Kane flung the torch at
the rest of the pack before he scrambled up the heap of
corpses to grab the edges of the doorway overhead.

He hauled himself up on his trembling forearms and
fell forward as he heard a chorus of snarls lurch towards
him. The ghouls were close to swarming out of the crypt
after him. Perhaps the corpses of their fellows were too
immediate a temptation, for Kane heard the ghouls begin
to feast on those instead. He dragged himself away from
the trapdoor and raised his head. He was at one side of
the church, surrounded by weather-beaten monuments
and their ragged shadows on the untended grass beneath
a full moon like a luminous primitive mask. Snow floated
through the chill air as if fragments were crumbling off
the moon. Where was Father Michael? Kane could deal
with him, but now it occurred to Kane that in the midst
of his encounter with the ghouls he had seemed to hear
a distant scream that might have been the priest's. Had
Father Michael fallen victim to his own unholy flock?
They might not be delayed too long by the scrawny
corpses underneath the trapdoor. Kane had risen onto
his haunches to shut the door and weigh it down with
stones when he became aware that he was not alone in
the churchyard.

The three men who had been watching his escape
closed in on him. They were almost as massive as the
stone figures silhouetted around them. Their faces were
overgrown with symbols composed of inflamed flesh, but
Kane recognised them. One face still boasted its tattoos,
entangled with Malachi's sigils. The second man retained
his luxuriant beard, and the third remained as bald as the
moon. All their eyes were as black as the sky, which had
turned cloudless now that there was no sun to obscure,

and all of them were grinning like wolves at some joke too cruel for mirth. As the bearded man stepped forward Kane saw a rounded object dangling from his fist. "Friend of yours?" the man asked Kane, and shied the missile at him.

It landed on the frozen earth beside Kane and rolled onto its back, staring up with eyes as empty as the sky around the moon. The neck had been crudely hacked from the body, and the mouth gaped wide in a mute protest. It was Father Michael's head. "We don't like priests," the bearded man explained.

"We don't like anyone that prays," said his tattooed companion.

"Was you at your prayers?" the bald man enquired of Kane with a jeering laugh.

"Better hurry up and say amen," the bearded man said, and then he peered at Kane's face. "Have a look at this, lads. Remember this one?"

The bald man crouched to stare at Kane, who saw that the occult symbols had even infested the shaved pate. In the moonlight it resembled an embroidered skullcap made of skin. His eyes widened as though to encompass more darkness as he identified Kane. "He's not a fighter," he said.

The third raider took some time to recognise Kane, relishing the process. "What are you doing here, Puritan?" he said, and the mass of tattoos and sigils around his mouth drew back lazily, peeling open a vicious grin.

Kane rose to his feet. His strength was returning, and he did not waver. He gazed into each face and saw only corruption, inscribed on the flesh and polluting the eyes to the depths of their souls. "So," he said, "you have given yourselves over to this evil, have you?"

The bald man grinned more broadly still, exposing

rotten teeth and blackened gums. "You should try," he said. "It gets you more than praying."

"Malachi will hold all this land soon enough," the bearded man declared and spat on a grave at the foot of a stone angel. "What's the point in you fighting?" he said and raised the bloody axe he bore in one thick fist.

The word, or the sight of Father Michael's blood on the axe, appeared to excite the bald man. "And the only thing round here is fighting," he said before wiping his mouth with the back of his hand.

An eager grin tugged the tattooed man's lips awry. It was clear that he was barely able to contain his anticipation. "But you don't do that," he said, "do you?"

A single consciousness seemed to be appraising Kane, but it did not belong to their leader. The Overlord's attention must be elsewhere, and Kane was faced by simple gleeful brutishness – the dull group intellect common to every mob that has found a scapegoat for its hatred. "Well," he said slowly and softly, "you know, I may just have changed my mind about that."

He watched understanding creep into the corrupted eyes. It failed to make the men wary of him; they seemed delighted that he was proposing to put up a fight. The tattooed man took a deliberate pace towards him and reached lazily for his sword. Before he could draw it Kane strode to meet him and seized the man's fist on the hilt. The man's eyes widened in furious surprise, and he wrenched at the weapon. He was striving to free it and his hand from Kane's grasp when Kane drove his knife deep into his adversary's right shoulder.

The man's eyes bulged with disbelief, and a snarl drew back his lips. His sword arm was useless now. Kane felt the fist grow slack as he sawed the blade through the man's shoulder towards his neck. Perhaps the pain was so great that it drove all capacity for thought out of his opponent's head. The man twisted his whole body to escape the blade, but he was turning towards it. The knife sliced across his shoulder and cut his throat wide open.

He staggered sideways, spitting gouts of blood, and crashed to the earth among the graves. As Kane drew his sword the bald man rushed at him, thrusting his own blade at Kane and roaring at the top of his voice. Whether the cry expressed his fury or was intended to daunt Kane, it had no effect on him. He parried the man's sword and met his onrush with the knife, plunging it between the ribs into the heart. A punch in the face sent the dying man backwards and left the dagger in Kane's grasp. As the raider sank to the frozen ground, clutching his chest in a vain attempt to stem the gush of blood, Kane turned on the bearded man.

His courage appeared to have left him as his companions had. He was already backing away, swinging the axe in front of him with such force that drops of blood flew from the blade, spattering monuments black in the moonlight. If the sweeps of the axe were meant to ward Kane off, they only enraged him. He stalked at the man and slashed his arm with the sword. The axe sprang from his hand and chopped into the earth. Kane seized the handle and, tugging the axe free, raised it high.

He was tempted to rid the earth of the bearded brute. Instead he turned the axe and clubbed the man to his knees with the flat of the blade. As the man tottered on the edge of consciousness Kane flung the axe away among the monuments and seized the man by the front of his stained leather jerkin. He dragged him to the trapdoor outside the church and threw him down, planting one foot on his chest as the man's head dangled backwards over the edge. A chorus of hungry snarling greeted the sight, and the bearded man twisted his head to peer into the crypt, and then gazed up fearfully at Kane. More than the moonlight turned his disfigured face pale. "What are they?" he gasped.

"They are your brothers and your sisters." Kane stared down at the man, whose very fear seemed bestial, and the mass of monstrous faces beneath him. "No," he said, "even they are better than you. They were cursed, but you chose to become part of this evil."

He rested the point of the sword on the man's throat and lifted the locket from his own neck. In the moonlight Meredith's face and her mother's looked drained of colour – of life. A snowflake settled on Meredith's lips like an icy kiss, and Kane brushed it away before lowering the locket towards his captive. "This girl," he said urgently. "Your kind took her."

The man shook his head so vigorously that it drew blood at the point of the sword. "I don't know her," he protested.

"Look well." Kane used his foot to shove the man back so that his shoulders were over the edge. As the man clawed at the frozen earth for support, Kane said "It is your only chance to save your pitiful life."

The ghouls snarled – they might have been agreeing wordlessly – and the bearded man stared down to see them leaping almost close enough to seize him. "Have you seen her?" Kane demanded.

The man turned his fearful face up and peered wildly at the locket. "Yes," he said. "Yes, I saw her."

Kane leaned on the man's chest until he felt ribs begin to crack. "Where have you seen her?"

The man licked his lips and made a last effort to struggle free before he had to respond. "She's dead."

"Dead?" The word tasted like ash in Kane's mouth.

"Don't you lie to me," he said through his teeth, and pricked the man's throat with the sword.

"I'm not." The man's eyes rolled from side to side in their distorted sockets. "No, I want to live," he pleaded. "I wouldn't lie. She's dead. I threw her out of the wagon myself."

Kane was hardly aware of speaking. He might have been listening to someone else recite the formula of a prayer. "She isn't dead."

"She is," the man cried and clutched at Kane's leg in sudden panic. "I told you what you wanted," he said like a betrayed child. "Let me go."

"Go," Kane said, less with anger than from the depths of an utter indifference born of despair, and shoved him over the edge. The man fell screaming into the crypt, where many taloned hands jerked up to catch him. As the screams grew more agonised, accompanied by the splintering of bones and by snarls muffled by feasting, Kane walked away without a backward glance. He came to a halt when the shadow of an angel laid a hand across his path. "She is gone," he said. "She is gone and I am lost." He raised his eyes to the angel as if he might find some hint of hope there, but the weathered face might have symbolised the decay of all his faith, and the white eyes were as unresponsive as the moon.

TWENTY-SEVEN

Kane rode through the dead land, leading two horses that had belonged to dead men. The fields were sheets of ice, spiky with lifeless grass and weeds like carvings of white ivory. Snow and wind and the endless winter had reduced the scattered trees and shrubs to bones picked clean even of colour. Patches of mist drifted across the fields, unable to rest or to fix on a shape, wandering like lost souls of the landscape. They were no more aimless than Kane. The chill of the sunless afternoon reached not just into his marrow but to the depths of his soul, finding little but emptiness there. It was no longer worth saving now that Meredith was dead.

When he saw smoke in the distance he thought a village was on fire. Such things had ceased to concern him, and he made for it only because it lay ahead. But the smoke came from chimneys, and a few minutes' weary ride brought him in sight of a small town. He no longer imagined that he was being guided by his destiny. That had abandoned him now that Meredith was dead.

A gradual slope descended to the town. At first Kane failed to grasp why the slope seemed unnaturally deserted, and then he realised that he would have expected to see children sliding down it on makeshift sledges and to hear their shouts and laughter. If there were any children in the town, they had been silenced. He could have been given no clearer sign that the land had been drained of life.

An archway led into the single street. Perhaps the solitary entrance had let the townsfolk believe that their town was defensible, but they would hardly think so now. It must have been a market town, though there were few traces left of this – just the remains of a few half-demolished stalls. As he passed beneath the arch Kane heard the desultory clank of a blacksmith's hammer and saw two men struggling to load a barrel onto a cart. Two women standing amid the frozen ruts of the street gazed up at him as though he might represent some hope, but glanced away hastily when they found none. Once their plight would have enraged him, but now it roused only indifference. It was the way of the world now – of Malachi's world.

The street ended at a wide square almost too irregular to earn the name. A motley assortment of cottages and larger buildings surrounded it, raising a haphazard roofline to the featureless grey sky. Every building was brown as dead grass. Apart from a man in drab clothes, who was winching a bucket up from a well, the only occupants of the square were several raiders. They stood outside an inn, laughing and cursing between gulps of ale from tankards. Either drunkenness had dulled their curiosity or the land was so much under Malachi's control that the presence of a lone rider did not trouble them, for they stared at Kane with no apparent interest. They turned away as he rode past them to stables next to the blacksmith's, where the man with the hammer peered hard at Kane over the sparks of the anvil.

The stable-master emerged into the square to greet Kane. He was slighter than the blacksmith, wiry and quick-eyed. "Good day to you," he said and glanced past Kane at the raiders. "You'll be stabling your horses."

"No," Kane said. "I want to sell them."

The man gave them an appraising look, and then his gaze hardened. He sent a second glance past Kane and reached a swift decision. "Bring them in here," he said low.

Kane dismounted and led the horses into the stables, less speedily than the stable-master appeared to like. A smell of hay and horse dung met him beneath the rafters. A line of stalls, fewer than half of them occupied, led to the back of the large room. A boy of about Samuel Crowthorn's age was shovelling out a stall, but the stable-master beckoned to him. "Go to your mother, Joseph," he said, "and tell her that I may be late."

The boy scratched his curly head in bewilderment. "But father – "

"Do as you're bid," his father said and made to cuff him across the ear.

As soon as the boy darted into the square, the stable-master led the horses to the far end of the passage alongside the stalls before turning to Kane. "How did you come by these animals?" he said just loud enough for Kane to hear.

"What does it matter?" said Kane.

"They bear the mark of Malachi." The stable-master pointed to the saddle and the harnesses, where Kane had failed to notice an embossed symbol – an oval filled with swarming flames, like a spyhole into Hell. "If you stole them…" the stable-master said and gazed unreadably at him.

"You cannot steal from dead men," Kane said.

The man frowned at Kane's weapons before peering down the passage, beyond which Kane heard the raiders crowd shouting into the tavern. As the square grew quiet the stable-master murmured "Did you kill them?"

Kane was done with boasting. He had no pride left, nor any reason to describe his exploits. As he responded only with a stare the stable-master said "We heard of a man such as you who has been hunting them."

Kane found no cause to reply to this either. Perhaps his muteness unnerved the stable-master, who said "You must hide, sir."

Kane discovered that he had not entirely lost his self-respect. "I hide from no man," he declared.

"The town is theirs." By now the stable-master was unable to keep his gaze on his listener. "All around here they hold sway," he said under his breath. "There are spies who work for them. They listen in the shadows and betray any who would fight back. If they know you are here – "

His furtiveness angered Kane. "I don't care who knows," he said so loud that a horse whinnied in a stall.

"But listen." The man laid a hand on Kane's arm. "There are those here who would fight," he murmured. "They are only waiting for enough men."

"Then let them fight," Kane said. "Pay me."

The stable-master withdrew his hand and turned it up as though still hoping for a reward. "Will you not join them?" he said so incredulously that he forgot to murmur.

"No," Kane said and held out his own hand. "Now pay me." In case he had left the man in any doubt, or with any vestige of hope in Kane, he said "Pay me enough to drink myself into oblivion." It was the nearest to a prayer that he had left in him.

TWENTY-EIGHT

The ground floor of the tavern was a room as large as a barn. Kane found a table to himself in the darkest corner and shouted for ale. The raiders had joined several of their fellows, and all the disfigured brutish faces glanced at his shout. Their indifference might have suggested they thought that, besides representing no threat, he was no better than they were, but even this notion failed to inflame him. He was there for one purpose only – to achieve stupor.

As soon as the landlord brought a tankard and a jug of ale Kane filled the tankard to the brim and quaffed the contents. The man gave him a doubtful look but pocketed the coins Kane slammed on the table. Once the landlord trudged away Kane gazed around the room. Dozens of men sat on rough benches at the oaken tables or stood in groups on the bare plank floor. Some he took for townsfolk, others for travellers breaking whatever journeys brought them to this defeated region, but there was little of the uproar he would have expected to hear in a tavern. Only the raiders were boisterous, while the rest of the drinkers kept an uneasy peace. The blurred murmur of conversations felt like a promise of insensibility, and Kane raised a mocking tankard to it before he gulped another mugful.

When the afternoon darkened he thought it was

matching his mood. Dusk crept into the tavern like a spy or a conspirator, and the landlord lit rush-lights on the tables. Kane welcomed the gloom, not just for letting him stay unobserved. He lifted the locket from around his neck and laid it open on the table. The tiny fragile portraits looked as weather-beaten as monuments, which was all they were now. Rain and snow had smudged Meredith's features and her mother's, so that they might have been depicting how his memories of them had already begun to fade, erased by ale. The unstable light blessed them with a kind of life, a cruel illusion. Kane felt unworthy even to pray for their souls, and he drained the tankard in the hope that the ale would wash away the last of his emotions. The jug was empty, and he planted it on the table with a blow that would have driven a nail deep into a coffin. It brought the landlord, who made to replenish the tankard from another jug, but Kane seized his arm. "Leave it all," he growled and threw a bag of coins in front of him. The landlord grabbed the bag and retreated as Kane refilled the tankard. Even when he downed the bitter contents he seemed incapable of recapturing the apathy that had felt within his reach. It was not just the interruption that had distracted him. Somebody was watching him.

He lifted his heavy head to glower about him. At some point the raiders had blundered bellowing out of the tavern, but few of the drinkers had taken the chance to raise their cowed voices. The pinched flames of the rush-lights flickered, lending every face a nervous twitch. The antics of the dim light made it harder for Kane to focus on his fellow topers, but in a few moments he located the watchers at a table close by. One looked youthful, lightly bearded and with dark hair trimmed relatively short, while his companion was bulkier, with a beard as thick and black as his unkempt hair. Neither of them seemed to pose a threat or to be of any other significance to Kane, and he let his gaze sink to the locket. As he fumbled to pick up the tankard his movement deflected the flame of the rush-light on the table, drawing a veil of shadow over the portraits. He was hoping that the ale would be as capable of veiling his thoughts when the bearded man said "Are you sure?"

"It is him." Apparently this was cause for excitement, however muted. "I knew it," the younger man said.

Kane did not look up, even when the pair left their table and slid onto the bench opposite him. Their arrival bowed the flame towards him, and he could almost have fancied that Meredith's face stirred. Once he might have hoped this meant she was still alive, but the sign was meaningless to him now. "Sir?" the younger man said.

Kane kept his head low and grasped the handle of the tankard. Surely it was clear that he must be left alone – that he would do whatever was needed to preserve his state. He cupped his hand about the locket, to conceal it or at least to ward off any curiosity about it, and the shadow of his fingers plunged the women's faces into blackness. "Captain Kane?" the man persisted.

Nobody had called Kane that for many months – nobody except Meredith. The man's words felt like a mocking echo of her appeals to Kane. The sight of her face buried in darkness weighed his gaze down, but he scowled beneath his brows at his unwelcome companion. "I'm Henry Telford," the man told him. "Don't you remember me?"

If the name and the determinedly youthful face had any meaning, it seemed as dim and unreliable as the flames all around Kane. As Kane gave his head a single effortful shake, Telford said "I was a mate on the *Tiercel*."

Kane remembered him now – remembered the voyage and the plundering and bloodshed that had waited at its end. Although the uninvited memories seemed prehistorically remote, they were part of Kane's journey to losing his soul. "Telford. Henry Telford," the man said doggedly. "You were the captain. You must remember."

His stocky colleague grimaced at Kane and tried to pull Telford away. "It is not him," he muttered. "He is no captain of men."

"It is, Garrick. It's Captain Kane," Telford insisted and lowered his voice. "He can lead us, believe me."

"Lead us where, Henry? To another tavern?" Garrick seemed close to spitting on the floor in disgust. "Look at him," he objected and leaned towards Kane. "My friend here says you're the greatest warrior he ever saw," he said. "I don't believe him."

A great weariness had overtaken Kane. His quest had exhausted not just his body but his soul, and it was an effort even to speak. "You should not," he said.

"There, Henry," Garrick said in bitter triumph. "You have heard it from the man's own lips."

"He is in his cups. A leader has no need to boast of his exploits," Telford said and appealed to Kane. "I know what you can do, Captain. I have seen it."

His persistence reawakened Kane's dull rage, and he grasped the front of Telford's tunic to haul him close. "Those were distant times," he said indistinctly. "I am no longer that man. She's dead now and my soul is forfeit."

Perhaps Telford took the faces in the locket to belong to Kane's wife and daughter, though Kane had none. Sympathy glimmered in Telford's eyes without ousting his determination. There was little sympathy in Garrick's as he muttered "He's no use to us or anybody. Leave him."

"No," Telford said with such force that it set the rush-light flaring. "Captain Kane," he said low but urgently, "we need a leader. We have to fight back against this evil. It must never rule this land."

Kane let go of him and fell back. His shoulders thumped the walls that formed the corner of the tavern, but either the impact was too dull to trouble him or the dullness was in his mind. "Then fight back!" he shouted.

It might have been a challenge not just to his uninvited companions but to anyone who would take issue with him. Everywhere in the gloom, faces turned to stare at him. All of them looked nervous of his words as well as agitated by the flickering light. Garrick made to rise from the bench, but Telford caught at his arm. Was Telford so stubborn that he meant to linger even now that Kane had drawn attention to him? "She's lost," Kane said, clutching at the table to lever himself to his feet. "And I lost her."

He leaned against one wall and groped for the locket, scraping the table with his nails until they snagged the chain. He pulled it towards him and succeeded in fumbling the chain around his neck. He shut the locket with a snap that sounded not just flat but empty and let it dangle against his chest, where it seemed to be reaching vainly for his heart. "I am to blame," he said and raised his voice once more. "Let them come and get me. I care not."

Even this outburst failed to daunt Telford. As Kane stumbled out of the corner, the man moved to support him or detain him. "Captain Kane..."

"Get out of my way," Kane bellowed and shoved him aside with such force that he sent himself staggering. "I swore to find her," he declared, "and I failed." He no longer knew whom he was addressing; it might have been the huddle of drinkers into whose midst he was reeling.

Several hands fended him off so vigorously that he fell against a table. He clutched at it and brought it down with him as he crashed to the floor. A rush-light fell in front of his face as his head struck the boards, and then the flame went out, or his consciousness did, or both. The last flicker of the flame could have signified the extinction of all light in the world, or perhaps it was an omen of the fires of Hell.

TWENTY-NINE

Kane lay on straw and imagined he was in a manger. He was as helpless as a baby and as innocent of any thoughts. Sounds and smells of animals surrounded him in the darkness of the barn. Otherwise he seemed to be alone, and he could find no reason to expend the effort it would take to focus his eyes if he should heave them open. As he sought to recapture the stupor from which his aching skull had roused him, a wooden frame creaked beneath him. This was at odds with his sense of his surroundings, and he struggled reluctantly towards the surface of his consciousness. There were his hands, even if they seemed almost too remote from his brain to belong to him. He groped at his eyelids and fumbled them wide and peered into the gloom.

He was not in a barn. The snorts and wordless snarls that had invaded his slumber belonged not to animals but to drunkards like him. The large room owed the smell of straw to the narrow mattresses on which the sleepers sprawled, and there was an underlying stench of sweat and urine and beery breath. Three ranks of pallets were lined up along the room with hardly an arm's length between the beds. The head of Kane's bed was against one wall, and he was lying several pallets distant from the door, which stood ajar, affording a feeble hint of illumination. In the past such a situation would have brought all his senses alert, but now he was not just stupefied by ale and by his fall; he could think of no reason to be wary on his own behalf. He was no longer worth it. He had come to the end of himself, and he wanted nothing other than insensibility, however it might be granted to him.

He could just hear the confused hubbub of the tavern down below, and someone was climbing the stairs. As torch-flames flickered in the doorway, he closed his eyes before the sight could fully waken him and drag him back into the unrewarding world. He heard the door groan wide, and then planks began to give beneath the weight of stealthy footfalls. They halted, and a low voice spoke. "No, that is not him."

The words sounded unwelcomely familiar. Were the searchers Telford and his men? Kane was determined that they would not rouse him. The chain of the locket dug into his neck, but he was not about to move. He confined himself to taking shallow breaths as a torch was lowered towards his face. He felt the heat on his forehead, and a glow bloomed within his eyelids. Before he would have had to breathe again, the glow diminished and the heat withdrew. He was waiting to hear the voice once more when a hand was clamped over his mouth.

The large hand bruised his lips, and it stank. Kane's eyes sprang wide to see a raider's blemished face leaning close to him. He was less indifferent to his own fate than he had tried to believe after all, and he sank his teeth into the hand, which tasted like tainted meat. He was too late. Hands had already fastened on his arms and legs, pinning him to the bed. The raider who had seized Kane's face roared in pain and punched him ferociously on the chin, stunning him afresh. The yell awoke most of the occupants of the room. Presumably the raider had silenced Kane in case anyone ventured to aid him, but the men on the pallets only watched fearfully or turned away, hiding their faces. Kane was relieved of his weapons and then hauled to his feet. Trampling on beds or kicking them aside, the raiders dragged Kane out of the room.

He was flung downstairs to cannon head first against a wall at the bend of the staircase. Before he could recover from the impact he was seized again and thrown down the remaining flight to sprawl on the floor of the tavern. The room was deserted. The noise he had taken to belong to drinkers was the nervous murmur of a crowd outside, where a fitful glow seemed to mimic the illumination of the rush-lights. In a moment Kane heard an agonised yell. A raider threw open the door of the tavern, and Kane saw the triumph of evil.

Two men lay screaming in the mud on the far side of the square, in a sunless daylight as grey as the driving rain. Each man was bound to a cross by his hands and feet, and raiders were nailing the hands to the wood. At every hammer-blow the fingers of the nailed hand tried convulsively to form a fist and then recoiled, falling back to await the next stroke. The man on the left strained to raise his torso as if he could somehow heave himself free, but was able only to lift his head. Around him the market stalls were ablaze, and the light played on his bearded face. He was Telford's companion Garrick. "Mercy," he pleaded.

The raider who was attending to him gave no sign of hearing him. A last blow of the hammer drove the nail flush with Garrick's palm, and then the raider stepped over the pinioned body to deal with the other hand. The man on the second cross seemed to have passed beyond words to screams as much of disbelief as pain, but his cries had no effect on his torturer. As two raiders dragged Kane on his knees across the tavern he saw that the second victim was the stable-master who had attempted to enlist him in the rebellion. Surely Kane was not responsible for the plight of either man, but he was overwhelmed by dull anger at their helplessness and his. His beaten body was as ineffectual as his soul. He was no more capable of rescuing the men than he had been of protecting Meredith.

The sounds of hammering ceased, but the screams were renewed as raiders hauled the crosses upright with ropes. Garrick's pleas were wordless now, and in moments they grew hopeless. As the raiders fixed the crosses in position, Kane's captors dragged him into the mud, and he saw a horseman watching him across the square – the masked Overlord. He spurred his horse past the crosses and, having allotted the victims an appraising glance, rode over to Kane. The raider at Kane's back dealt his captive's head a blow with the side of his fist to teach him deference, but the masked rider held up one gloved hand. He dismounted and fixed his gaze on Kane. Gouts of rain streamed down the leather mask but left the eyes untouched, and their blackness betrayed no emotion. When Kane responded with a stare smouldering with rage, the Overlord took him by the chin to lift his head.

His grasp was almost gentle. It seemed somehow secretive, and the leather glove felt like a chill wet substitute for flesh. Kane could not judge what it might contain in the way of a hand. He suffered its grip and met the eyes behind the mask, though he might as well have been staring into the uttermost depths of space. His own eyes had begun to sting with fatigue and the relentless downpour by the time the Overlord spoke. "Solomon Kane," he said.

For the first time Kane heard the voice beyond the mask. It was little more than a whisper as cold and sharp as the rain. It was not just muffled by the mask; it seemed lacking in shape, close to mouthless. "Do you know me, Solomon?" it said.

The suggestion of familiarity revolted Kane. If he had not been so stunned and enfeebled he would have struggled free of the leathery grasp. "I know you for a foul servant of evil," he said with all the force he could recover.

The head bent towards him, and Kane had a grotesque sense of having somehow disappointed his interrogator. "Malachi cannot be defeated," the thin voice said. "Join us, Solomon."

Kane lifted his face into the rain, and the gloved hand helped him. Kane was making sure his answer would be heard throughout the square. "Never," he declared.

The gloved hand gripped his face, and the black gaze seemed to plumb his soul. "Join us," his captor hissed, "and be saved."

Kane's answer was almost a shout. "I will have no part in your foulness."

"Then you are lost." As the Overlord let go of Kane, he might have been relinquishing any trace of humanity that had remained in him, hidden by the mask. "You will die here," he said, "and then your true suffering will begin."

He turned his back and mounted his horse as a raider stepped in front of Kane. The livid symbols on his dripping face seemed to work his mouth. "This man cannot save you," he shouted to the townsfolk, who had been herded into a corner of the square. "He is nothing."

Two of his fellows seized Kane by the shoulders and dragged him, still kneeling, across the square. Between the two crucified men, who had fallen silent from exhaustion or from loss of blood, a cross lay supine in the mud. Perhaps it was Kane's destiny, which had lain in wait for him. Though he did his best to struggle, he could not prevent his captors from forcing him onto his back on the cross. A cord was passed around his torso, binding him to the central shaft so securely that the rope bruised his flesh. A raider stretched Kane's right arm to its full length while a second man knelt on the other and stooped to Kane's left hand. Kane clenched his fist, but the raider prised it open. He leaned his weight on the fingers and dug an iron nail into Kane's palm, piercing skin and flesh.

The first hammer-blow drove the nail so deep that when the man released Kane's fingers, their anguished convulsion could not dislodge it. Kane clenched his teeth to bite back a cry and glared at the man from the depths of his soul. Another stroke of the hammer sent the nail between the tendons of his hand to lodge in the cross, and a third blow pinned his hand to the wood.

Only instinct – the will to cling to life before it drained away, to prolong even the suffering that kept him alive – made Kane close his other hand. The raider levered the fingers back and thrust a nail deep into the palm. A blow of the hammer drove the nail through flesh and gristle with a crunch that seemed to resonate throughout Kane's body, or the outrage did. Kane ground his teeth until his jaws ached, but the pain was no distraction from the blaze of agony in his hands. A final stroke crushed the palm under the metal head and flattened the tendons against the crossbeam. The raider stood back to take a moment's pride in his work, and then the cross was hauled up from the mud.

If Kane had imagined that he had reached the peak of his torment, he was stripped of the illusion at once. The rope that bound him to the central shaft did not entirely support him, and his weight tugged at his nailed hands.

His clenched jaws throbbed, and his bulging eyes wept
with rain. As the square fell away beneath him, he could
hardly separate the tilting of the cross from the vertigo
his agony brought on. The cross wobbled vertical and
then steadied in the socket that had been dug for it.
Every movement shot a fresh pain through his hands,
but he managed to hold a solitary notion in his mind:
his torment was not meaningless if it prevented any
worse from befalling the townsfolk. His soul was
lost along with Meredith, but at least he would have
succeeded in leaving some good in the world.

The Overlord rode to the foot of the cross and gazed
up at him. He might almost have been sharing Kane's
thoughts; certainly some preoccupation detained him
while Kane drew a shuddering breath. The mask might
have been displaying his inhuman disinterest as he
turned his horse away, voicing his decision through the
mouth of a raider. "Burn this town to ashes," he said.

So Kane had presumed too much even now, and he
was nothing after all, just as the raider had informed
the townsfolk. He was incapable of helping anyone;
he could only bring evil upon them. His eyes grew
blurred, no less with agony than rain, as he witnessed
the destruction of the town. Raiders smashed windows
and threw blazing brands into every house, and some
drove a wagon on fire into the stables. He was reminded
of breaching the doors of the obsidian African castle.
It seemed a lifetime ago – another man's lifetime – but
it was one of many stages on Kane's journey into the
embrace of evil. Soon the entire town was ablaze, and
flames leapt from the upper windows, which were
level with Kane's face. He thought the flames were
beckoning him to a greater fire – one that would never
be extinguished. He turned his face up to the heavens,

but no sign of redemption was to be found there. Just as the sun had forsaken the sky, so all light had forsaken his soul, and he could only wait for the darkness to take possession of him.

THIRTY

Meredith was drenched by the constant rain and spattered with mud. Her fingers ached from clutching at the bars of the cage, and her head swam with the incessant jolting of the wagon on the stony road. Her hair was loosely glued to her face, and her clothes clung to her like a waterlogged shroud. She had to keep dashing rain out of her eyes, although all she saw were leafless trees advancing through the downpour. She was so cold that she could no longer recall how it felt to be touched by the sun. Above all, however, she felt ashamed of herself.

It seemed that deep down she had hoped for some privilege. She had been captured by the Overlord himself, after all. She would have been glad if the reward of her apparent importance had been a quick death, to take her to her family in Heaven. It was wrong to hope to die – far worse to pray for it, however secretly – and she might have concluded that her plight was a punishment from God. In any case it was naïve to expect so immediate an end when the Overlord had gone to such lengths to find her. Whatever she was marked for lay ahead.

She was in the foremost wagon of three, where she had been escorted by two raiders and the Overlord himself. Not only this suggested a mockery of prestige. Most of the captives were in the other cages, apparently to ensure

that Meredith was not crushed to death, and the cart
was guarded throughout the interminable journey by
four mounted raiders, leaving two alongside each of the
vehicles behind. It was plain that her treatment had made
her unwelcome, and her fellow captives had glimpsed the
mark on her hand as well. None of them would speak
to her; perhaps they believed she was associated with
the evil that had them in its grasp. She could not have
dissuaded them, whatever Captain Kane had said. She
had been touched by corruption, and the insensibility of
her marked hand felt like the start of the death of her
soul. The dullness seemed to be overtaking her thoughts
when she saw that the forest was thinning ahead.

At first she could see nothing beyond the trees except a
grey veil of rain. As the wagon emerged from the denuded
forest the veil retreated across an expanse of sodden
fields, revealing black clouds on the horizon. It was not
a storm ahead; they were masses of smoke. The horses
plodded onwards and the wagon lurched over muddy
ruts, and in a few minutes she saw another plundered
town on fire.

While many of the buildings had collapsed, the entrance
to the town – a stone arch – stood firm. As the wagons
trundled down a slope, a band of raiders drove their
captives through the arch to meet them. The guards
unlocked two of the cages and forced back the occupants
to make room for more, but left the foremost cage
unopened. Meredith sensed how her companions resented
being made to seem favoured by evil. She alone was, and
she felt more outcast still – abandoned by her fellows and,
she was even more ashamed to think, perhaps by God.

The cages were slammed and locked, and the wagons
resumed their journey. The foremost horses shied a
little as they passed between the blazing ruins, but the

driver quelled them cruelly with his whip. The women in the other cages hid their children's faces from the conflagration. Perhaps this was the only road west, but Meredith wondered if the raiders were taking a wicked delight in confronting the prisoners with the destruction of their homes – and then she saw that they were being shown far worse. The smoke hovering over the ruins had drifted low as if weighted by the rain, but now it parted raggedly to reveal the heart of the town.

It might have been a diabolical parody of Calvary. Surrounded on every side by fire, three men had been crucified in the town square. Blood trickled down their arms and dripped from their nailed hands into the mud. All three heads were bowed, and Meredith hoped that God had granted them peace. She breathed an entreaty on their behalf as the wagon lumbered across the square, and then she seized the bars of the cage and peered through the rain. Although the face of the victim on the central cross was almost hidden by bedraggled locks of hair, above which the downpour sprouted from his scalp like a translucent spiky crown, she thought she recognised him.

His fists clenched in what might have been a final convulsion. His torso strained against its bonds in an attempt to take the weight off his pierced hands, and his head wavered erect. Some of the hair trailed back from his face, and Meredith cried "Solomon."

The driver of the wagon turned to stare at her, and then he whipped the horses into a reluctant trot. The cage was past the crosses before Meredith could repeat her appeal. Captain Kane had not opened his eyes; he seemed unaware of anything around him. His head sank as though the strength was draining from him with his blood. Meredith struggled to the back of the cage, heedless of the muttered protests of her fellow captives.

She grabbed the bars and sucked in a breath that felt like inhaling rain. As she did so Captain Kane's head lolled to one side, and his mouth fell slackly open. "Solomon," she cried, but the wagon was leaving the sight of his limp body behind, and with it the last mockery of her hope.

THIRTY-ONE

Before Kane closed his eyes the world began to leave him. The walls of the burning houses wavered as if they were no more permanent than the rain, and the faces of the raiders seemed close to abandoning their shapes like waxen masks on fire. Perhaps all this was an illusion produced by the waves of heat that even the downpour could not quench, but Kane thought he had come to the end of his senses. A black pall drifted across his vision, and the stench of smoke filled his nostrils. In a while the stink dissipated, but his sight stayed dark. It could show him nothing that would comfort him, and so he let his eyelids fall shut and bowed his head.

He felt all his sensations withdraw from him – the vicious gusts of rain in his face, the rope that bruised his body as it lashed him to the cross, the dull ache that extended along his arms to link him with the anguish of his nailed hands. A surge of that agony reached for him, to return him to his torment on the cross. His head rose in protest, and he struggled to lever up his body against its bonds to relieve the burden on his hands. As his head pounded with the effort, he imagined that he heard his name.

The blood in his ears was louder. It thumped like a funeral drum while he strove to lift himself even an inch without using his arms. He managed to sustain the posture for a very few seconds, and then all his weight dragged at his hands. The swelling agony brought faintness in its wake, and the torment grew remote as Kane's consciousness drew into itself. He was scarcely aware that his head was drooping onto his chest. It tilted to one side, and his mouth gaped as though it was preparing to expel its final breath. He was urging oblivion to engulf him when someone called his name.

The cry was desperate, almost prayerful. It was so hoarse and shrill that he could hardly believe it was the voice he had never expected to hear again in this life. Was Meredith inviting him to join her in the next world, or was this some diabolical trick? In any case he need not regain his senses, and he was blissfully close to leaving them behind when the voice cried out once more. "Solomon!" it beseeched him.

Kane shook his head dully and opened his blurred eyes, and his sensations flooded back – the onslaught of rain, the clinging icy chill, the aches that racked his exhausted body, the anguish that pierced his hands. He strained his eyes back into focus and peered wearily through the rain and thick drifts of smoke. A train of prison carts was splashing sluggishly through the mud of the ruined square. Faces clustered behind the bars, too closely for Kane's enfeebled vision to tell them apart – and then he caught sight of a lone figure at the back of the first wagon. He squeezed his eyes shut to rid them of rain, and stared until they felt like cinders embedded in his skull. His vision swam with the agony in his hands, and then it fastened on the captive's face. At that distance the face was no larger than her image in the locket, but it was unmistakable. "Meredith," Kane blurted.

His voice was so weak that he feared it would not reach her. All the same, she thrust her face against the bars as if she yearned to force it between them. "Solomon," she pleaded. It might have been a prayer for him, reduced to its heartfelt essence. A raider scowled towards Kane and struck the bars with his whip. The spectacle enraged Kane, who felt as if his helpless anguish had given him back his voice. "Meredith," he yelled.

She heard him and responded, even as she was borne out of the square. In a moment the horses passed beyond a blazing cottage, and in a few more the wagon was hidden too. As flames reared up to cut her off from Kane, Meredith cried out his name.

The agony that seized him then was not merely physical; it pierced to the depths of his soul. The vow he had made to her parents felt like a reopened wound more grievous than his crucifixion. He would not forsake her while he was capable of drawing breath. He braced himself against the cross and tensed all the muscles of his right arm, and then he hauled it away from the crossbeam. "God give me strength," he said through his clenched teeth.

It was both a prayer and a snarl of atrocious pain. Sweat indistinguishable from the downpour streamed over his forehead and stung his eyes. His arm shuddered with the dreadful effort, and he felt the hole in his palm gape wider. The head of the nail was not much broader than the shaft, and he dragged it through his hand, tearing flesh and parting gristle. He felt the nail snag on a tendon before it pulled free. The hand fell away from the cross, throbbing like an injury too huge for definition.

Much of Kane's weight was on his left hand now. The nail ripped through its palm, grinding against a tendon. The hand jerked free, and for a moment he was supported by the rope around the upright of the cross. It was not meant for such a purpose, and perhaps it was rotten with the constant rain. It snapped like a hawser in a typhoon, and Kane fell from the cross to sprawl on his side in the mud.

Though he could barely see for pain, he made out half a dozen blurred shapes advancing on him. Perhaps they thought him superhuman to come at him in such numbers, but he was only a man. He managed to struggle onto all fours with an effort that made his head reel and his limbs shake. Even if he could have sprung at the raiders, what would that achieve? He had no weapon, and his hands were useless. He could only raise his head in a final gesture of defiance as a hulking shape tramped forward, raising a massive axe.

The axe came swooping down, and blood spurted high into the downpour. The axe missed Kane by inches and dropped from the raider's grasp. The blood was not Kane's. The raider slumped on his face in the mud, to reveal Telford and the sword with which he had dispatched the man. A band of men had entered the square while all attention was on Kane, and now they rushed upon the raiders, running swords through them or chopping them down. Telford almost decapitated a raider before helping Kane to his feet. "Captain Kane," he murmured and put an arm around his shoulders. But the last effort had proved too much for Kane, who was not even aware of reeling against him. The world went out like a snuffed candle, and then Kane knew nothing at all.

THIRTY-TWO

Kane heard murmuring and could not understand a word. He thought the voice might be praying for him. It was a woman's voice, and almost as soft as an absence of sensation – the absence that had Kane in its gentle embrace. He was only just awake, and it seemed to him that his body was staying asleep. It must need to sleep in order to recuperate, and he ought not to rouse it until it was healed. If he had been granted peace at last, surely it must come from God, and to reject it would be a sin. "A elfyntodd dwyr sinddyn duw cerrig yr fferllurig nwyn..." The voice beside him was soothing him, and he need not interpret the words.

But there were other voices. Several men were speaking in some enclosed space that surrounded them with stony echoes. "We need him whatever his past sins were." Did Kane recognise that voice? "To swap one evil for another seems like folly," came a response, and a different speaker remarked "Set a devil to fight a devil." Kane was attempting to regain the blessed state of unawareness when a man protested "He killed his own brother."

They were discussing Kane – judging his life. Only God could do that, and he was not ready to be judged. "Os syriaeth ech saffaer tu fewr echlyn mor, necrombor llun..." The woman's voice seemed to be seeking to lull him, but he would not be sent back to oblivion. Was she trying to cast a spell over him? His soul revolted at the thought, and in a moment he was fully awake.

He was lying on a makeshift bed against the wall of a cave. The mattress and the pillow were rougher than he had imagined, though any bed would have been a comfort. Bandages held objects that felt cool and moist against his palms and the backs of his hands, where he detected no other sensation. A rush-light stood on a shelf of rock next to the bed, showing Kane the woman who was seated beside him, leaning close to him. A canvas cap and a few straggling locks of grey hair framed her wrinkled face. A lifetime's worth of lines had gathered at the corners of her lips, but her greenish eyes were more ancient still, or some aspect of them was. As Kane fixed his gaze on her, she began to speak in English. "Earth and fire, stone and water..."

If this was meant to reassure him about the nature of her incantations, it merely enraged him. "Keep your filthy pagan magic away from me," Kane snarled and would have clenched his fists except for fear of injuring them afresh.

The sound of his voice silenced the men in the outer cave. The old woman gripped her stick with fingers as knurled as the wood and sat haughtily upright like a sceptred queen. "It is my pagan magic that has healed you," she declared.

Kane dragged out his hands from beneath the coarse blankets. Even when he turned them palms upward, no blood was visible on the bandages. "This is God's work alone," he said.

"There's more power here than your Christian god." The old woman's gaze strayed around the cave as though she might be speaking of the prehistoric stone. "You would do well to remember that," she told Kane.

"It is evil," Kane said doggedly. "Christ came to earth to drive it out and all the other Devil's works."

"Some would name you as evil, Captain Kane."

Not just the form of address but the memories of wickedness that it revived left Kane unwilling to respond. "You," the old woman persisted, "who came down from the cross and returned from the dead."

Anger at the suggestion almost robbed Kane of speech. "What do you say of me, witch?" he muttered.

The old woman gave him a pitying look. "Did you not know that you were dead?"

"Those are the Devil's words. They cannot trick me." More fiercely still Kane said "I am no Christ. I am but God's avenger on earth."

"Did your father not send you forth?" The old woman gazed into his eyes as if she was searching his soul. "Did your life not change when you were taken to a high place and shown all that could have been yours?" she said. "Have you not made a pilgrimage through the wilderness? Did you not mean to atone for the actions of others by your crucifixion? Do you not seek to cast out a demon and perform a miracle?"

"Your casuistry will not sway me, witch. There is one Christ and one alone," Kane said. "He has always been and always shall be."

"Your Christ was not the first to rise from the dead when it was time. This land has its own ancient ways." The old woman grasped her stick and rose effortfully to her feet. "Draw what powers you must," she said and left Kane with a look of renewed pity. "You need not know them."

Kane watched her trudge out of the cave, leaning on the stick. She passed from sight beyond an array of swords in sheaths that were propped against the wall, and then he heard her in the outer cavern. "I have done what you asked," she said without pride. "His body is healed."

It was plain that she was making no claims for his soul. "What do you see of our future?" a voice said, and Kane recognised Telford's.

"Your champion will lead you into blood and darkness," the old woman said. "Are you ready for that?"

Telford had no audible response. Fortune-telling was the Devil's snare, forbidden by the Bible. Kane heard the hollow plodding of the stick recede and emerge into the open. Telford and his men had resumed their discussion, too low for Kane to hear. Kane brought up his hands to examine them afresh and saw his own breath in the chill air. It might have been a sign of his return to life. He had experienced no pain in his hands since regaining consciousness, and so he risked flexing the fingers. Except for the dragging of the bandages against whatever substance they contained, there seemed to be no hindrance at all.

He picked at the knot on his left wrist with his fingernails and uncovered the hand. A lump of some unfamiliar herb or root had been pressed against each side. When he removed them he saw that the hole through the hand had entirely closed up, leaving only scars. The same was the case with his right hand. He clenched them and then opened the fists wide. They were as supple as they had ever been, but the action emphasised the marks like stigmata, so that for a moment he felt at the mercy of the old woman's impious comparison. He had to believe the healing came from God, whoever God might have employed as His instrument. Meredith had used herbs to heal Kane, after all. The thought of her made Kane sit up, careless of his state.

He was naked to the waist. His body did not waver,

and his dizziness quickly passed. He pushed away the blanket and lowered his legs to the stone floor. He stood up without faltering and found the bag of his provisions in a corner of the cave. He was pulling on his shirt when Telford called "Captain Kane?"

Kane advanced to the mouth of the cave. Beyond it was a cavern several times the size. Telford and a handful of his followers were gathered near a fire over which a cooking pot dangled from a stand, and dozens of men were scattered through the cavern. Telford saw Kane and hurried to him. "What are you doing?" he protested. "You need to rest."

"It is not over." Kane clenched his fists, which felt like strength revived. "She is not dead."

"But you are barely healed." When Kane ignored this Telford said "We are too few to fight Malachi's men."

"Then remain where you are safe," Kane told him. "For myself I cannot."

"Just wait a little," Telford said and caught him by an arm.

Kane closed a hand around Telford's throat and shoved him against the cave wall. "I do not ask you to come with me," he growled. "Nor do I want you to."

Several men started forward and hesitated, apparently uncertain how to defend their leader. In Kane's days of privateering, his men would have cut down anyone who threatened him. Then a stocky bearded man advanced to stand next to Telford. "You may not want it," he said, "but we will."

He bore scars of battle, and met Kane's gaze without aggressiveness but equally without fear. "This lad has promised us you will destroy the evil," he said, "and we're here to fight with you."

His companions murmured in agreement, and Kane

saw their eyes gleaming with resolve that began to match his own. He slackened his grip on Telford's neck but kept his hand there. "Promised," he enquired, "have you?"

"That's what you want, isn't it?" Telford lifted his right shoulder in a shrug and smiled with that half of his mouth. "To end this?"

Kane wanted nothing else. "Yes," he vowed.

"Then let us help you."

Kane demurred for a moment and then let go of him. If the men were set on battling Malachi, they would at least be no hindrance – they might well help clear the way for Kane to reach his foe. He inclined his head and stepped back, sensing relief on every side of him. "If you will not rest you should eat," Telford said.

Kane was troubled by a question that he should already have asked. "How long have I been here?"

"Some days," Telford told him, but would not be drawn further on the subject. "Come, we shall talk as we eat. Let me introduce you to our company."

He handed Kane a metal plate as the men gathered near the fire. The bearded man was named Mcness, and Telford identified others as Kane broke bread with them. The revival of his strength had brought hunger with it, and he wolfed down a portion of the stew from the pot and did not refuse a second. Many of the men were younger than Mcness – even than Telford. Kane read courage in every youthful face, and a necessary apprehension too, but neither quality seemed to have been tempered by experience. His reflections prompted him to ask "What do you know of Malachi?"

"He was a priest," Telford said. "A priest and a healer."

"He grew weary of healing his flock," said Mcness, "and even of saving their souls."

"It's said he looked too long into the mirror," Telford said.

"We should have no truck with mirrors." This came from Caldicott, one of the youngest of the men. "They do not show the soul," he declared.

"If you look into a glass at midnight," Mcness said, "they say it will be the Devil that looks back."

As several men crossed themselves Telford said "It was so with Malachi. Some of his flock saw him at the glass when God-fearing men should be sleeping God's sleep. They heard him speaking to the mirror, and they say the mirror spoke to him."

"The Devil did," said Mcness. "He offered Malachi the power to rule the land and all who live there in exchange for his soul."

"Now Malachi enslaves our people," Caldicott said fiercely, driving a fist into his open palm. "He corrupts the land."

"He drains everything of life," said Fletcher, another beardless youth. "Some say he has the power to hide the sun from us and bring eternal winter."

None of this seemed to help Kane. He felt as though his adversary had stolen into the cave, attracted by the rumours or infiltrating the discussion with them. The cave was lit by torches, and some of the younger men had begun to glance about at the shadows that flapped at the edge of the light. The shadows might have been the wings of great demons crouching in the gloom. Kane was about to speak, to dispel the devilish illusion, when Telford said "And that masked rider, he is the iron fist who commands his army and spreads his poison through the land."

"They say he has no face beneath the mask," said Fletcher. "They say the sight would shrivel a man's soul. Even yours, Captain Kane."

"He can possess you with his touch," said Caldicott.

"It's true. I've seen it."

"It is the healer's power gone bad," Mcness said low. "It no longer heals men's flesh but infects it, and the soul."

The demoralising rumours had gathered in the cave once more, and Kane tried to drive them out. "If we kill him Malachi will be vulnerable," he said.

"Easier said than done, my friend," said Mcness.

"He will fall. He is but a man," Kane vowed. "Only God can grant eternal life."

All the same, he was reminded of the eyes behind the mask – the black inhumanity that had stared out at him. Surely it showed that the Overlord was less than a man, a shell that could be smashed like one. "Enough of him," he said. "Do you know where this Malachi is?"

"He makes his lair in the west," Mcness told him.

"Then my travels have been leading me there." Kane could not help recalling the abbot's words about him. "Does this lair have a name?"

"That is no secret," Telford said. "It is on the coast less than a day's journey hence. Its name is Axmouth Castle."

"No." Kane felt as though every shadow of his past had swarmed into the cave. As the torchlight shuddered at some unidentifiable movement – perhaps his own shiver at the chill that had taken hold of him – the shadows pranced derisively around him and above him. "No," he said like a repetition of a prayer, "that cannot be."

"There is no doubt," Telford said, frowning at him. "Do you know the place?"

"I grew up there." Kane found it hard to speak. "My father was lord of Axmouth," he said.

"There is no lord there now," said Telford.

"I did not know he had died." Kane bowed his head and stared into the shadows. If he had obeyed his father's wishes all those years ago, might the Kanes still be lords of Axmouth? Marcus would still be alive, and surely even he would have defended their father against any attack. Kane could have thought that his entire life since leaving Axmouth had been contrived to lead him back there, to the site of his first slaughter – and then he managed to turn some of his trapped rage away from himself. "No lord save Malachi, you mean," he said, and rose to his feet. "Now this must end."

Telford and his men gazed up at him. He saw hope in many eyes, and a stirring of valour. "All of you gather your weapons," he urged. "We will take the fight to him."

Telford expelled a breath that blanched the air in front of him. "We aren't ready," he protested.

"Nor is Malachi," said Kane.

"But they are legion. We are too few."

"Ah, come on!" Kane was sure there were no cowards in the cave. "You have seen me take cities with less," he said.

Memories flared up in Telford's eyes and left a fierce fire in them. He squared his shoulders and made for the store of weapons. Mcness followed at once, and most of their companions did. "But how can we hope to get through the front gates?" Caldicott asked anyone who might respond.

"You forget I was born here." Kane took the sword that Telford handed him. He closed one fist around the scabbard, the other on the hilt. The solidity and weight felt capable of anchoring him in the present, relieving him of the distractions of his past, at least until he had fulfilled his vow. "I have no intention of going through the gates," he said.

THIRTY-THREE

When they heard footsteps somewhere above them, all the women in the cell looked up. Some of them glanced across the stone corridor at Meredith, alone in her cell. The footfalls descended the steps to the dungeons, and the women huddled closer together. The light of torches set in brackets between the cells flickered in their eyes, mimicking their apprehension, and the shadows of the bars snatched at the women like a net. The footsteps halted at the end of the passage, where Meredith heard a mutter of brutish voices, which was succeeded by a rattle of keys and the clatter of one in a lock. She knew the footsteps had entered a cell when she heard a wail of protest rising to a scream. The women ventured to the bars and peered along the corridor as the door to the other cell clanged shut. "They've taken Martha," one whispered loud enough for Meredith to hear.

They stayed at the bars while the screams receded upwards. Some of them were glaring at Meredith now. She heard the captive's feet thumping the steps as the woman was dragged away. The cries passed along an upper corridor and were interrupted by the slam of a great door. Meredith knew this was not the end, and sensed that she was far from alone in holding her breath. Eventually there came a cry that might have expressed outrage and terror beyond words. It was so shrill and so appalled that, despite the distance, it seemed to pierce Meredith's consciousness. All too gradually it ebbed away and dwindled into silence, and she wondered if the victim simply had no more strength to scream. Meredith retreated into the gloom of her cell and sat on the edge of the rough bench that served as a bed, but the women continued to watch her. "See how she casts the evil eye upon us," one murmured and made a gesture to ward off Meredith's gaze.

"I am just a prisoner like yourselves," Meredith protested. "I am no witch."

"Like ourselves, are you?" another woman jeered. "Why then do they treat you like a princess?"

Meredith hugged herself in a vain attempt to keep out the subterranean stony chill. Her movement scared a rat, which had been making for the remains of food on Meredith's plate. It darted into a hole in the wall, where the glint of its eyes was still visible. "You think a princess would be kept in a cell," Meredith said.

"You don't have to share it with us commoners," a third woman retorted. "Somebody thinks you're above the rest of us."

"We can see nothing special about you," said the first speaker. "Tell us how you are."

Meredith closed her fist over her blemished insensible palm, only to realise that she should not have drawn attention to it. "She's hiding the mark," a new voice declared. "She has been marked by the Devil."

"Show us your hand, witch," the first speaker cried.

"I have told you I am not a witch," Meredith said and clenched her senseless fist. "My parents brought me up to fear God, and I will never betray them."

"Where are they now?" a woman demanded.

"The raiders slew my family." For a moment the faces

Meredith saw in the uncertain light did not belong to the women. "My father and my brother," she said as if she were praying for them. "My little brother too."

"Tell us why you were left alive." With a sneer the questioner added "If you dare."

Meredith dug her nails into her palm but could feel nothing. "God help me," she said, "I wish I knew. I do not deserve to live now they are gone."

"Leave God's name out of your devil's mouth," a woman cried. "Show us the mark."

Meredith did not feel her hand unclench, but she found it had done so. For a moment the dimness obscured it, and then a torch flared beyond the bars, illuminating the tendrilled blotch on her palm. Some of the women groaned in disgust, and all of them crossed themselves. "Is that why you were spared?" one of them accused Meredith.

She could not deny it, and there was nothing else that she wanted to say. As she bowed her head, the rat emerged from its lair. "It is the mark of Malachi," she heard someone whisper. "He sets his signs in the flesh of all who follow him."

"Why just her hand?" someone else muttered. "She doesn't look like any raider."

There was a pause and then a gasp of understanding. "They have put her down here with us as a spy."

A woman let out a moan of dismay. "What has she heard? What will they do to us?"

"She heard Martha speak out against Malachi and lead a prayer for our deliverance," another one declared. "That's why Martha was taken."

"I am neither a spy nor a witch. Please believe me." Meredith lifted her head, but this time the rat did not retreat as far as the wall. "You said yourselves they have set me apart. Why would they do that if they wanted me to spy on you?"

"So that nobody would see you spying," a woman answered with a triumphant mirthless laugh.

"But you've seen that I spoke to nobody," Meredith pleaded. "How could I have betrayed your friend?"

The laugh that greeted this was bitterer still, and several women joined in. "We don't know all the ways of your master," one said, "but we know he lives within his creatures like a parasite and shares every one of their thoughts."

"He is not my master," Meredith said desperately. "None shares my thoughts but God."

"She's blaspheming again," a woman cried. "She will bring evil down upon us."

"Just as she did on her kin," said another.

"She fouls the air we breathe," the oldest woman shrieked and spat through the bars of the cell. "We do not want her near us."

"Take her to her master," one woman shouted to the guards along the corridor.

"Or lock her in here with us," another suggested, "so we can give her a reward on earth."

"Stop the row," a guard yelled and started towards the cell.

He had taken no more than a pace when he halted. A heavy deliberate tread was descending the steps. The women glowered at Meredith as though she had summoned the newcomer. She heard the tread enter the corridor, but no words were exchanged. Why were the guards so silent? The women stared along the corridor, and she saw their faces stiffen. They had grown expressionless, but all at once she wondered if she could believe who they were seeing. Might it be Captain Kane, somehow rescued from the cross? Might God have helped him honour his undertaking to keep her safe because he had made it out of faith? She had despaired of ever seeing him again, but despair was a sin. Prayer was the answer to it, and she breathed one as the purposeful tread approached along the corridor.

She saw a tall shadow turn towards her, and then it swelled massive and ominous. Before its owner appeared she knew he was not Captain Kane. The rat fled squealing as the figure gestured with one black-gloved hand for a jailer to unlock Meredith's cell. Despair had seized her again, so that she felt she was being held helpless by the eyes in the impassive mask.

THIRTY-FOUR

Kane had ridden almost within sight of the castle before he was sure where he was. He meant to keep Telford and his men well clear of any road, having expected to remember the land around Axmouth, but nothing seemed familiar. If it had not been for the view of the sea beyond the cliffs, he might have believed they had strayed into some blighted region that he had never known and would never want to know. It was not just the unrelenting rain that obscured the landscape, or the years that had changed it and stolen his memories, or guilt that prevented him from recognising his home. More darkness lurked in the forests around Axmouth than the absence of the sun could quite account for. Perhaps only rain had turned the trees grey as fungus, although many of the trunks looked rotten as the limbs of corpses abandoned on a battlefield, but the darkness clung to the open fields too, where the vegetation seemed in danger of merging into a single undifferentiated mass, drowned beyond any possibility of growth. The gloom did not belong simply to the veils of rain; it might have been hopelessness rendered palpable, for it fastened itself to the soul. Worst of all were the hollows into which the route forced the riders to descend, since the miasma lingered thickest there. It might have been an essence of the corruption of the land; it seemed to soften the ground beneath the horses' hooves, so that they felt in danger of sinking slowly but inexorably into a bottomless marsh. Each time the horses seemed to have more of a struggle to climb the upward slope, as though they too were enervated by the murk, dragged down by it. More than once Kane felt the hooves of his steed slither backwards on the slimy grass, and had the impression that the miasma was reaching for him, closing around him as the corrupted earth would. Each of those moments felt like the start of an eternity of despair – of an utter blackness that had already laid claim to his soul.

He coaxed his panting horse to the top of a last treacherous slope and saw a wall ahead, on the far side of a swampy meadow. The wall led across the cliff top, following the irregularities of the land until it vanished into the murk. The rough old stones looked beaten down by rain, plumed as they were by dead bedraggled weeds, but the view gave Kane back his sense of purpose. Beyond the wall he would be able to see his home.

He rode across the sodden meadow, where every muffled hoofbeat seemed to rouse a chill that gathered deep in him, and dismounted near the wall. "Leave the horses," he said. "We cannot ride from here." He watched his companions turn their steeds loose, and then he tramped through the mud to the wall. The sight beyond it caught at his soul.

Axmouth Castle stood on a hill, commanding the slopes in every direction and the sea beneath the cliff. Towers guarded both ends of the massive edifice, and a great central tower rose at the far side of the courtyard. Several thin spires crowned the tower above an enormous arched window, and as a boy Kane used to think the castle was a crown the landscape should be proud to wear. Now he could imagine that it was crouching on the hill like a monstrous toad or spider, or some diabolical hybrid of both – a nameless thing that had made the land its lair. A pall of black cloud hovered over it, as though it had drawn the darkness down to veil its shame or to conceal the horrors to which it played host. Crows flapped within the pall as though it was growing lively and more solid. Raiders swarmed about the castle like an unholy brood to which it had given birth, and a train of prison carts was crawling along the road to the gates, bearing its nourishment. The spectacle revolted Kane, and he had to master his fury. "Follow me," he said and turned towards the cliff.

He used the wall for cover until he reached the end, and then he glanced towards Axmouth. As far as he could see, the raiders were still unaware of him and Telford's men. Beyond the wall a Celtic cross might have been marking the absence of a grave. That was where Marcus had fallen – had been flung to his death. Over the years the cross had fallen askew; it might even be sinking into the saturated earth. It seemed neglected, abandoned to the darkness that had claimed the land. Kane dragged his gaze away and looked over the edge of the cliff.

The path he had followed alongside the wall continued down the cliff face, but not as he remembered. Either it had seemed wider to his boyish eyes or it had been narrowed by erosion, and his memory had not suggested it was so precipitous. It was less than two feet wide, and composed of mud as well as rock. Waves lashed the jagged rocks two hundred feet below, as if a gigantic fanged mouth were foaming with savage hunger. "This is the only way," Kane said and stepped down.

Caldicott was behind him. The youth hesitated on the brink until Mcness murmured "Stay close to Captain Kane, lad." The veteran followed Caldicott as soon as the youth ventured forward, clutching at a protrusion of the cliff. Kane would have told him not to look down, but failure to choose his footing would be at least as great a risk. "Walk where I walk," Kane said and risked adding "God does not mean us to fall."

He heard at least one man mutter a quick prayer before setting foot on the path, and Kane almost echoed the words aloud. The storm that had Axmouth for its heart seemed bent on dislodging the men from the cliff. Gusts of rain lashed them, and water streamed down the cliff face to lie deep in the hollows of the path. The earth underfoot was hardly firmer than a marsh, and the rocks were not much less slippery than ice. Every step Kane took felt like a fresh peril, a threat of plunging to the rocks where he had left the broken body of his brother. The vicious icy winds drove the waves higher against the rocks, as if the frenzied sea were eager to engulf him. The curtain of rain across the bay was almost black, obscuring all sense of the rest of the world, shutting him in with the scene of his brother's death. Despondency saturated the atmosphere, and only the thought of his vow kept it at bay. He had despaired once, but he would not give way to it again while there was the least chance of saving Meredith. He picked his way doggedly forward, dashing rain from his eyes, until he heard Caldicott expel a shaky breath. Ahead a section of the cliff had sloughed away, halving the width of the path.

The narrowed stretch was at least a hundred yards long, and irregular with rocks embedded in mud. "Put your trust in God," Kane told the youth and took the first constricted step. There was barely room to shuffle forward with one foot in front of the other while his face came close to chafing against the rock. Parts of the path sloped out and down, so that he had to grasp every handhold he could find, however slippery. Once a handful came away, and a breathless silence measured its fall before it clattered on the rocks. After that he tested every hold and flung away any loose chunks of the cliff that came to hand. He was almost at the end of the narrow ledge when Caldicott's foot slipped on a rock.

The young man gasped and made a desperate grab for Kane. His foot slithered down the muddy cliff, and he lurched into space. Kane was already hearing the youth's cry as he fell – it sounded very much like his own brother's – when Mcness seized Caldicott by the scruff of the neck and hauled him back onto the path. "We need you, lad," he growled. "Don't leave us."

"I can't," Caldicott said, his teeth chattering. "I can't do this."

"Not far now." Kane grasped a projection of the cliff face with his right hand so as to extend his left to Caldicott. "You'll be fine," he said.

Caldicott faltered and then stumbled forward. If Kane had not caught hold of him, he would have lost his footing once more. Kane gripped the handhold and dragged Caldicott towards him until the youth regained his balance. "Easy, boy," he said. "Do you want to die?"

Caldicott gritted his teeth until the muscles stood out from his rainswept face. He held Kane's gaze, and when he was able to speak evenly he said "Not till we're inside the castle."

Kane helped him onto the broader stretch of path. The way was still treacherous, and he was watching every step he took when Caldicott murmured "Are you sure this will take us in?"

"It will," Kane said and pointed. "There is our route."

Perhaps the men did not immediately understand. The path traversed the cliff face just above a rounded opening from which foul liquid trickled, staining the rock. A wind brought the stench of the passage, and Mcness gave a disgusted grunt. "You want us to go in through the shithole?" he complained.

Unexpectedly, it was Fletcher who answered. "Would you rather fight your way in through the gates?"

"I'd rather wade through blood than shit," Mcness said. "Can this really be the best way?"

"If we are to have surprise for our ally," Kane told him. "Without it even we may be too few."

"Then lead on, Captain Kane," Mcness said with a gruff rueful laugh, and Kane turned his face towards the open sewer. At least he had suppressed the retort he had been close to offering: that however unpleasant the route might prove, it would lead them to far worse.

THIRTY-FIVE

Meredith expected her captors to drag her from the cell. Once he had unlocked the door and pushed it open, however, the jailer stepped aside. The Overlord did not move towards her, but the shadows of the bars seemed to act on his behalf, plucking impalpably at her as if the simple repetition could entice her forth. Meredith stayed seated on the edge of the rudimentary bed. "What do you want of me?" she whispered, careless whether she was heard.

The jailer answered for his master. The words sounded as though a cave had found a voice. "Do you not know?"

Meredith saw the women watching her across the corridor – saw their eagerness to learn that she was implicated in the evil that had seized them. "I do not," she said.

This earned her a chorus of jeering from the other cell. At first it was wary, but when neither the jailer nor the Overlord turned on the women it grew louder. "What is she?" the oldest woman demanded. "Why is she here?"

"She has been chosen," said the voice that possessed the jailer.

"Chosen!" The jeers grew more derisive as the old woman said "Is she Malachi's harlot?"

"She will bring him what he most desires."

Meredith gripped the wooden frame of the bed with

both hands and stared at the Overlord. "I shall not," she said.

Her response silenced the women, and she grew tense as the Overlord fixed his black gaze on her. He did not stir except to hold up one black-gloved hand as the jailer took a menacing step towards her. The hand sank and turned upwards before it crooked its long forefinger like a black worm writhing slowly in the air. It was summoning Meredith.

She clamped her hands on the edge of the bed and pressed all her weight down on the unyielding mattress. She told herself that her captors would have to drag the bed with her at least as far as the door of the cell – and then she felt something take her by the left hand. It felt almost as insubstantial as the restless shadows of the bars, and yet it had a kind of power. It might have been composed of cobwebs, tugging feebly but insistently at her, growing stronger by imperceptible degrees. Perhaps the idea of being enmeshed by a spider made her fingers open in revulsion, recoiling from the bed. But no, her repugnance had a deeper source. The sensation of a spidery grasp had not just settled on her hand. It was under her skin, clutching softly at her flesh.

She stared in loathing at her hand. It felt as though the tendrilled stigma had not merely corrupted her flesh but taken control of it. She thrust out the hand at arm's length, but the gesture of repudiation could not save her. All her consciousness seemed to home in on her blemished hand, so that she was only peripherally aware of letting go of the bed and rising to her feet. The insensibility of her marked flesh had spread to her mind. Even the derision of her fellow prisoners at the spectacle of her marching mechanically to the door of the cell, one hand extended like a beggar's, could not return her to herself.

Once she was in the corridor the jailer slammed the door. It clanged like a cracked bell and sent the torch-flames leaping in celebration of Meredith's emergence. Perhaps the sound or the flaring light reawakened her awareness, unless the Overlord had no further need to exert his power over her. He did not even point to the steps from the dungeons, simply turning his masked head towards them. At least she was able to think again, however sluggishly. She had to be alert for the slightest opportunity to escape.

The Overlord and the jailer paced her to the steps. Prisoners reviled her as she passed their cells; more than one spat through the bars at her. She could not bear to leave them so debased by hatred. "I will pray for you all while I live," she said.

"Will you intercede for us with your friend the Devil?" a woman cried.

"We have no need of your kind of prayers," another declared. "May God strike you dead the moment you open your mouth."

It seemed suddenly crucial for Meredith to demonstrate that she could make a sign of the cross. She was raising her left hand before she realised that it was not the one she used. It ought still to belong to God as much as its counterpart did, and she was determined to use both. She seized its wrist with her right hand to force it downwards and then up and sideways. She had almost completed the sign when, to her horror, she saw that she was not just sketching a cross backwards but inverting it. Her left hand had tricked her into thinking she was in control of it instead of the reverse. She snatched away her right hand and struck herself with it – her aching forehead, her famished belly, her left shoulder and the other. However passionate the sign might be, she felt as though she had made it too late. Too much of her body was at odds with her soul; her left hand lying against her hip was as cold and flabby as a toad. Her fellow prisoners had observed her difficulties and were unconvinced by the sign she had finally made. Their jeers pursued her all the way along the corridor, and their contempt seemed capable of stealing her breath.

The jailer remained in the passage. As Meredith reached the steps, the Overlord was at her back. The steps curved until she grew dizzy with climbing. The light of a solitary ensconced torch threw her nervous shadow ahead of her, and she saw it clamber up the last steps and disappear into a wide corridor. It appeared to have escaped, and dare she take that as a portent? She tensed her whole body in the hope of outdistancing the Overlord, and then it went as slack as her marked hand. Two raiders were ready for her in the corridor.

As she left the steps the two disfigured brutes moved to flank her while the Overlord strode ahead. Her escorts paced her so closely that she smelled their rank sweat and stale meaty breath. The corridor was lit by torches, which showed that the stone floor was blackened by muddy footprints numerous enough for an army of the raiders. Great tapestries cloaked the walls, but the images seemed so distorted that Meredith preferred not to examine them too closely. Perhaps only the unstable light made the heroic figures looked diseased, their flesh grey and spongy as if fungus had invaded the woven material, but the saints were worse; their faces were distorted by grimaces that appeared to shift slyly when she glanced at them, and the signs their hands were making seemed not just occult but obscene. Had Malachi's evil infested everything here? The succession of tapestries was interrupted by doorways, beyond which Meredith had no desire to look.

Those doors that were open showed blackness unrelieved except by the light from the corridor, and she thought the illumination did not reach far enough, instead flinching from the dark with every flicker, unless that darkness kept darting forward, eager to snuff out the light. The darkness looked altogether too sentient, however shapeless, and she was almost glad when the corridor brought her to a pair of double doors. At least light was visible beyond them.

Otherwise they were not reassuring. They stood more than three times the height of a man. In the uncertain torchlight they resembled the hide of a great reptile, scaly with square panels that were studded with diamond-shaped bosses the size of her hand. As the Overlord strode to the doors the light shivered, lengthening the shadows of the bosses, so that it seemed the reptile had drawn an enormous silent breath at the sight of Meredith. Beside each door stood an oval mirror set in a frame unpleasantly similar to tatters of dead flesh. The mirrors were taller than Meredith and darker than the reflection of the corridor should be. Something other than darkness might have been stirring under the glass, but she had no wish to see it clearer. She watched the masked figure grasp an iron ring on the left door with both hands and twist it to push the door wide.

Beyond it was a great hall. Two ranks of mirrors like the pair that flanked the doors led through an antechamber. Many torches on metal stands were ranged about the tiled floor of the main room, and candles were even more numerous. Once it must have been a noble room, but now it seemed to have been transformed into a parody both of a chapel and a throne room, with a colossal flat stone planted like an altar before the throne. At first this was all Meredith could see for the dazzle, but she had the impression that more darkness had gathered within the great room than the torches and candles could altogether eliminate. A chill impalpable miasma seemed to settle over her soul. Then her captors seized her arms and urged her through the antechamber. She glimpsed movements in the mirrors that she had no time to distinguish, because she was seeing far too much ahead of them.

The round stone was indeed an altar. A ceremonial knife lay on it, glistening with blood. Blood stained the grooved surface of the altar, which was broader than a man was tall. The grooves united in a single gory channel that led down the side of the altar to a circular orifice in the tiled floor. Meredith could not mistake the fate of the prisoners who had been dragged from the cells, but she had a sense of something yet more impious. Was it only the light that made the rim of the pit appear to work like the lips of a great round mouth? She could have thought that the hole had not been dug out of the stone – that it had opened of itself, as though the evil that made the castle its lair had possessed the very fabric of the building. Her captors marched her forward, and she saw the figure that was seated on the throne beyond the altar.

He was attired like a potentate, in sumptuous robes the red of drying blood. His head was lowered, intent on some thought that Meredith was instinctively grateful to be unable to guess. In a moment he looked up, and his long white hand let go of his jaw. The thin cruel face was just as pallid. An unnaturally high forehead was emphasised by a widow's peak, and locks of oily black hair trailed over his shoulders. Meredith had seen blackness in the eyes of his minions, but it was nothing to the Stygian dark that confronted her now. She might have been gazing into the depths of a void beyond the farthest stars, and the void was staring back.

He considered her for a few moments and then raised an indolent hand. He might have been lazily brushing away an insect rather than indicating Meredith's fate. Even the Overlord had grown deferential in the presence of his master. He stalked forward as the raiders forced Meredith towards the altar. She was already struggling, and she redoubled her efforts when she glimpsed the contents of the pit in the floor. In a sense the pit was empty; it contained only an exposed section of the foundations, but the material was no longer rock. It was raw and porous and appeared to be steeped in blood, and Meredith was almost sure that it quivered with a feeble pulse. Then her captors swung her around, and she saw what she had been distracted from noticing – a prison cage to the left of the altar.

The Overlord unlocked the door, and the raiders shoved Meredith into the cage. As she stumbled across the floor she heard the key grind in the lock. The raiders retreated towards the antechamber, and their leader followed them. The door beyond the avenue of mirrors shut with a massive slam, and flames bowed as if they were making obeisance to the occupant of the throne. Shadows scurried into all the corners of the great hall, where they seemed to peer fearfully forth to observe him. They might have been enacting Meredith's dread, but she would not yield to it. She stepped forward to grip the bars and stare at him.

In a moment she found she could neither look away nor breathe. She was seeing more and worse than him. A heap that might have been composed of discoloured refuse towered on either side of the throne. She saw hands protruding from each heap, and grimacing faces embedded in the tangle of flesh. The bloodless cadavers were not simply piled up; they appeared to be in the process of merging together. Nor was their arrangement entirely haphazard; it suggested some occult meaning that Meredith was glad to be unable to grasp. She could have thought the charnel sculptures were attempts to decorate the lair of the evil that had made Axmouth its home, and she did her best to focus all her loathing in her glare at him.

Perhaps it provoked him. As she managed to regain her breaths, he rose from the throne with a sinuous motion that brought to mind a great lizard slithering off a rock. His robe flowed about him, concealing his form as he crossed the floor with a silent reptilian tread. He paused beside the altar and rubbed a long finger over the bloody surface as if he were searching for dust. He put the finger in his practically lipless mouth and licked it clean before pacing to Meredith.

She held onto the bars and struggled not to shudder. While he was beyond the altar she had seen that his face was decorated with dozens of straight lines, and now she saw their nature. They were lines of some magical text inscribed on the flesh, as though his face were a page of a grimoire. They were in no alphabet Meredith recognised, but she had an uneasy sense that his eyes were able to convey the meaning, unless his actions would. His left temple bore a large raw sigil that might have been the Devil's brand. Was he aware of her thoughts? His eyes glittered with black delight, and he passed his pale tongue over his lips as if savouring a taste or anticipating an experience. Meredith had the impression that the darkness of which his eyes were no more than a symbol was reaching for her, closing its insidious oppressive embrace around her. She was striving to fend it off with a prayer when she heard a distant scream.

The sorcerer seemed eager to relish her reaction.

Meredith choked down her distress as the screams of protest grew less remote and more desperate. Somebody was being brought up from the dungeons, and Meredith knew she was about to witness one more slaughter. Soon the victim was dragged between the mirrors through the antechamber. The light fluttered with the screams, as if the torches were paying the woman a derisive tribute. She fell silent as two raiders bore her into the great hall, where she blinked in terror at the altar and the sorcerer and then stared with abhorrence at Meredith. She was the woman who had accused Meredith of witchcraft, and her hatred gave her back her voice. "Did you choose me for your entertainment? Has he put you there to watch?"

"I believe I am being saved for worse," Meredith said.

She had not thought it until she spoke, and she wished she had taken time to find another answer. She would not have been surprised if the woman had retorted that it was no more than Meredith deserved, but perhaps she had grasped Meredith's plight at last. As the raiders dragged the woman to the altar Meredith called urgently "What is your name? Tell me your name."

"Anne," the woman cried as if it let her cling to a scrap of her sense of self. "Anne Cooper."

"I will pray for you, Anne," Meredith promised, and dared to go further. "Let my prayer carry you to God."

She began to pray as the raiders spread-eagled Anne Cooper on the altar, gripping her wrists and ankles. She had to raise her voice when the woman's screams grew louder as the sorcerer picked up the ceremonial knife. He removed the ragged cap that Anne still wore and laid it on her chest as gently as a seducer. He took hold of a fistful of her hair, in which streaks of grey were visible among the raven locks. Whatever cares had silvered them and etched premature lines in her face, they were at an end for her. Pulling her head back to the full extent of the neck, the sorcerer cut her throat from ear to ear.

Her shriek of incredulous protest almost blotted out Meredith's prayer. Soon the scream weakened, growing clogged and liquid. The sorcerer gestured the raiders away and planted a hand on Anne's heart as she flailed at the altar with all her limbs. He was holding her in position, but he might have been squeezing forth the gouts of blood by leaning all his weight on her. The blood coursed through the grooves in the altar and streamed down the channel into the pit in the floor. Meredith was just able to make out the bottom of the pit – more than she would have preferred. There was no doubt now that it was pulsing like a monstrous heart, and she seemed to sense the presence of whatever it was helping to enliven, as yet invisible but so close that the room grew miasmatic with its imminence. She glimpsed movements in the antechamber, and risked an apprehensive glance. Every one of the mirrors that she could see contained a hideous shape. They had come to the surface to watch the sacrifice.

She would not look again. She kept her gaze on Anne Cooper and managed not to falter in her prayer. Anne's struggles grew feebler, and her cries subsided to a choking gurgle. As the last of her blood drained away into the heart of the corrupted place, her body drew into itself as though reverting to its unborn state. A parting breath rattled in her throat, and then her face grew slack and empty, just as the rest of her did. Meredith sent a prayer to follow her – to accompany her, she hoped. "Amen," Meredith said.

The sorcerer lifted his head to enjoy her behaviour. His reptilian tongue flickered out to part his lips and shape a wicked smile. "Amen," he echoed.

His voice was soft yet shrill as the hiss of a snake. It sounded like the icy darkness in his eyes rendered audible, and sent an uncontrollable shiver through Meredith. All her outrage and dismay seemed to be reduced to a single question. "Why are you doing this?" she cried.

He extended his long fingers towards her and brought his hands almost together. He might have been parodying prayer or demonstrating the mechanism of a trap. "He will come," he said.

THIRTY-SIX

"Keep climbing, lad," Mcness told Caldicott. "Nearly there."

Kane held onto the rungs set in the streaming wall and looked down. Now that he and the men were almost at the surface they had doused their torches, and the only light came through the grating overhead. Caldicott was clinging to the rungs beneath Kane, and Mcness was below the youth's feet in the vertical passage. The younger man looked grimly determined even though whey-faced. Kane listened hard but could hear no sound above him besides the constant hiss and drip of rain. He was about to raise the grating when he heard another noise beyond it. "Wait," he muttered.

"Wait," Caldicott whispered, and the word was repeated by a succession of low voices into the depths of the sewer.

In a moment Kane identified the sound in the courtyard – the rumbling of the portcullis. It gave way to the trundling of heavy wheels, and he heard wails of despair. There was no mistaking the arrival of another prison wagon. "Hold fast," said Kane.

Versions of the command were passed down into the dimness. It might have been an hour or more since the first of the men had lowered themselves from the cliff path to clamber into the mouth of the sewer. Their efforts were rewarded by a trudge through the noisome passage. Caldicott and several of his young companions had vomited, so that Kane was afraid that if they had to tarry in the sewer they would be little use as fighters. The dull thunder of wheels grew louder, and he saw them roll ponderously past within inches of the grating. Then a prisoner looked down and saw him.

Kane clenched his fists on the rungs and held himself absolutely still – even his face, even his eyes. The woman's downcast gaze was lingering on him, trying to establish what was there. Although she seemed bewildered, she was opening her mouth, but the cart lumbered out of sight before he heard her speak. In a moment the boots of a raider shook the grating, and Kane grasped the hilt of his sword. Mud fell through the grating to spatter his upturned face, and then the raider had tramped past. Perhaps the woman's senses were too blunted by her plight for her to comprehend what she had seen, or perhaps she was fearful of drawing attention by speaking. Kane heard the great inner doors of the courtyard groan open, and the cart and the raiders passed within. Their dogged sounds receded, and the doors shut with a massive slam.

Once he was sure that the courtyard was deserted Kane gripped the topmost rung and planted his hand against the grating. He pushed and pushed harder, and then shoved with all his strength, but the cover did not stir. Rust and, he suspected, the weight of passing wagons had wedged it into its metal frame. He thrust the fingers of both hands through the mesh and braced his feet on a rung, and then he levered at the grating with every muscle he could bring to bear. It shifted reluctantly, grinding against the frame. With another shove that involved his entire body Kane dislodged it, and it reared up with a squeal of metal.

Kane supported himself with one hand on the muddy earth of the courtyard and held the grating with the other while he made sure that nobody was approaching to investigate the sound. At last he climbed higher and let the hinged cover drop to the ground with a muted thud before he clambered up into the rain. He blinked his eyes clear as he rose to his feet, and then he glared around him. "Dear God," he breathed.

The courtyard was ornamented with death. Human skulls were impaled on stakes thrust in the mud, and strings of skulls like an ogre's jewellery dangled from the walls that enclosed the yard. The longest strings hung above the inner entrance, and Kane wondered if they were meant as a hideous greeting to the caged prisoners, an indication of their fate. He saw all this not just by the dismal light that seeped through the black clouds but by the glow of a wagon that had been overturned and set on fire. The pointless destruction seemed like the act of an idiot child, and Kane thought it showed how mindless the raiders had grown, or how corrupted by Malachi's influence, which had left them unable to achieve anything but ruination. Kane was scarcely aware that his companions had joined him in the courtyard until Caldicott spoke. "Was this your home?"

"Explains a lot," Mcness said as if he was finding what humour he could.

"When Malachi's head is on a spike," said Kane, "it will be once more."

"Where will we find him?" Fletcher said.

Kane's answer tasted sour in his mouth. "I believe he will have taken the great hall."

"And how are we getting in there?" Mcness was anxious to learn.

"There is a way up through the dungeons," Kane said before a noise distracted him.

At first he could neither identify nor locate the sound. He might have fancied that it was the rattle of a monstrous snake or the clatter of a gourd that was being shaken in some ritual. A mass of smoke rose from the blazing wagon to hover above the courtyard as though the source of the rhythmical staccato had summoned it for concealment. Rain raked at the smoke, and as the mass grew thinner Kane made out a small figure on the wooden balcony above the inner entrance. It was the little girl whom Meredith had rescued from the ruined village – the witch.

She leaned over the balcony to simper at him. She was flanked by human skulls on poles, and she was brandishing a skull, shaking it to produce the sharp dead sound. The smoke drifted aside and the wagon blazed up, casting her shadow on the wall behind her. It was taller than the girl, unstable and deformed. As it pranced with the movement of the flames it seemed almost as gleeful as her voice. "Welcome home," she cried, "Solomon Kane."

The shadow was betraying her nature, Kane thought – revealing her true self. It seemed to shiver with delight as it imitated the girl in holding a skull high. As she shook the skull again, reawakening its lifeless chatter, he wondered if she meant to show him the fate she wished upon him. Or was she giving a signal? The idea sent his hand to his dagger just as she flung the skull at him.

The missile was still flying through the air when he launched the dagger at her with all his force and skill. He felt as if he was using the weapon as much on Meredith's behalf as his own. It sailed end over end and pierced the girl's chest like an arrow, throwing her backwards and pinning her to the wall. Her face appeared to crumple with a childish disbelief not far short of petulant, and in less than a breath the features grew ancient and wizened, dried up by evil as well as by age. The face worked and then flew apart – the entire dwarfish body did, blackening as it separated into fragments. They were crows, which emitted harsh desolate cries while they flapped up to merge with the pall of cloud that loomed over Axmouth.

The skull had shattered on the ground in front of Kane. The contents had spilled out of the smashed cranium, and he was unnerved to see that the object lying in the mud was a withered brain. Was it shrunken so small and hard because the victim's soul had been stolen or subjected to some worse atrocity? Kane had no time to wonder. Perhaps the shaking of the skull had indeed been a signal, or silencing it had. He was about to lead the way to the dungeons when another door burst open, and raider after raider stormed forth.

Their faces were so disfigured by sigils that they were scarcely human, and there was nothing in their eyes but death. Kane unsheathed his sword and strode to meet them, cutting one brute down before the man could lift his own blade, impaling another through the heart, almost severing the arm of a third. Mcness was beside him, laying about himself with an axe. Telford and the others moved to flank them, and Kane saw that the youngest had all the fervour of youth. Caldicott was among the bravest, his sickness forgotten or conquered, as he took on two adversaries at once, hacking and stabbing like a veteran. All finesse was abandoned, and Kane thought sheer fierce determination might win the day. Then the inner doors swung open, expelling fire and smoke like an exhalation from Hell, and the Overlord stalked into the courtyard.

His advent seemed to possess his minions with redoubled fury. Kane saw the blow of a raider's sword cleave through one man's blade and send him staggering backwards. The masked figure was striding straight at Kane. Caldicott and Fletcher ran to intercept him, but he parried their blows with a single two-handed sweep of his sword. It sliced through Fletcher's neck, having disarmed Caldicott, whom the Overlord seized by the throat. Before Kane could reach him, a twist of the black-gloved hand snapped Caldicott's neck like a flimsy branch.

The Overlord flung Caldicott's body into the mud like a child throwing away a broken doll. Kane saw raiders swarming out of the doorway, and fell back alongside his companions. "Telford, get your men inside," he urged. "We cannot win this."

As Telford glanced at him in something too close to despair, the Overlord came at Kane. One of the raiders was in his way, but not for long. The Overlord thrust his sword through him from behind and swung the twitching body away from him with such force that it slid from the point of the blade and crumpled into the mud. "Go, Telford," Kane shouted over the clangour of blades and the cries of the wounded. "Take your men and free the prisoners if you can." He had scarcely finished speaking when the Overlord was upon him.

Kane's muscles were already aching from the combat, and his adversary's strength seemed close to inhuman. A blow of the sword almost jarred Kane's weapon from his hand. He parried another vicious stroke two-handed, and a third. Every impact shivered through his arms, weakening them further, and the blows were so relentless that he had no opportunity to reply with a lunge of his own. The wounds in his palms felt in danger of reopening. He was forced to retreat, and barely able to manoeuvre towards the castle rather than be driven to the outer entrance. He blocked a stroke so fierce that it numbed his arms and sent him stumbling almost against the wall – and then he realised where chance or instinct had brought him.

He was at the steps that led down to the dungeons. Before he had time to catch his breath, another blow reverberated through his sword and bruised every joint in his fingers. The impact threw him off his footing, and he fell backwards down the steps, barely staying on his feet. Several raiders saw his fall and converged on him. He was trapped if the door behind him failed to open. He groped for the heavy ring in the door and twisted it, bruising his fingers afresh. Scales of rust flaked away in his grasp, but he felt no other movement. The Overlord started down the steps, raising his bloody sword, and his minions followed. They were almost within a blade's length of Kane when the metal ring shifted with a grinding squeal, and the door swung inwards.

It let him into a rough stone corridor illuminated by a solitary torch. He slammed the door with such force that the torch-flame streamed away from him. Was there no bar to hold the door? In the tremulous light he could see none – and then a shadow outlined a length of wood lying by the wall. He dropped it into the sockets just as several bodies thumped against the door.

The bar was as thick as a child's wrist and made of solid oak. Nevertheless Kane heard it tremble in the sockets. Another onslaught shook it visibly, and a third extracted a groan of protest. The wood had felt moist, so that Kane wondered if it had grown rotten with the corruption that had gathered within Axmouth. Perhaps the stairway afforded the raiders too little space to mount a decisive assault, because he heard their tread retreat into the courtyard. They would mean to track him down, and he hurried along the corridor.

While he knew that the steps led to the dungeons, he had never used the route. The corridor was ominously silent, so that he could have feared the prisoners had all been slain. It brought him to a junction with a passage that took him some way towards the great hall but ended at an intersection. More than one of the corridors there was unlit, and skulls glimmered in the dimness. He must be among the ancestral vaults. The passage to the great hall was the darkest, and Kane lifted a torch from a bracket. Sword at the ready in his other aching hand, he advanced along the corridor.

A face bobbed out of the darkness to watch him – its remains did. It was a skull in a niche. No eyes were turning to observe him; they were shadows in the holes where eyes used to be. Surely only the unsteadiness of the light made the oppressive darkness ahead seem disinclined to give way. He heard claws scrabbling beyond the light, but surely they belonged to rats, one of which – a loathsomely fat specimen, its pelt glistening with moisture – he saw disappear into a hole in the wall. The corridor bent sharply, and he saw torchlight at the end. He was making for it when he heard a rush of heavy footsteps, and raiders crowded into view ahead.

Even Kane could not overcome so many. He stood where he was, steadying his sword and the torch. At first he thought the raiders had been sent after him, but they must be reinforcements for the battle in the courtyard. They were brutishly intent on their mission, and passed the junction without noticing Kane. Their sounds receded, and then the silence was complete except for the flapping of torch-flames. No, there was another noise, though it scarcely dared to be audible. Someone was whimpering.

Kane strode to the junction. Across the passage along which the raiders had stampeded, steps led downwards.

As he made for the arched entrance, which was guarded by a skull on a shelf, he could feel how dank the depths were. At the foot of the steps a corridor was fitfully illuminated by guttering torches that sent up oily smoke to blacken the stone roof. On both sides of the corridor fearful faces peered between the bars of cells at the new light that was descending towards them. Kane held it high and strained his eyes. "Meredith," he called.

Nobody answered him. As he set foot in the passage the faces flinched into the dimness as though the torch was too bright for them, unless they were afraid of Kane. "I will not harm you," he said and made for the nearest cell, which was opposite an empty one. He laid the torch on the floor outside and raised the locket on its chain around his neck. "Have you seen this girl?" he said, cradling the open locket on his palm.

The women in the cell ventured to the bars and narrowed their eyes at the portrait of Meredith. Kane seemed to glimpse wariness before the oldest woman spoke. "She is not here."

"I am certain she was brought to Axmouth. Do none of you know where she is?"

"She is not here," another woman said, and her cellmates muttered in agreement. Kane saw nervousness in their eyes, and he was about to question it when it turned to naked fear. Some of the women cried out, and some even found words, but they were too late. Whoever had crept behind Kane had snatched the pistol from his belt and thrust the muzzle against his back.

Kane could not fail now, having come so far. He whirled around to knock the assailant's hand aside. The man was a jailer, his broad face a mass of livid symbols under the low brow. His dull eyes widened as though the blackness within them had swollen with surprise in the instant before Kane's blade slashed his throat open. He wobbled backwards, clutching at the wound, and collapsed to the floor as Kane seized the pistol from him.

Kane could not wait for him to die. Three blows of the sword finished him off. Kane detached the keys from the jailer's belt and straightened up to listen. It seemed that the man was the only guard down here, and Kane risked raising his voice once more. "Meredith," he called. "Meredith."

It brought no response. Kane found the key that unlocked the first cell and swung the door wide. "You're free," he said.

The women gazed at him as if their captivity had drained them of understanding, and certainly of will. "Go now," Kane urged them. "Take care which way you go. The raiders may be occupied elsewhere."

The women emerged one by one from the cell, sidling past him as though they had some reason to be fearful of him. As they fled up the steps he unlocked the next door. Though he showed every prisoner Meredith's portrait, none would admit to having seen her. He heard their footsteps dwindle along an upper corridor, but no sounds to suggest that the fugitives had been recaptured or slain. He had done all he could on their behalf, he thought as he unlocked the last cell.

THIRTY-SEVEN

At first Kane thought the occupant of the cell was dead. The man lay half crouched on a bed of filthy straw in one dim corner. Apart from a mug of water and a tin plate of half-eaten food on the stained wet floor close to the prisoner's bare feet, there was nothing else in the cell. A hole in the floor served as a privy. The man's face was turned to the wall as if he could not bear the stench from the hole or the sight of his situation, but Kane made out that he was old and frail. The strands of unkempt hair that trailed over the shoulders of his ragged shirt were every colour of tarnished gold. He did not react to the sound of the key in the lock, but as Kane pushed the door wide he saw the prisoner take a breath, so feeble that it looked reluctant. "Come, old man," Kane said urgently. "You are free."

He heard a laboured breath that might have been a sigh. The prisoner kept his face averted and crouched closer to the wall as though he was ashamed to be seen. When he spoke his voice was barely audible, whether from disuse or determination to be left alone. "I cannot leave," he said.

Kane was desperate to find Meredith, but he could not abandon such a defenceless captive. "Let me help you," he said and stepped into the cell.

The flame of the nearest torch jerked back and forth

with his movement. The shadows of the bars toppled across the floor of the cell as if to produce an illusion of freedom, and Kane heard the sluggish rattle of a heavy chain. The old man was chained to the wall. Kane found the restraint wickedly excessive, and it infuriated him. "Why are you chained?" he demanded.

"For my sins." With a kind of guilty stubbornness the old man added "I have said I cannot leave."

A thick manacle was fitted around his thin wrist, so tightly that Kane could have imagined it had shrunk as the prisoner starved. "These are just chains," he said. "They can be broken."

The old man huddled into the corner as if he had made it some kind of refuge. "Even without them," he said, "I would stay."

Kane stared at the walls glistening with moisture, the noisome hole gaping in the floor at the chain's length, the crude bed of rank straw, the food hardly fit for a wild beast, the darkness that seemed eager to overwhelm the uncertain light and engulf the cell. "Dear God, why?" he said.

The old man let out a sigh that sounded like an attempt to have done with breathing. "This was my home."

Kane peered at the emaciated figure. Worn and hoarse and enfeebled though the voice was, it was not altogether unfamiliar. "Father?" he said in disbelief.

The old man's shoulders hunched as though he wanted to crouch into himself – to vanish if he could. They sagged with a convulsive shudder, and he turned to blink at Kane. "Solomon?" he wondered aloud.

Kane gazed at him and could find no words. More than the years had drained the vitality from Josiah's face. The yellowed skin was little more than a tissue over the bones, which looked close to showing through. Lines deeper than scars were etched in his forehead, which bore scabs left by violence. His eyes were haunted, darkened by memories or by the struggle to keep them at bay. It was apparent that moving his head caused him pain, and Kane suspected that even returning to consciousness had. Kane swallowed hard and was about to speak when Josiah said "Are you another phantom sent to torment me?"

"I am real," Kane said and had to steady his voice. "I am alive. I am your son."

"I thought I had lost you forever." Josiah reached out painfully but stopped short of touching Kane's face. "You were still a boy," he murmured, "when..."

His voice fell away as his hand did, and Kane was overtaken by a surge of guilt and grief indistinguishable from rage. If he had not left Axmouth because of his pride – if he had not robbed his father of the protection that Marcus would surely have given him – the old man would never have been reduced to this abject state. Kane closed his bruised hands around the chain and wrenched at the ring set in the wall. He hauled at it until his muscles throbbed – until the strain felt capable of reopening the wounds in his palms – but the ring stayed as firm as the rock in which it was embedded. "You will never break them, Solomon," his father said.

"I am not the boy who left you," Kane protested and heaved at the chain while his shoulders shook.

"I see you are not." Josiah's eyes seemed close to growing blurred, and he narrowed them to regain control. "It makes no matter," he said. "No man could break them. They are spun with dark magic as much as with metal."

Kane became aware that the chill of the links was spreading up his arms as if it would fasten on the whole of him. He let go of the chain with an oath and gazed helplessly at his father. "How may I free you?" he pleaded.

"You cannot break my bonds," Josiah said. "Do not try, Solomon. Do not waste your strength."

Kane made to embrace him in the hope of affording him some comfort, but the old man winced away from him. Perhaps his body was too painful to suffer any contact, unless he was loath to be held by his son. Kane went down on his knees in front of him and gazed as deep into his eyes as he could. "I have carried so much guilt for what I did," he said.

Josiah raised one infirm hand as if to sweep the confession aside, but Kane was not so readily absolved. "I never meant for Marcus to fall," he said. "I never meant for him to die."

The old man's eyes had grown more haunted, so that Kane felt guiltier still. "Your brother did not die," Josiah said. "If he had, this nightmare would never have begun."

"He did not?" Such a flood of emotion overwhelmed Kane that it felt as though a dam composed of all his years away from Axmouth had burst, and he scarcely grasped what his father had also said. "Thank God," Kane murmured. "He is alive."

"Do not blame God." For an instant the old sternness hardened Josiah's eyes. "It is not through God's will that he survived," he said.

Kane felt rebuked in more ways than he understood. "What do you mean?"

"He was terribly injured by the fall." Before Kane could take this as an accusation that Josiah had waited all these years to make, his father said "He did not die, but nor would he wake."

"And now…" Kane had to prompt.

"No surgeon could help him, nor any priest, and so – "

With an effort that appeared to send a shudder through his emaciated frame, Josiah admitted "I brought the sorcerer here."

"Malachi?" Kane spat the name as if he were expelling poison from his body. "You brought him here to Axmouth?"

"Speak his name softly, my son." Josiah glanced uneasily past Kane as the shadows of the bars seemed to grope like elongated fingers for the men. "He hears everything within these walls," he whispered. "His power has passed into the very stone."

Surely the torchlight had been agitated only by a draught. Kane was heartened to be called his father's son once more but dismayed to see Josiah so fearful, and appalled to hear him talk of Malachi in a hushed tone that ought to be reserved for God. "Let him hear," Kane said so loud that the bars appeared to quiver with his shout; at least, their shadows did. "Let him know I have come to destroy him."

Josiah gazed at Kane as if he wondered whether it was not too late to hope. "What did he do to my brother?" Kane said without lowering his voice.

"They said he was a healer. I did not know then where his powers came from." Josiah gave his head a solitary painful shake and said "Or perhaps I chose not to know."

"Was he not a priest?" Kane said.

"Aye, so he claimed, but what devil does he serve? I offered him everything I had," the old man said and gazed about at the pittance that remained to him. "Everything, if he would bring Marcus back to me. I could not lose another son."

Kane wanted to respond that his father had never truly lost him, but was afraid of presuming too much. He might have bowed his head in shame if Josiah had not spoken. "He succeeded, Solomon," he said. "He reached into the darkness with his magic and his mirrors and brought Marcus back."

"Where is Marcus now?"

"He was changed, Solomon." Josiah shook his head again as if he wished he could turn his face to the wall. "You know he was never gentle," he said. "You know it all too well. I have often wondered if I made him so. I only sought to raise you both as men."

His gaze seemed to be searching for the past and finding none to comfort him. He spoke as if each word gave him pain. "His strength came from the worst of him. I no longer know my son."

"Was it Marcus who imprisoned you?" When Josiah would not answer Kane said "Where is he? Tell me where he is."

"I cannot say, Solomon." Kane thought he understood his father's reluctance – a last attempt to protect one or both of his sons – until Josiah said "He goes abroad on his master's errands. For a time the sorcerer was content to work his evil here in Axmouth, but now he seeks to claim the entire land for whatever devil he serves." With an effort that shook his frail body and jangled the links of the chain he added "His face was so damaged by the fall that he hides it behind a mask."

"No," Kane said in disbelief that felt like desperation. "That cannot be my brother."

"It is, Solomon." With a gentleness that surpassed despair Josiah said "The leader of the raiders is your brother or what remains of him. He obeys only the will of the sorcerer."

Kane recalled how the Overlord's voice had emerged from the mouths of his minions – recalled the eyes from which all traces of humanity, however depraved, seemed to have been drained. "That is not Marcus," he insisted doggedly. "Some demon has possessed him."

"He does not just lead the raiders. He infects all who follow him." Josiah laid his free hand over the chained one as if this was the nearest he could come to prayer. "I believe that deep within himself he is still my son," he said, "and so he may yet be saved."

Kane did not know and could not answer. He watched his father's eyes grow less resigned and more determined, and at last Josiah spoke. "Now you must do one thing for me, Solomon."

"Ask and it will be done," Kane vowed at once.

"You must end my life."

Kane would have retreated across the cell, taking all his weapons out of Josiah's reach, if he had not been on his knees. "No," he cried, and it felt like a prayer.

"You must, Solomon." His father stretched out a hand that had regained its steadiness and drew a pistol from Kane's belt. "We both have our sins to answer for," he said. "I am ready to answer for mine."

"But not like this," Kane pleaded. "Let me deal with Malachi, and then – "

"My son, you do not understand." Josiah grasped the barrel of the pistol with both hands and pressed the muzzle to his heart with all the fervour of a zealot clutching at a holy relic. "I invited him in," he whispered, "and while I am alive he will remain. He keeps me here because it gives him power, and he will never let me die. Kill me and you may lessen his grip on the land. Otherwise I fear you will never defeat him."

He held the pistol against his chest with his manacled hand while he reached for his son's with the other. Kane resisted, but his father guided his finger to the trigger, so delicately that it felt like tenderness – more than Kane had ever experienced from him. "Do this one thing for me as my son," Josiah murmured, "and you will bring me peace."

He met Kane's gaze without wavering, and Kane saw a prayer in his eyes. Though he could not have put it into words he seemed to share it, and for those moments he was aware of nothing else. He could not have said which of them pulled the trigger. He thought the explosion should have resounded throughout the corridors and shaken the castle to its foundations, but it was as muted as the single blow of a muffled drum. The pistol jerked in his fist as Josiah took a swift sharp breath, which he released as a faltering sigh. His mouth stayed open like a sleeper's, and the lines of his face seemed to soften. Kane glimpsed fire in the old eyes, but it was the reflection of the torchlight. He touched his fingers to the lids and drew them gently down, and then he rose to his feet, squaring his shoulders as though his grief were a physical burden. "May God take you to Him. You have suffered enough," he declared and strode out of the cell.

THIRTY-EIGHT

"Malachi!" Kane roared. "Malachi!"

The flame of the torch that lit his way out of the dungeons seemed to flinch from his shout or his rage. There was no point in attempting to be stealthy; his father had made this clear, and Kane wanted Malachi to know that his nemesis was upon him. He stalked along the subterranean passage, his swords ready in his hands. If his fists ached, it was not so much from the pains of battle as with a yearning to spill blood – Malachi's blood. He heard sounds of conflict ahead, and there was a great light beyond a bend of the corridor.

From the bend Kane saw three corridors leading from a junction. All of them were strewn with lengths of blazing timber. Telford and a few men were battling raiders at the junction. Most of the disfigured creatures were on the far side of the blaze, but Kane saw that it would not hold them off for long. A raider was creeping up behind Telford, a dagger in his hand. With a shout Kane darted at him, and as the raider turned Kane slashed his throat so viciously that he almost decapitated him. "Captain Kane," Telford cried. "Help us, for God's sake."

Kane strode to join him. The passages were scattered with the bodies of raiders, dead or mortally wounded, but Kane saw fewer than a dozen of his men still standing. "Is this all you have left?" he demanded.

"All," Telford said, and there was accusation in his voice.

"The prisoners are free," Kane said in case Telford thought his men had fought in vain. "Except for Meredith. Free her if you find her, and I shall. I go to pay my debts."

As Telford stared at him in little more than desperation Kane heard a shot, and a youth beside them collapsed to the floor, blood jetting from his neck. "This is your folly," Telford protested.

"Just keep them back," Kane urged him and his men. "Just a few more moments. I think I can end this with a single blow."

He saw resolution flare up in the eyes of some of the younger men. It could scarcely be called hope. He had often observed it in battle – the grim resolve of men who were looking their own death in the face and who chose to fight on while they lived, to take as many of their adversaries with them as they could in their last moments on earth. "I am proud to have fought beside you," he said and turned away from them.

He knew where he must go. The passage to the right was narrowed by blazing lengths of wood piled against the stone walls, but he strode between them. No raiders were to be seen. At the limit of the jerking light, steps led upwards. The dimness of the stairway felt like the adumbration of a greater darkness, which Kane seemed to sense waiting for him. He tramped fast up the steps to a door and twisted the iron ring to haul it wide.

It showed him a broad corridor leading to the great hall. Although he recognised the corridor, it seemed dreadfully transformed. Tendrils of some glistening substance had invaded the tapestries on the walls, distorting the faces and gestures of heroes and saints. In the unreliable torchlight the caricatures of figures seemed eager to display an unnatural liveliness, to participate in some ungodly celebration. The corridor felt as cold and secret as a cavern far beneath the earth. Shadows massed in the gloom beneath the roof, where they crawled and flapped and groped about as if the blackness was searching for a shape in which it could grow solid and fall on its victim. As a boy Kane had felt dwarfed by the corridor, but he was no longer a boy. He would be master of Axmouth, and he strode to the great hall.

The passage ended at a space several times its width – the lobby of the hall. It was dominated by a pair of doors that might have been designed to daunt all who stood before them. The iron bosses with which they were studded no longer lent them the appearance of a shield; now the doors resembled enormous slabs of reptilian flesh that were borrowing breath from the shadows. They were flanked by torches taller than a man, and beside either torch an oval mirror towered, propped on skeletal legs. The torch-flames flickered in the mirrors like the elongated vertical pupils of a reptile's eyes, but Kane sensed worse in the depths of the glass. None of this had the power to deter him, and he strode to the doors. "Malachi," he shouted, hammering three times on them with the hilt of a sword. "Malachi, I'm here. Isn't this what you want?"

The name seemed to conjure forth a silence as chill and indifferent as the farthest reaches of space. Even the sounds of conflict had ceased, unless the unnatural stillness had somehow cut them off from Kane. It felt as if the whole of Axmouth were holding a breath, or did it feel more like the utter absence of breath? He had a gradual but insidious impression that it was growing more palpable, gathering substance behind him, unless the darkness that lurked everywhere in Axmouth was.

A faint noise made him turn, a noise like a single breath emerging from many mouths. Under cover of the silence that had blotted out his senses, dozens of the raiders had closed in behind him.

The sight enraged him – their skulking presence did, and his own unwariness, and the brutish unanimity of the corrupted faces watching him. Kane lifted his swords high and stretched his arms out on both sides of him. "Come on," he snarled.

As they took a concerted pace forward, so ponderous that it seemed to shake the stone floor, Kane heard a sound behind him. It was slow and massive and inexorable, and it brought an icy insubstantial clutch to the back of his neck. It felt as though ice were forming there, and as he swung around, his breath visibly preceded him. The doors to the great hall were standing wide.

A rank of oval mirrors towered on either side of the antechamber. Each mirror was held in a frame as tattered as rotten skin and supported by thin struts like fleshless limbs. Kane had seen their sort before, and now they symbolised a past he had hoped to leave behind. Nevertheless he advanced between them at once. As soon as he was past the doors they slammed together, shutting out the raiders, who had never meant to slay him. They had been deployed to leave him nowhere else to go except the hall.

The echoes of the slam fled into the corners of the great room, to be swallowed by the shadows. The light of torches lined up along the antechamber continued to prance as Kane strode on. The flames might have been celebrating his arrival, but their antics left the depths of all the mirrors dark. He could have been passing between two rows of pools grown impossibly vertical in defiance of the laws of God, and he felt as if inhabitants of the dimensionless dark were observing him. While this troubled him, he saw worse ahead.

He had reached the heart of the evil that had invaded Axmouth. The glow of myriad torches and candles seemed to take a wicked pride in displaying it to him. A figure draped in bejewelled robes of dull crimson occupied the massive seat from which Josiah had pronounced judgement on the youthful Kane. The figure's head was bowed, no doubt in contemplation of some fresh malevolence, so that Kane saw nothing of the face except a pallor veiled by ropy locks of hair that trailed from the oily pate. The creature had made Axmouth not merely his abode but a monstrous lair, for the corpses of his victims were piled behind his throne and on either side – bloodless heaps in which the individual bodies had grown indistinguishable, though limbs and hands and the remains of agonised faces were visible within the masses of corruption. Kane had the dreadful notion that the soundless cries the mouths still appeared to be uttering might be intended as an oblation – that the whole charnel arrangement was an aspect of an occult ritual. He saw where the victims had met their deaths, on a bloodstained altar placed before the throne as if to honour the occupant – an altar so primitive that it could only invoke an ancient evil. Kane's gorge rose at the defilement of his ancestral hall. He was ready to shout a challenge to the figure on the throne as he emerged from the antechamber – and then he saw what else the hall contained. To his left was a prison cage, and in the cage was Meredith.

She was crouched on the floor, hugging herself in search of comfort or warmth, but she looked up at the sound of Kane's tread. Perhaps she was unable at first to focus her eyes, unless she was afraid to believe what she was seeing. Her face cleared, and she wavered to her feet and stumbled to the bars. "Captain Kane," she cried. "You came for me."

"I vowed I would," said Kane.

"I prayed you would come." Meredith gripped the bars while Kane tramped around the cage to find the lock. "Sometimes I thought..." Her eyes grew moist with an anguished memory as she said "I was afraid you might have died."

"Not while my vow had to be kept," Kane said.

He was lifting a sword to break the padlock when Meredith's gaze strayed past him and her lips parted in dismay. "He will come," she said almost to herself, and then she threw her hands out as if she wanted to fend off a sight or to seize hold of Kane. "Solomon," she cried, "it's a trap."

Kane whirled about to see the occupant of the throne raising his head. The languorous fluid motion put Kane in mind of a cobra. Until the long pale hand relinquished the chin, he might have fancied that the sorcerer was holding up a white mask. The elongated sharp-nosed face was practically lipless, and it was horizontally striped from the extravagantly high forehead to the pointed chin. Eyes from which blackness seemed to have erased all humanity gazed straight ahead as if they were fixed in the sockets. Perhaps this was a parody of meditation; the sorcerer's words suggested as much. "Long is the road that the pilgrim walks in the name of his devotion," he said, but it might have been a stone that spoke, so cold and hollow was his voice. "Yet longer still is the journey home to the land of his fathers."

The voice seemed to seep into Kane as though it meant to gather in his soul. "I have been waiting for you," Malachi said, and his depthless gaze found Kane's eyes. His thin lips twisted in a mocking smile that could hardly have been more grotesque if a reptile had essayed the expression. "Do you like what I've done to the place?" he said.

"It will look fairer when your head is on a spike above the gates." This fell short of conveying Kane's wrath, and he stalked past the altar, raising both his swords. "You are not fit to occupy my father's chair," he shouted.

"Your father was a child." The sorcerer did not move except to fold his long hands together in a mockery of supplication. "A pathetic fool," he said, "who made a pact with the Devil."

His voice felt like a dank fog that was settling over Kane's soul in an attempt to suffocate all hope. Kane was close enough to see that the lines inscribed on the elongated face consisted of occult symbols. Whatever they represented or invoked, Kane could have thought their power was reaching for him through Malachi's words. He was distracted by the sight of a gaping pit in the floor beside the altar – a hole edged with bloodstains and exposing a porous crimson mass larger than a man. A slow pulse passed through it, and Kane seemed to sense the monstrous heartbeat spreading almost imperceptibly through the fabric of the great hall. "You tricked him," he said through his teeth. "You, who were a man of God."

"He betrayed you, Solomon Kane." Malachi's lips pinched together in a colourless sneer. "Your soul is damned," he said in vicious glee.

"I damned myself. Do not dare to blame my father. I sinned, and now I shall redeem my soul." He needed to say none of this to Malachi – it felt like being tricked. "Get up!" he yelled.

"Are you still the good loyal son?" Malachi's lips worked as if they were savouring their contempt, and

Kane rushed at him.

The sorcerer reared up and slithered out of the chair. The movement seemed close to boneless – as sinuous as a snake. As the robe fell about him, Kane saw that he appeared to be unarmed. He felt no compunction over cutting such a creature down, but as Kane slashed two-bladed at him, Malachi clapped his hands together and jabbed them at the floor. He might have been miming an inverted prayer, and the effect was immediate. The space in front of Kane seemed to be sucked into itself, and his swords sliced through a shapeless impalpable mass – a cloud of black smoke as tall as the sorcerer. It was a trick that an illusionist might have performed to astound simpletons or children, and it aggravated Kane's rage. He swung around to glare about the hall. "Malachi," he shouted. "Malachi, show yourself."

Nothing but the sluggish flutter of torchlight and candle-flames answered him. Only shadows were creeping about near the walls beyond the columns and ducking out of sight behind the stained altar. "Malachi, you coward," Kane roared, but there was no response. He was wasting his time and Meredith's. With a last glare all around him he strode to the cage.

Meredith had been watching him silently but apprehensively. As he reached the padlocked door she whispered "Don't you understand yet? It's a trap."

"What trap?" Kane demanded.

"They only marked me so that you would come." Meredith gripped her hands together as if she wished she could squeeze her palm clean. "The Devil wants you, Solomon."

"The Devil can take me soon enough," Kane declared and smashed the padlock with the hilt of his sword. The staple of the padlock was trapped in the hasp of the door. He wrenched at it and managed to free the staple from the slot, which the blow of the sword had distorted. The padlock clattered on the floor, and Kane made to throw the door wide. He was reflecting on the wilful pointlessness of evil – on how much carnage and destruction had been perpetrated simply in order to entice him home – when Meredith screamed. She might have been voicing his outrage for him, or his sudden agony. The blade of a sword had pierced his left shoulder and was protruding in front of him.

THIRTY-NINE

As Kane attempted to drag himself free of the blade his assailant drove it deeper, and Kane felt it grind against his collar bone. He clenched his teeth until his head throbbed, and overcame a wave of nausea as he succeeded in keeping both hands clamped on his swords. Before he could wield either of them, his adversary hurled him aside. Skewered on the weapon, Kane was swung away from Meredith with such force that it hurled him off the blade to sprawl many paces away from the cage. The fall inflamed the pain in his shoulder, making his head swim, but he crouched around to face his assailant. The man had not followed him; he stood dangerously close to Meredith, his sword upraised in triumph or anticipating victory. He was the Overlord of the raiders. He was Kane's brother.

His eyes showed no more emotion than the mask did. Kane could have thought that Malachi himself was observing him through the eyeholes, but he spoke as he struggled onto one knee. "Listen to me, Marcus."

The only answer was an inarticulate snarl from within the mask. Kane might have concluded that the sorcerer's influence had reduced Marcus to brutishness – to the simple savage instinct to kill – but he had to believe that his brother could still be reached somehow. "You do not have to do this," he insisted. "Our father is dead. Malachi has no power here any more."

Some of this seemed to affect Marcus, who rushed forward with another wordless roar, swinging his sword high to deal a fatal blow. Kane heard Meredith cry "Oh God, Solomon." It sounded too close to despair. He had not endured so much to abandon her now – it would make a mockery of his vow and her faith. He braced himself on his knee and brought his swords up just in time to meet the descending stroke.

The impact almost overbalanced him. It shivered along the blades and sent a dull ache through his arms. It seemed to widen the wound in his shoulder, which felt as if a claw had dug deep. Perhaps the prospect of leaving Meredith at the mercy of the sorcerer lent him strength. Much of it was in his right arm, but he managed to regain his feet. The swords disengaged, and Kane barely had the chance to draw a breath before Marcus resumed the attack.

Kane parried the scything blow, but it made his shoulder blaze with pain. Marcus came after him, chopping at him with stroke after powerful stroke, giving him no opportunity to fight back and little to defend himself. Soon his left arm was too weakened to help him block the strokes. He had to rely on the other while he sought to wound Marcus with the blade in his left hand – sought only to disable him. Each attempt renewed the agony in his shoulder, and each one fell short of its goal. He was being driven back towards the antechamber, and he could have thought the aim was to deliver him to the raiders outside. He was closer to a worse peril, which he glimpsed once Marcus forced him to retreat between the mirrors. On both sides of him the glass stirred like water that was growing less stagnant, and he had the impression of shapes rising from the unplumbed depths – tall scrawny figures with little to their lengthy faces except round lipless mouths that fastened on the insides of the mirrors. Marcus gave him no time to glance at them until a great two-handed stroke drove Kane close to a mirror, and two arms sprang forth from the glass to seize him.

He glimpsed the hands before they closed around his throat. The grey fleshless fingers were segmented like the limbs of insects, and abominably long. He strained his body forward as they strove to drag him into the mirror – he hacked at them with both his swords, but they did not relent. They were drawing him inexorably within the frame, and he felt the transformed glass parting to receive him. It was colder than ice and lethargically fluid as a swamp. The sensation revolted him, and he sawed at the creature's right wrist with all his strength. In moments the hand was separated from the arm, but it clung to his throat, more than ever like an insect, while he stabbed at its partner and wrenched himself free. He saw the mutilated limbs disappear into the mirror as though they had sunk into a marsh while he prised the fingers from his neck and flung the severed hand away. It twitched on the floor and almost succeeded in inching towards him before it grew still.

Marcus had watched with inhuman detachment, but now he advanced to trap Kane in the avenue of mirrors. Beyond him Kane saw Meredith ease open the door of her prison. She darted around the cage and retreated behind one of the columns supporting the roof. Had Malachi seen her, wherever he was? How could she escape from the hall? Kane's brother cut viciously at him, and Kane barely avoided the blow. Now he was between another pair of mirrors, and shapes moved eagerly to wait for him to stray closer. "Where is your master?" he shouted. "Is he hiding in the shadow?"

"His master indeed," Malachi said. "Your brother is the lord of Axmouth. He is the heir, but he is subject to my will."

His insidious stony voice seemed to emerge from every corner of the hall. At first Kane could not locate him, and then he saw the sorcerer beside the high seat, one hand resting indolently on its arm in token of ownership. His thin contemptuous smile suggested that he had been waiting to be noticed, having rendered himself not so much invisible as indistinguishable from his surroundings, impossible for the observer's mind to grasp. The trick of vanishing in a cloud of smoke had been merely a disdainful exhibition of his magic, conveying his scorn for his audience. "Why should I hide from you, Solomon Kane?" he said.

Marcus had halted like a puppet whose manipulator was preoccupied elsewhere. When Kane attempted to dodge past him, however, Marcus drove him back with a lethal sweep of the sword. "Then fight me, you coward," Kane shouted at Malachi. "Fight me like a man."

"Why should I stain my hands? I have my champion. I shall set brother against brother." Malachi lifted one long finger as if he were tugging the string of a puppet. "I want you here," he said.

Kane glimpsed movement beyond a column, and willed Meredith not to betray her whereabouts. He held Malachi's gaze with a fierceness born of loathing. "Have you staged this for your entertainment?" he demanded. "Or do you need me to complete your dominion? I will never kneel before you, Malachi."

"You are of no consequence to me." The sorcerer's voice took on the tone of a sermon. "Every step you took," he said, "every pain you suffered, was punishment for your sins."

Kane might have thought that Malachi had rediscovered his priesthood if it had not been for the derision apparent on the pallid face. "My master will have your soul," Malachi hissed.

"Is your master as much of a coward as you?" Kane shouted in some desperation. "Is he afraid even to be seen?"

"He has no need to show himself." Malachi made a sign that might have been an impious benediction, unless it was meant to ward off the vision Kane had called to mind. "See what he has sent to claim you," the sorcerer said and glided to the darkest corner of the hall.

Less of the light reached into the corner than its distance from the nearest flames could quite account for. An object as tall as the lofty ceiling stood in the gloom. Malachi turned to it, his robes whirling, and whipped off the enormous discoloured canvas that covered it. He might have been performing his last and greatest trick, but the theatricality gave Kane no comfort. "Dear God," he breathed.

Malachi had uncovered an oval mirror at least five times his height. For a moment Kane thought the glass contained only the reflections of the flames that filled the hall, but the reddish glow was too intense, and it had too defined and purposeful a shape. It was growing – it was advancing to the surface of the mirror, to claw at the glass. As the talons screeched over it, leaving claw marks within, Kane saw that it was a colossus made of fire and molten scaly flesh. "Your soul is damned," Malachi gloated, "and this demon will not fail to drag you down to Hell."

He stood with his back to the mirror like a showman introducing an exhibit. Kane willed the claws to reach down and rend the sorcerer to shreds. Instead they raked the glass again, and he saw Meredith flinch at the piercing screech that seemed to scrape at the nerves of his teeth. The sound roused Marcus, and he swung his sword at Kane, who dodged back. The blade sliced through the air scant inches short of his face, and he retreated further without thinking. It brought him within arm's length of a mirror.

He heard an unnaturally liquid sound behind him, and knew it for the sound of inhuman fingers parting transformed glass as they writhed forth to seize him. Before he could dodge out of their reach, Marcus swung the sword down at him. Kane ducked aside barely in time, avoiding the clutch of the denizen of the mirror as well. Marcus was unable to halt the sweep of the blade, which struck the mirror.

There was a clang like a blow on a great anvil, and the mirror shattered along its entire length. Instead of scattering over the floor the fragments imploded into a lightless void, bearing the shards of the inhabitant, which jerked in spasms even as they vanished. In a moment the tattered oval frame contained nothing but bare discoloured wood. "Not the mirrors!" Malachi cried, and his voice had grown shrill.

The command appeared to disconcert Marcus, or the destruction of the mirror did. He faltered long enough for Kane to dart past him, out of the antechamber. With a frustrated almost bestial roar Marcus pursued him into the open space between the avenue of mirrors and the altar. At least Kane could manoeuvre here – could retreat as his brother came relentlessly at him, dealing stroke after murderous stroke. Even staying clear of them had begun to sap Kane's strength. When he blocked them with the sword in his right hand, the impacts shivered through his body and jabbed deep into his wounded shoulder. Then his brother's sword sliced into Kane's right arm, and the new wound seemed to open wider as Kane gripped the hilt of his weapon before it could fall from his hand. He backed away from another deadly stroke, not swiftly enough. His brother's sword slashed across Kane's breast, laying it open almost to the bone.

Kane stumbled backwards and heard Meredith cry out with fear for him. In the midst of the combat he had almost forgotten her, and his awareness of her peril seemed to lend him strength. He stood his ground, and as Marcus cut at him with a two-handed sweep of the blade Kane blocked it with the sword in his right hand. The clash of steel reverberated through him, throbbing in his wounded arm and chest and shoulder. They felt as though red-hot coals had been embedded deep in his flesh. Nevertheless he had managed to ward off the blow, and at once he put all his weight behind the sword in his left hand.

The thrust redoubled the agony in his shoulder, but the blade found his brother's heart and pierced deep. Marcus gave vent to a bellow of disbelief, which sounded baffled enough to have come from an overgrown child. The wound was not fatal yet; it seemed not even to have weakened him. He seized Kane by the throat and dragged his brother to him, driving the blade deeper into himself, an action not merely defiant but close to mindless. He glared at Kane with utter hatred and lifted him off his feet, choking him. There was no room for Kane to wield his sword, which was trapped between their bodies, or to twist the other blade. His head swam and the world turned black. He felt as if the ability to think were being squeezed out of his mind, and only instinct was left to him. It made him reach out and snatch off his brother's mask.

The face was not merely unrecognisable. It had little claim to be described as a face at all; it was a wound, imperfectly healed. Part of the jaw had been torn off by the fall on the rocks, and some of the bone was still exposed. The left eye socket was too large, and a section of the bony rim was visible. The entire left side of the face was clenched into a permanent grimace by its withered skin, the product of Malachi's healing. The bald misshapen pate looked raw, as if the scalp had been ripped away by the fall from the cliff. Perhaps Marcus retained some trace of his old vanity, which had made him don the mask. Certainly he was infuriated to have his face revealed, and he hurled Kane away from him.

Kane landed on his back, close to a torch on a stand. The fall almost jarred the sword out of his grasp. He scarcely had time to rise into a crouch before Marcus strode towards him, hefting the sword like an executioner's axe. "Brother, stop," Kane exhorted him. "Brother."

If the repeated word affected Marcus at all, it was only to inflame his hatred. He lifted the sword above his mutilated head with both hands to deal the final blow. Kane lurched to his feet, and as he rose he grabbed the torch from the stand. Before Marcus could strike, Kane thrust the torch at him.

The flaming end struck him in the chest, and the heat glued it to the leather of his jerkin. Oil from the brand spilled down him, and in moments he was ablaze. He roared even louder than the flames that had begun to consume him. His torso burned like a barrel of pitch, and his legs were twin pillars of flame, but he tramped doggedly at Kane, slashing almost blindly at him. In a confusion of grief and fury Kane stabbed him with the sword. He had to run him through before Marcus sank to the remains of his knees. He raised his head from the conflagration of himself, and Kane thought he glimpsed a trace of renewed humanity in his eyes, as if the fire had purged him of at least some of the evil. He might even have been offering his neck for the coup de grace. "Rest in peace, my brother," Kane murmured like a prayer, and gripped his sword with both hands and struck with all his power.

The stroke severed Marcus's head. The decapitated body tottered and then toppled forward to lie propped on the hilt of the sword in its chest, its hands outstretched as if it were making a hideous obeisance to the bloodstained altar. Kane's rage was focused on Malachi now, and he was turning away from the blazing remains when he caught sight of a movement that should not be taking place. Something more solid than blood, and with more of a shape, was emerging from the stump of the neck. "What is this abomination?" Kane said through his teeth.

He watched in loathing as it crawled forth. Perhaps the flames were driving it out of the body that had been its lair, unless it no longer found the body useful. Its taloned fingers came first, spindly digits that writhed in the air and then clawed at the floor. Gaunt grey arms followed, and a long livid head as bald as a maggot. At first the motions were so tentative that Kane might almost have been witnessing a grotesque parody of birth, but with every moment they grew more purposeful. The demon lifted its head, showing Kane the little it had for a face – eyes black as a crow's and a circular mouth. He had seen those eyes before, glaring out of the mask.

He waited until the creature dropped to the floor, spattering the stone with Marcus's blood. As it prepared to spring up or scuttle away on all fours he trampled on it, pinning it to the floor and splintering its ribs. It screeched like an injured raven and gibbered sounds that might have been words, though not in any language Kane recognised or would want to understand. He chopped at the neck and then sawed two-handed through it, and kicked away the severed head, which continued to screech until the body finished twitching. "Go back to the Hell that gave you birth," Kane snarled and was turning to find Malachi when he heard Meredith scream.

FORTY

As soon as Meredith dodged behind the column she began to pray for Captain Kane. She would have prayed aloud if it might not have alerted Malachi. She had cried out when the demon in the avenue of mirrors had caught hold of Kane, but she had to be silent now – had to believe that her silence would help to conceal her. She could only hope that Malachi had not observed her flight, wherever he might be. She dared not risk making for the doors out of the great hall in case the horde of raiders was still out there, even though freeing her from the cage had cost Kane a grievous wound. She could do nothing except pray that he would survive the combat, after which they might escape from Axmouth together. Then he raised his voice to taunt the sorcerer, and Malachi answered him.

He was somewhere near the throne, out of Meredith's sight. She saw Kane's challenge halt his brother, as though it had interrupted Malachi's power over his puppet. She heard Malachi refuse to fight Kane, and thought he was as much of a coward as he had been called. She heard him meet Kane's gibes with words, and prayed that the lull in the combat would give Kane the chance to elude the mirrors and their demonic inhabitants – but he was still trapped among them by his monstrous brother. Then he extended his challenge to Malachi's master, and she heard the sorcerer's response.

She could not quite see what Malachi did then. By peering warily around the column she was able to make out that he had uncovered an enormous oval mirror in the darkest corner of the hall. Something stirred within the glass – something as gigantic, glowing like an open furnace. This was all she could distinguish from her vantage point, and she withdrew hastily behind the column as Malachi turned away from the mirror. In a moment an atrocious glassy screech resounded through the hall. The sorcerer was calling to Kane, threatening him with a demon, and Meredith was dismayed to see one reach for him in the avenue of mirrors. Before she could cry out a warning he sidestepped a blow of his brother's sword, which smashed the glass. "Not the mirrors!" Malachi yelled.

The panic in his voice felt like an answer to Meredith's prayers, and so did seeing Captain Kane take advantage of the diversion to dart past his brother. His masked adversary swung around at once and followed him into the open space by the altar. Meredith clenched her hands together to intensify her prayers, although it felt as if she were striving vainly to press some sensation back into her marked palm. She gripped her knuckles until the fingers ached – just the fingers of her right hand. She kept her desperate prayers silent while she watched Kane give ground, parrying his brother's strokes but never managing to deal blows of his own. She stifled a cry when his assailant's sword cut into his arm, but she was unable to stay mute when another sweep of the blade slashed his chest open. She had barely cried out before a hand closed over her face.

It was as cold and soft as a slug, and smelled of some unholy incense. The long pallid fingers writhed over her lips, pinching them shut, as Malachi's face craned gleefully over her shoulder. However pulpy his flesh was, his clutch was as strong as a python's. She could not move her bruised lips as his other arm slid sinuously around her waist and lifted her off her feet as though she weighed no more than a child. When she tried to kick and claw at him, his robe enfolded her so tightly that it could have been responding to his will. Her helpless struggles brought her close to exhaustion as he carried her to the enormous mirror. As she began to discern a titanic fiery shape within the glass he turned to watch the combat, holding Meredith in front of him.

Captain Kane had succeeded in striking a blow, and his sword was protruding from his brother's heart. It seemed not to lessen the sorcerous power that possessed him. He was lifting Kane by his throat into the air, but flung him to the floor once Kane pulled off the mask, revealing a face more appropriate to a corpse long gone in decay. Meredith strove to find words for a prayer, however stifled, as the smells of incense and cold corrupted flesh almost overwhelmed her senses. As the unmasked figure moved to finish him off, Kane set it on fire with a torch and then wielded his sword. At last his adversary collapsed like a burning scarecrow, and Kane released him from his suffering with a headsman's stroke of the sword. At the sight of the fall of his champion, Malachi twisted furiously to face the great mirror, taking Meredith with him. "It is time," he hissed.

Meredith saw a monstrous face loom down from the height of the mirror – fanged jaws vast enough to hold a man between them, red lurid eyes whose smallness suggested how tiny the savage brain might be. Malachi seized her right arm and stretched it out before him. "Only your innocent blood will release him," he said and licked his thin lips with his colourless tongue. Snatching the knife from the altar, he cut Meredith's arm open.

It was not just the pain that made her cry out. Malachi had fastened his lips on the wound. His tongue crawled wormlike over it as he sucked her blood, and she felt as if he were seeking to batten on her soul as well. When he raised his head his mouth looked as rouged as any harlot's, obscenely vivid against the unhealthy pallor of his skin. His head jerked like a snake's towards the mirror, and he spat on the glass.

Meredith saw the mixture of blood and spittle splash the mirror. She might have fancied that the world had been diabolically inverted, because instead of running down the glass, the liquid began to climb. It spread tendrils across the mirror as it raced upwards, until it seemed the glass itself was imbuing it with eagerness. It was no longer on the surface; it was merging with the glass, effecting some alchemical transformation. Malachi stepped aside, dragging Meredith with him, as the glass bulged like an enormous transparent sack.

It grew molten with the heat of the shape that was pushing it outwards. It stretched thin, and then it tore asunder like a reptile's egg, and the monster it had hatched burst forth. It stank like a furnace whose very bricks were burning. Its molten core – all that it had for a heart and guts – was visible between its exposed ribs. Flames flared around the haphazard chitinous scales that patched its torso. Its colossal arms and legs were covered with material that might have been armour or a carapace like a titanic insect's. A gigantic chain was wrapped around its trunk. It emerged into the great hall with a tread that shook the floor and vibrated as far as the antechamber, where a torch rattled in its stand. As Malachi released a hiss of pleasure at the spectacle, the demon turned its sluggish monumental head and lowered it towards him and Meredith.

The prognathous face resembled the skull of some unholy hybrid of a beast and an insect. Horns curved backwards from the hinges of the jaw to bristle above the flaming skull. The fire that surmounted the cranium might have been parodying a halo or a crown of thorns. Flames filled the gaping mouth and dripped from the jaws, and the eyes were twin pits of flame. It seemed impossible that they could see, but the demon sensed it had not found its quarry. It swung its ponderous head towards Captain Kane, and Meredith began to pray more fervently than she had ever prayed in her life.

FORTY-ONE

Kane saw that Malachi had dragged Meredith to the mirror like a sacrifice to its colossal denizen. The sorcerer cut her arm open and sucked greedily at the wound. The sight lent Kane the strength of loathing, and he was striding forward when Malachi spat the mouthful of blood on the mirror. It rushed up the glass like a scarlet vine, its ascent diabolically accelerated. It fastened parasitically on the mirror and seemed to thin the glass, which ballooned as if reality itself were giving way – as if the laws of God were. The demonic head that was forcing the mirror outwards dwarfed Meredith and her captor. The sorcerer had stepped deferentially aside, taking the injured girl with him, and Kane saw that she was still in mortal danger. Before he could reach Malachi or even challenge him the mirror split apart down the entire length of the oval, and its colossal inhabitant lumbered forth.

As first it appeared to be making straight for Kane with a determination as monolithic as its form. Then it noticed the girl and Malachi beside the mirror, which had sunk back into the frame, regaining its blackness. Did the demon sense Meredith's wound or the mark on her palm? The titanic head turned with the ponderousness of a landslide, and the fanged rudimentary face bent towards her, drooling fire. It must have found her unworthy of attention, for it reared up almost to the ceiling and came for Kane. "My God," he breathed, "only You can help me now."

He had no more time for prayer. The demon was lowering its head to find him, and it was as though an erupting volcano had stooped towards him. He thought its brain might be as undeveloped as the monstrous insectoid skull, which seemed to have no use for flesh, but then what need did such a creature have of the ability to think? If it had any purpose other than to claim Kane, it was to embody the essence of the Hell to which it would deliver him. Fire dribbled from its horned jaws, and its small eyes flared like coals as though expressing a cretinous delight in having identified him. Perhaps it was a fighter's instinct, but also a last hope of divine intervention, that made Kane raise his sword.

The colossus was swifter than he had assumed. An incandescent fist swooped down at him like a meteor, and if he had not dodged backwards he would have been crushed to pulp. The blow shattered a section of the floor yards wide as if the stone were as flimsy as shell. Fragments of molten stone flew up from the impact, and one landed on Kane's arm, burning into his flesh until he brushed it away. Without pause the demon rose to its full dreadful height and came after him.

Each of its strides was equal to half a dozen of Kane's. He thought of luring it out of the great hall – perhaps he could elude it in the corridors or find some means of destroying it there – but then he saw that it would only have to stoop and reach its arm through the antechamber to seize him in its molten grasp before he could reach the doors. He dashed towards the columns that supported the roof on the left side of the hall, and felt the floor shudder under the pursuing tread. He felt heat on his back as though a furnace had gaped wide behind him. He had barely dodged beyond a column when the demon swung a massive arm at him.

It could have been lunging to catch him, unless this was a gesture of frustrated almost mindless rage. The arm smashed through the column, dislodging a chunk of stone that left a gap as large as Kane was tall. The giant fist would have closed around him if he had not already retreated towards the next pillar. He ran along the line of columns until they hid him from the demon, and tried desperately to plan. Three rose windows overlooked the columns, but they were too high for him to reach. A gargantuan footstep shook the column at his back, and he imagined he was hidden until blazing scaly fingers, each one larger than his arm, groped around the column to find him.

He was put in mind of an imbecilic child searching for a lost doll. His eyes began to smart and grow desiccated with the appalling heat. When he backed away, the titan hand followed him. The demon knew where he was. It would find him wherever he hid, and he had a sense that it was playing a wicked idiotic game with him. At least the idea gave him back his rage. It was time to bring the ignominious game to an end, and he strode into the open.

He was only just swift enough. The blazing hand snatched at him, and as it missed, the arm pulverised a section of the column. Rubble crashed to the floor behind Kane, and shards of stone hit his back like grapeshot. He ignored them and his wounds as he headed for the enormous oval mirror. The sorcerer had moved in front of it, pinning Meredith to him. As he met Kane's eyes he raised the knife to hold it almost negligently against her throat. "Stop," Kane shouted.

"The girl has served her purpose," Malachi said,

tracing a line over her throat with the knife.

"Then you have no need of her." Kane heard and felt a massive footstep crunch the rubble at his back. "Let her go," he said. "You can have my soul."

"Why do you risk everything to save her?" The sibilant voice seemed to hiss with amusement. "Even your soul," Malachi said.

For a moment Kane had engaged his attention, but it drifted away as Malachi gazed at the demon. Another footstep shook the floor, and Kane felt the heat seize hold of him and heard the clank of an enormous chain. The demon was about to wield it, to strike Kane down or to bind him with the red-hot links, a first taste of the eternal torture that awaited him. He saw a drop of blood trickle down Meredith's neck from the point of the knife as she stifled a cry. He had one chance to make a difference to her in his final moments, but almost no time to think how. If Malachi's power was bound up with the mirrors, perhaps destroying the largest might lessen his power, but would closing the portal not leave the demon at large – leave Meredith at its mercy? There was only one way Kane could hope to release her and to mitigate her danger. He snatched his pistol from his belt as a final immense footstep shuddered through the floor. It was so close that it sprinkled him with fire, and he felt the hair on the nape of his neck begin to smoulder. "I made a promise. I must keep it," he said and pulled the trigger.

The shot struck Malachi in the centre of his forehead. The thin lips stretched wide in a grimace that resembled an unpronounced curse, and the knife clattered to the floor. The arm that had been holding Meredith jerked away, its fingers writhing in convulsive rage, and she darted out of reach, to the side of the mirror. She seemed not to know where to look – at Kane or at the spectacle of Malachi. The gout of blood that had sprung from his forehead was rising above him to stream into the mirror. He was not dead yet, for he uttered an appalled shriek as his body started to blacken and tatter and disintegrate. All the corruption it housed was overwhelming it, and it flew apart in a sluggish explosion of putrefied scraps that were sucked into the blackness of the mirror. Meredith backed away, and Kane thanked God that she was out of range of the process. He was not, however. A fiery hurricane had risen at his back and was rushing into the mirror.

Flaming chunks and particles of fire raced past Kane, and he knew that the demon was bursting apart as Malachi had. He would have been reassured if the violence of it had not threatened to overwhelm him. Before he could attempt to dodge aside, he was raised helplessly into the air, to hover in the midst of the onslaught of fire. Why was it not carrying him onwards? It seemed to lift his arms from his sides and extend them as far as they could reach, so that he could have imagined he was still on the cross. The storm of flame and molten matter rushed past him, not quite touching him, and all at once he understood that the force that had raised him up to crucify him in the heart of the firestorm had nothing to do with the mirror.

It was a kind of purification. He felt as if his sins were being seared from him at last – as if, although the fire was bypassing his flesh, it was penetrating his soul. It gave him a foretaste of eternity, and while it endured it was timeless. At last every iota of fire was swallowed by the mirror, and the power that was holding Kane aloft released him. As he crumpled to the floor the mirror turned black, and it seemed the world did.

FORTY-TWO

Kane was at peace. It was more than an absence of sensation; he had no need of feelings any longer. If there was a gentle light, it showed him nothing that would trouble him; it showed him nothing at all. He might have believed that time had ended for him, since he had no means of measuring it and no desire to do so. Perhaps that was a definition of eternity, but it did not require him to put it into words. He was giving up the last of his thoughts – it seemed to him that any doubts would depart with them – when he heard a distant voice.

It had spoken his name. At first he thought it was praying for him, and then he grasped that it was also calling to him. He had not yet earned peace after all, and he fancied that the voice was summoning him back into the world to continue his task. It returned his senses to him. The light was less constant than he had imagined, and as he glimpsed its flickering he felt soft rain on his upturned face. He was lying on his back on stone, and as the awareness took hold of him, so did the pain of his wounds. That opened his eyes, and he saw Meredith.

She was kneeling beside him, and the rain was her tears. As he met her gaze and held it she wiped her eyes. "Solomon," she said once more. "It's gone. You sent the demon back, and it took Malachi instead."

"Your father told me that if I saved you my soul would

be redeemed." As he spoke Kane was recapturing his memories and his sense of himself. "I have, and it is," he said. "The Devil's claim on me is no more."

He had more to say, but he heard the doors to the antechamber open wide. Meredith helped him raise his head as Telford and a few of his men came into the great hall. "The guards have fallen," Telford said. "Axmouth is yours, Captain Kane."

Meredith supported Kane while he struggled to his feet. He steadied himself with an arm around her shoulders, and then he took hold of her left hand. The mark imprinted by the witch had gone, and the palm looked renewed – reborn. "You destroyed the evil," Meredith murmured. "Thank you, Captain Kane."

"Thank God." Kane stumbled to the altar and leaned a fist on it as he stared into the pit in the floor. Its contents had petrified, reverting to the stone of Axmouth, although the bottom of the pit was dark with the blood it had consumed. He remembered sensing that the fabric of the castle was corrupted, possessed with unholy vitality, but he had no such impression now. He saw shadows growing restless beyond the columns of the hall, but they were merely the companions of the torchlight and the candle-flames. Through a window he caught sight of the glint of a star, and knew that the pall no longer loured over Axmouth. He gazed at his father's chair and could see only the heaps of entangled cadavers that flanked it like tributes. Nor could he avoid seeing his brother's charred and mutilated remains, profaned by the demonic parasite that lay nearby in an attitude that parodied its host's. Marcus looked shrunken, reduced to his boyhood stature. "It is not over," Kane said almost to himself.

Telford came to stand by him. "What must be done? Shall we destroy the altar?"

"And every mirror," Kane said. "Let no man look within them."

"It shall be as you say." Telford gazed aghast at the corpses of Malachi's sacrifices. "And however long it takes," he said, "each victim shall have a Christian burial."

"The guards too," said Kane. "The demons will have left them."

"Will there never be an end to it?" one of Telford's comrades muttered. "Some of us died fighting them."

"And Captain Kane offered up his soul to fight the evil," Meredith cried.

Kane felt unworthy of her impassioned defence – he had let her brothers and her father be slaughtered, after all. "The fight goes on," he said.

He pushed himself away from the altar and wavered where he stood. Telford grasped his arm, and Meredith hurried to him. "You are wounded," she protested. "Stay and let me heal you."

"God bless you, Meredith," Kane said and leaned on them both. "And then I must go forth again," he said. "I have my work to finish."

FORTY-THREE

—◆—

The top of the cliff was the green of sunlit grass after months of rain. Only the two elongated heaps of rock beside the Celtic cross introduced a sombre note. Except for a flotilla of white clouds along the horizon of the sea, the azure sky was clear. A sun like a token of a pure eternal light stood above the gentle waves. A breeze that smelled as salty as a voyage crossed the bay and rustled the grass that had already set about softening the outlines of the mounds of rock. Kane stood for a long time between the mounds, deep in thought and prayer. At last he raised his head and spoke as if those who lay hidden before him could hear him. "Brother, forgive me for all that I did to you," he said. "Father, I have kept my promise. Meredith is returned to her mother."

A movement over Axmouth caught his eye. Birds were wheeling in the sky above the castle – birds as white as the crows had been black. They were gulls, which flew with plaintive cries across the cliffs and out to sea. "The demon is gone," Kane said. "It is banished to the shadows along with the sorcerer who cursed us all."

He could see just one shadow on the cliff top – the shadow of the cross. It was a sign, and Kane knew what it had to mean to him. "Evil is not so easily defeated," he said. "I know I will have to fight again."

He seemed to hear a whisper of response. It was the

wind in the grass, a murmur so wordless that it might have been encouraging him or issuing a challenge. "I am a very different man now," he said. "Through all my travels, all the things I've seen and done, I have found my purpose."

For a long breath he gazed towards Axmouth. The castle was his home now, and perhaps in time he would return. He had kept his pledge to Meredith's parents, and now it was time to commit himself to another oath. He said a last prayer over the graves and left them with a sign of the cross before mounting his horse. "There was a time when the world was plunging into darkness," he reflected. "A time of witchcraft and sorcery, when no one stood against evil." He let his gaze rest on the graves while he remembered the events that had led there – his masked brother laying his hands on his followers to infect them with evil, his father imprisoned as much by having yielded to temptation as by the chains in the dungeon. The memories lent power to his vow, and so did the knowledge that he was the last of his line, its only champion. "That time is over," he declared and was positive that God could hear him. Spurring his horse, he rode to find whatever might await him.

THE END

ABOUT THE AUTHOR

The *Oxford Companion to English Literature* describes Ramsey Campbell as "Britain's most respected living horror writer". He has been given more awards than any other writer in the field, including the Grand Master Award of the World Horror Convention, the Lifetime Achievement Award of the Horror Writers Association and the Living Legend Award of the International Horror Guild. Among his novels are *The Face That Must Die*, *Incarnate*, *Midnight Sun*, *The Count of Eleven*, *Silent Children*, *The Darkest Part of the Woods*, *The Overnight*, *Secret Story*, *The Grin of the Dark*, *Thieving Fear* and *Creatures of the Pool*. Forthcoming is *The Seven Days of Cain*. His collections include *Waking Nightmares*, *Alone with the Horrors*, *Ghosts and Grisly Things*, *Told by the Dead* and *Just Behind You*, and his non-fiction is collected as *Ramsey Campbell, Probably*. His novels *The Nameless* and *Pact of the Fathers* have been filmed in Spain. His regular columns appear in *Prism*, *All Hallows*, *Dead Reckonings* and *Video Watchdog*. He is the President of the British Fantasy Society and of the Society of Fantastic Films.

Ramsey Campbell lives on Merseyside with his wife Jenny. His pleasures include classical music, good food and wine, and whatever's in that pipe. His web site is at www.ramseycampbell.com.

AVAILABLE NOW

RUNESCAPE: BETRAYAL AT FALADOR
T.S. Church

In the Kingdom of Asgarnia, the Knights of
Falador are beacons of order and chivalry, but
their dominance is threatened by the forces of
chaos which plot to shatter the time of peace.

When a mysterious young woman suddenly
appears in the city of Falador in the teeth of a
storm, her arrival launches a chain of events that
will alter the fate of the kingdom forever.

Unless the knights can solve the riddle of Kara-
Meir, everything they hold dear may be lost.

Set in the world of *RuneScape*—the world's
most popular free online role-playing game.

ISBN: 9781848567221

AVAILABLE NOW

RUNESCAPE: RETURN TO CANIFIS
T.S. Church

Varrock is the greatest human city in the world,
yet its people are disappearing, spirited away to
Morytania, the land where vampires rule.

When the King is forced to send representatives to Canifis,
in the dark realm of Morytania, he selects the now-famous
heroine Kara-Meir, as well as Gar'rth, unique in his
knowledge of the land of the dead. They are accompanied
by Theodore, Doric the dwarf, the wizard Castimir, and
the barbarian priestess Arisha, on a mission that will
force Gar'rth to confront his werewolf heritage, and will
reveal secrets that will test their loyalties to the limit.

For the price of failure in Morytania is far worse than
death: if their mission fails, then a new King will rule in
Varrock, who is lord of both the living and the dead.

Set in the world of *RuneScape*—the world's
most popular free online role-playing game.

ISBN: 9781848567276

AVAILABLE NOW

THE FURTHER ADVENTURES
OF SHERLOCK HOLMES

SÉANCE FOR A VAMPIRE
Fred Saberhagen

When two suspect psychics offer Ambrose Altamont
and his wife the opportunity to contact their recently
deceased daughter, the aristocrat hires Sherlock Holmes to
expose their hoax. The resulting chaos leaves one of the
fraudulent spiritualists dead. With Holmes missing, Watson
has no choice but to summon the only one who might be
able to help—Holmes's vampire cousin, Prince Dracula.

ISBN: 9781848566774

AVAILABLE NOW

**THE FURTHER ADVENTURES
OF SHERLOCK HOLMES**

DR. JEKYLL AND MR. HOLMES
Loren D. Estleman

When Sir Danvers Carew is brutally murdered, the
Queen herself calls Sherlock Holmes to investigate.
In the course of his enquiries, the esteemed detective
is struck by the strange link between the highly
respectable Dr. Henry Jekyll and the immoral,
debauched Edward Hyde. Can he work out what it
is that connects the two men or is it mystery even
beyond the skills of the great Sherlock Holmes?

ISBN: 9781848567474

AVAILABLE NOW

THE FURTHER ADVENTURES
OF SHERLOCK HOLMES

THE WHITECHAPEL HORRORS
Edward B. Hanna

Terror reigns on the streets of Whitechapel where horrific
murders are being committed. Sherlock Holmes believes
he knows the identity of the killer—Jack the Ripper.
But as he delves deeper, Holmes realizes that revealing
the murderer puts much more at stake than merely
putting a psychopath behind bars. In this unique case,
Holmes is faced with the greatest dilemma of his career.

ISBN: 9781848567498

AVAILABLE NOW

**THE FURTHER ADVENTURES
OF SHERLOCK HOLMES**

THE GIANT RAT OF SUMATRA
Richard L. Boyer

In deference to Sherlock Holmes's wishes, Dr Watson
kept the tale of The Giant Rat of Sumatra a secret.
However, before he died he arranged that the bizarre
story of the giant rat should be held in the vaults of a
London bank until all the protagonists were dead...

ISBN: 9781848568600

AVAILABLE NOW

**THE FURTHER ADVENTURES
OF SHERLOCK HOLMES**

THE ANGEL OF THE OPERA
Sam Siciliano

Paris 1890. Sherlock Holmes is summoned across
the English Channel to the famous Opera House.
Once there, he is challenged to discover the true
motivations and secrets of the notorious phantom,
who rules its depths with passion and defiance.

ISBN: 9781848568617

COMING JUNE 1011

**THE FURTHER ADVENTURES
OF SHERLOCK HOLMES**

THE PEERLESS PEER
Philip José Farmer

Holmes and Watson take to the skies in the quest of the
nefarious Von Bork and his weapon of dread... A night
sky aerial engagement with the deadly Fokker nearly
claims three brilliant lives... And an historic alliance is
formed, whereby Baker Street's enigmatic mystery-solver
and Greystoke, the noble savage, peer of the realm and
lord of the jungle, team up to bring down the hellish hun!

ISBN: 9780857681201

COMING AUGUST 2011

**THE FURTHER ADVENTURES
OF SHERLOCK HOLMES SERIES**

THE STAR OF INDIA
Carole Buggé

Holmes and Watson find themselves caught up in
a complex chess board of a problem, involving a
clandestine love affair and the disappearance of a priceless
sapphire. Professor James Moriarty is back to tease and
torment, leading the duo on a chase through the dark
and dangerous back streets of London and beyond.

ISBN: 9780857681218

COMING SEPTEMBER 2011

THE FURTHER ADVENTURES
OF SHERLOCK HOLMES SERIES

THE BREATH OF GOD
Guy Adams

A body is found crushed to death in the London
snow. There are no footprints anywhere near. It is
almost as if the man was killed by the air itself. This
is the first in a series of attacks that sees a handful
of London's most prominent occultists murdered.
While pursuing the case, Holmes and Watson have
to travel to Scotland to meet with the one person
they have been told can help: Aleister Crowley.

ISBN: 9780857682826